FOU

DOGS

MISSING

For my parents

FOUR DOGS MISSING

RHYS GARD

echo
PUBLISHING

echo
PUBLISHING

An imprint of Bonnier Books UK
Level 45, World Square,
680 George Street
Sydney NSW 2000
www.echopublishing.com.au

Bonnier Books UK
4th Floor, Victoria House,
Bloomsbury Square
London WC1B 4DA
www.bonnierbooks.co.uk

First published in 2023

Printed and bound in Australia by Griffin Press

The paper this book is printed on is certified against
the Forest Stewardship Council® Standards.
Griffin Press holds chain of custody certification
SCS-COC-001185. FSC® promotes environmentally
responsible, socially beneficial and economically viable
management of the world's forests.

Editor: Alexandra Nahlous
Page design and typesetting: Shaun Jury
Cover designer: Design by Committee
Front cover image: Back side view of a man with skinny jeans and jeans jacket
walking/running uphill off road at countryside in autumn,
background/sunset, by Ricca Novia/Shutterstock
Back cover image: Vineyard, by Neale Cousland/Bigstock

A catalogue entry for this book is available from the National Library of
Australia

ISBN: 9781760687724 (paperback)
ISBN: 9781760687731 (ebook)

echo_publishing
echo_publishing
echopublishingaustralia

About the author

Rhys Gard is a writer and a chef. Between careers, he studied English and Film at the University of New South Wales. He has worked as a journalist, marketer, wine writer and restaurateur.

He lives in Mudgee. *Four Dogs Missing* is his first novel.

'And you should not let yourself be confused in your solitude by the fact that there is some thing in you that wants to move out of it.'

— Rainer Maria Rilke, Letters to a Young Poet

1.

The navy van veered into the mouth of the driveway and stopped suddenly. Oliver emerged from the wine shed a couple of hundred metres away to investigate. A plume of smoke smouldered from the kombi's exhaust, and he caught a whiff of sulphur – another lost tourist, no doubt, trying to find a cellar door that'd still pour a tipple this late in the afternoon. He watched the distant figure step from the van and push open the gate to his vineyard.

The gate that said 'PRIVATE'.

Perfect, Oliver thought. *Do people not read signs anymore, or do they just not give a fuck?*

He walked from the shed towards his cottage, closer to the driveway, admiring his surroundings. Oliver loved Mudgee in the middle of autumn. The weather was still kind and his grapes had been picked and crushed into barrels. Looking out across the open landscape, the view of the mountains never failed to cheer him. The old vines were yellowing, and a copse of maples and liquidambars were losing leaves, floating and settling across a small patch of lawn beside the house. Oliver had already prepared his speech to deliver to the man making his way up the driveway: *No cellar door here, sorry, mate. You'll have to go up further to Vernon & Sons, but I have a feeling they've punched the clock for today.*

The driver opened the door and stepped onto the gravel, and Oliver froze.

The man wore his hair the same way that he did: slightly long fringe pushed to the right. Identical nose and almond-shaped eyes. Oliver felt like someone had placed a mirror directly in front of his face. The winemaker tried to speak, but nothing came out. He was in shock.

'I wanted to call,' the lookalike said, stretching languidly like a cat that had been cooped up for hours. 'Apparently you have a phone, but no one would give me the number. I couldn't even get an email for the vineyard.'

'No distractions like that out here,' Oliver said. For some reason, he was wary about approaching. It had been a long time. Fifteen years? 'I was just heading in for a shower before a wine show.'

The other man smiled, looking over Oliver's tattered jeans and the burgundy stains smudged on his shirt, as though he knew what Oliver was thinking. 'I can come back?' he offered.

Oliver paused – it sounded strange to hear his own voice coming from someone else's mouth. 'No,' he said. 'I'd invite you along, but there'd be too many questions.' He pointed towards the house. 'Why don't you go in?'

The visitor grabbed a large weathered suitcase from the back of the van and rolled it behind him as he followed Oliver inside. The cottage smelled of sandalwood and faintly of the garlic Oliver had fried with green vegetables and butter for lunch.

'Nice place, Oli.' The man looked at the paintings adorning the walls in the living room. Thick brushstrokes. Oils. Vineyards.

Coastal landscapes. Abstract. All worth a pretty penny and all painted by their mother. Theo unzipped the suitcase and produced a bottle of whisky. 'I was going to bring wine, but I thought that'd be like carrying coals to Newcastle.'

Oliver grinned, realising how much he'd missed Theo's sense of humour, his penchant for outdated idioms. 'There's food in the fridge if you're hungry,' he said, moving towards the bathroom.

In the shower, Oliver thought about what in his own life had changed since he'd last seen Theo. It would have been almost twenty years since they'd been close. Twenty years since they'd stolen cigarettes and snuck porn magazines into their bedroom; decades since they'd ridden their bikes up and down the street and around the block until dusk. Once upon a time, they'd shared everything: books, comics, games, clothes, friends, enemies. Then overnight, everything had changed.

When he emerged from the shower, his doppelgänger was smoking a cigarette on the balcony. He'd always envied his twin's ability to be content with quietness, with boredom. Oliver had ensured his life was filled with purposeful things to do – busyness – to avoid too many moments of silence. He couldn't help but notice how different they were as he watched Theo stare into the sky with an indolence Oliver could never manage in himself.

***

'Where have you been?' Gabe said as he lowered himself into Oliver's car, ignoring his seatbelt. 'You hate being late.'

'A random kombi just pulled up in the driveway.'

'Tourists. They're everywhere this week,' Gabe said.

'I thought the same, but then Theo jumped out.'

'Fuck.' Gabe whistled, long and loud, before flicking a curl of grey hair from his face and pushing his glasses to the bridge of his nose. 'It's been a while.'

'Longer than I've known you.' Oliver exhaled. 'No phone call, no letter, no messages to say he's coming.'

'In fairness,' Gabe said, 'you're not an easy man to get in touch with. How long is he staying?'

Oliver shrugged. 'It was a big suitcase.'

He manoeuvred the car into one of the last vacant spaces. A cluster of Mudgee winemakers and growers congregated near the door of the pavilion. Oliver groaned.

'Don't be like that,' Gabe said. 'You win something almost every year. It'd be rude not to show up.'

'Can't I just claim I don't play well with others and hermit away from promotional responsibilities altogether?'

Gabe put a finger in the air threateningly, but ruined the effect with a smile. 'You already do. You know this is basically the only event I ask you to attend.'

Oliver rolled his eyes and unstrapped his seatbelt.

'And one more thing,' Gabe said.

'Yeah. I'll be nice.'

Gabe paused. 'Just be wary of Theo. I know it's been a while, but remember, we've built this brand without him.'

Oliver wondered if Gabe knew something about Theo that he didn't. But what? As far as he could tell, Theo had never even set foot in Mudgee.

'He's not a criminal, Gabe,' Oliver mumbled eventually. 'He's my twin brother.'

***

Theo walked around the house like someone who had just checked into a hotel. He pawed through the bathroom drawers and kitchen cabinets, moseying from room to room. Then he sat down on a lounge chair for a moment and took a breath. His phone started to vibrate in his pocket, but he ignored it. Bugger him – if Harold wanted a fight, let him drive over here for it. Theo couldn't help but think the scumbag would show up sooner or later.

The afternoon wasn't anything at all like Theo had imagined. He'd concocted many potential meeting scenarios on the drive into Mudgee. How did he think it would *really* go down? Theo wasn't sure. One thing was certain: he hadn't expected to meet briefly with his brother and for Oliver to leave again so abruptly. It was a jolt – his twin brother there in front of him after so many years. Seeing how much he'd aged; how alike they were, even now.

Taking the whisky from the bag, Theo swigged, glancing at his mother's paintings for a moment before closing his eyes. One sentence kept sliding into his head, dislodging itself from his brain and falling into his mouth. He spoke it quietly to himself. 'Why did it take you so long?'

He picked up the bag and walked down the hallway to the office. There was a Royal typewriter, books on Champagne, Piedmont and Bordeaux, some papers and a *Gourmet Traveller Wine* magazine. A packet of cigarettes on a shelf. A thin layer of dust. Theo took a few books of his own from his bag and put them on top of the desk, before slipping his diary under some paperbacks.

From beneath his packed clothes, he pulled out two parcels wrapped in brown butcher's paper and set them on the desk. He glanced out the window to make sure no one was watching. The property was eerily quiet, the only sounds that of a truck shifting through its gears in the distance and the occasional cawing of birds behind the house. Was it risky to come here now? Perhaps. Yet Theo knew he didn't have much choice. Despite the danger, the message had compelled him to drive to the vineyard, to Oliver.

Beside the desk was a chest of drawers. It was wooden, shabby, a restored antique with a colourful past. Theo pulled the large bottom drawer out altogether, exposing the floor below. He placed the two perfectly wrapped paintings on the floor in the back left-hand corner, before once again sliding the drawer onto its tracks. It had been, since the twins were children, an agreed-upon hiding place for anything they wanted to keep from prying eyes. Theo couldn't remember it ever letting them down. Stowing Julia's paintings under Oliver's drawer felt like the right thing to do. If anything happened to him, he knew Oliver would eventually find the canvases; they belonged to him as much as they did to Theo.

The air outside was crisp. Clouds loomed in the sky. The world felt so much bigger in the bush – even when you were surrounded by mountains. Theo walked across the small patch of grass towards what he assumed to be the wine shed. Sliding open the door, which let out a gentle groan, he stepped inside. There were oak barrels everywhere. Tanks, hoses, boxes, crates. In true Oliver fashion, everything was meticulously kept. There was a large barn door at the end of the room. Theo glanced around and wondered if there were any cameras. He thought that the door might be locked, but it slipped open. Inside were tables lined with sealed wine bottles, all bereft of labels. There was something peculiar about the scenario, but Theo couldn't quite put his finger on exactly what it was. Grabbing a bottle, he casually twirled it in his hands before arranging it alongside the others again. His handprints tattooed the bottle; the rest of the glass surface was heavily freckled with dust.

In the corner of the room, against the inside wall, was a piano.

It looked familiar. Ancient. The name *Bösendorfer* printed in golden glyphs on the open hood. He guessed it was the same piano their mother had inherited from their grandmother. Oliver must have hunted it down and bought it after everything had been sold.

Why did it take you so long?

There was a metronome atop the piano. Theo remembered it from when he'd learned to play a lifetime ago. He set it in motion and listened to the ticking pulse through the room.

Tick.

  Tick.

    Tick.

      Tick.

        Tick.

          Tick.

            Tick.

***

Gabe grabbed them each a glass of prosecco as they joined a group beside the door.

'Are my eyes failing me ... Oliver Wingfield in public?' a gruff, sarcastic voice said loudly.

'Hello, Murray.'

Snowy-haired and loutish, somewhere in his early fifties, Murray was dressed in a suit that was twice as formal as anyone else's attire. After a decade spent managing neighbouring vineyards, he and Oliver still couldn't see eye to eye on pretty much anything.

'Must be going to win something, if you've come out past the front gate,' he almost spat.

Oliver took a sip of wine, keeping his cool. 'Didn't your mother ever tell you not to do up both jacket buttons?' He shouldn't be

7

getting into a useless argument with Murray today, but he couldn't help himself. When Murray didn't reply, Oliver said, 'You know, if I'd known you'd be here, I would have stayed at home.'

He smiled to himself, imagining the confusion he'd elicit if he'd brought Theo. Maybe he should employ his brother to attend events and competitions on his behalf?

'So, you're not agoraphobic,' Murray said, talking over Gabe, who had tried to change the subject. 'Just antisocial?'

'Most people just go for "arsehole".'

'I'll drink to that,' said Murray and raised his glass.

Oliver ambled to the bar, tipped down the last of the bubbly and grabbed a glass of something white. A woody chardonnay, judging by the smell. Some kind of brash nectarine-and-almond aroma. He tried to hide his contempt; he would have failed miserably at poker.

Oliver hadn't planned on making enemies when he'd moved to Mudgee, but it had happened organically enough. He held views on wine that others didn't particularly agree with. Purity and perfectionism over profit, for one. It certainly wasn't always the smartest way to run a business, but it meant he'd held onto his integrity and was still doing well. Murray and his younger brother, Charlie, didn't like Oliver's opinions. Didn't like the way he ostracised himself from their ethos. They didn't like that he didn't want to be in their circle. The Vernons had been growing grapes for generations – and in their view, Oliver was simply a rich city kid who'd blown into town with no ties binding him to anything. After Oliver's second vintage in Mudgee, when people started paying attention to his wine, Murray and Charlie had started the rumour that Oliver was a Balmoral boy experimenting with Daddy's money. He'd never bothered – or cared enough – to correct them.

Oliver looked around the pavilion. There was a string quartet plodding through a rendition of 'Eleanor Rigby'. Penny was supposed to be helping tend the bar, but he couldn't see her anywhere. Gabe and Murray were still standing together, both chortling, a woman beside them sharing an anecdote with overbearing enthusiasm. Oliver couldn't help but wonder why someone as sage as Gabe Aitken could keep company with someone as lowbrow as Murray Vernon. Although, he reminded himself, arbitrary things connected people, and in the case of his vineyard manager and his neighbour, it was their mutual diversion: watching racehorses gallop past the post.

'How's the chardonnay?'

He jumped slightly, recognising Clare's raspy voice before turning around. While she sounded her fifty years, she had the air of someone easily a decade younger, with her liquorice-black hair and the bright pendant earrings she wore. They had spent the morning tasting a few of Oliver's wines and entering data into the program they'd set up in the cloud.

'Not half as good as yours,' he replied honestly.

'Don't know our tricks, do they, darling?'

Oliver cringed. It reminded him of a wine show a year earlier – one Gabe had made him attend – where a lady had approached Oliver and Clare, politely interrogating them with byzantine questions about biodynamics and the technology company they co-owned with Orson Denver.

'Oliver, you trained with Mr Denver in California?' the stranger had asked him.

'We both did.'

'And you helped him develop microclimate weather stations? I know it's all very mysterious, but I really want the same technology for my vineyard. To know all of your tricks. I think you really need to sell it. People will pay big money.'

'We'll have to ask the boss about that one,' Oliver had said, smiling then making an excuse to leave for the bathroom.

Oliver nodded at Clare, coming back to the present. 'Speaking of tricks, have you heard from Orson, lately?'

Clare looked up abstractedly at the ceiling. 'Don't think that I have. Why do you ask?'

'After you left this morning, I noticed he hasn't updated his data for a few days, which isn't like him.'

'Valerie might have finally scored that holiday she's been pestering him about for years.'

'Yeah,' Oliver said, unconvinced. 'Maybe.'

He watched Gabe weave between a gaggle of journalists, some taking photos of winemakers in a novelty over-sized polaroid frame. He stood in the distance, waving Oliver and Clare over, and shunting them into a group of people Oliver barely knew.

'Oliver, I'd like you to meet John Geraghty, the Minister for Industry and Trade.'

They locked eyes and Oliver realised he recognised the man. Was certain he'd seen him before, he just couldn't pinpoint where. He was tall and banal in a typical old, white politician way. Salt-and-pepper hair, short back and sides. Slightly overweight, clean shaven. As soon as Gabe had finished his sentence, a woman pushed in and hugged Geraghty, unintentionally pushing the Minister away from Oliver. There was a sudden assault of spicy perfume.

'God, I hate her,' Gabe said, snubbing the pair. 'Someone needs to tell her a rosé should be a pale salmon colour, not a rich vermillion.'

'You'll have to take her to Provence,' Oliver said. 'Show her how it's done.'

'Her?' Gabe said. 'And an old queen like me? Please.'

***

While the mayor stood at the lectern and waxed lyrical about Mudgee wines, Oliver thought about his twin brother and the last time they'd spoken. He'd still been studying viticulture and oenology, or maybe he'd only just graduated.

During their adolescence, Theo had harboured an implicit envy of Oliver. From the time they were young, Oliver had had direction, a goal, determination. He was going to become a great winemaker. And Theo? Theo had had no idea. In fact, no one had any ideas about Theodore. Oliver had tried to help him find his passion, but he'd had little luck. Oliver's ambitions were fixed while Theo's were pliable. One week his brother wanted to be a chef, the next he was obsessed with computers. Theo enrolled in a four-year degree in music and science, only to drop out after six months to travel the world.

'And on that note, I'd like to invite the Minister for Industry and Trade, Mr John Geraghty, to present the trophy for Winemaker of the Year.'

The crowd applauded half-heartedly as Geraghty made his way to the podium. The mayor continued: 'Every year, we give this trophy to the winemaker in Mudgee who really showcases our region in all its glory. Who ...'

Oliver thought back to the last day he'd seen Theo. He had driven him to the airport in Sydney, catching every red light on the way. His brother had kept looking at his watch as they'd stopped and started along Gardeners Road.

'How long are you going away for?'

'I don't know,' Theo had said, shrugging his shoulders. 'I've only bought a one-way ticket.'

'So, you're just going to travel till you run out of cash?'

Theo had gazed at the bottle of water in his hand, picking at the corner of the label with his fingernail. 'Yeah, pretty much. I don't really have any plans.'

'It worries me.'

'What? Exploring the world and having a life?'

Oliver had looked ahead. The light finally had blinked green and they'd begun moving, albeit slowly.

'No, the nihilistic attitude. It's like you don't care what you do or what anyone else thinks.'

Theo had sat up in his seat. 'It's not like I've really got too many people to worry about.'

'What about me?' Oliver had pressed.

'Come on. You've never really cared what I want.'

'Get fucked.'

'I'm serious. Do you know how hard it's been for me?'

'Hard how?'

'Ever since. It's all been about him. About *us*. It should be about Mum. Why did everyone get it so fucking wrong?'

Oliver remembered that Theo had closed his eyes like someone had stabbed him, as though he was hiding considerable pain. This was, Oliver had thought, the first time Theo had ever admitted to feeling anything about their mother at all. He had been, up until then, a closed book. They'd started moving faster, the traffic thinning out. Without warning, Theo had unstrapped his seatbelt and flung open the passenger door.

'What the *fuck*!'

Theo had thrown a leg out of the car. Oliver had looked into the rear-view mirror; there was a long line of traffic in their wake. Cold air was punching in, smacking Oliver in the face.

Theo had begun giggling before he'd snapped the door closed again. Oliver had slowed down. People on the footpath were staring at them.

'Relax. I was just going to walk. Thought I might get there faster.'

Oliver had exhaled, gripping the steering wheel harder.

'Stop stressing,' Theo had said. 'You're such a worrywart. I'll send you a postcard. If you're feeling generous you can send me a bottle of vino. When you're a hotshot winemaker.'

At that moment, Oliver had wanted to shout at his brother. Tell him that he knew what had happened when they were seventeen. Tell Theo that he knew, after everything they'd been through, that his own twin brother had betrayed him.

Shaking off the memory, Oliver took a deep breath and looked up at the stage. Gabe poked him in the stomach, as if in anticipation. Maybe to bring him back to the present.

'—and that's why the judges' decision was unanimous. This year's Winemaker of the Year is Oliver Wingfield, of Four Dogs Missing Wines. Here's hoping you find them soon, mate.' The crowd broke into thunderous laughter.

Oliver hated crowds, hated speeches even more, but Gabe grabbed his arm and they began sauntering together to the lectern. As his vineyard manager, Gabe was effectively the only conduit Oliver had to the public.

While he nodded at the crowd and listened to Gabe speak about how grateful they were, Oliver thought of the conversation he'd had with his brother on the way to the airport. What was said, but more pertinently, what wasn't. Theo had proffered an awkward goodbye before getting out of the car and boarding a plane to London. Oliver had waited for a call or a postcard, but nothing had arrived. Later, he'd heard through friends that his brother was living in Thailand and was considering becoming a Buddhist monk.

Theo had not seen or said another word to Oliver until he'd arrived in Mudgee and stood there in his brother's driveway, looking and sounding so much like him that it hurt.

2.

'What fancy bit of brass have you got there?'

Oliver placed the trophy on the table and winced; he'd meant to leave it in the car. 'Barely fancy. More like an encouragement award.'

Theo rolled his eyes. 'What does it say?'

Oliver squinted, pretending to study the inscription. 'Stop being a reclusive fuck and open a cellar door. Our local tourism depends on it.'

'Sounds like you won big,' Theo said. The television was flashing. Bette Davis in scenes from a black-and-white film from the fifties.

'Good to see the old tele still works.' Oliver seldom turned it on. 'Speakers shat themselves, though.'

'Looks like you prefer the record player.'

'Yep.'

'So, nothing's changed.'

Oliver poured them wine. 'Pretty much. Life's easier that way. Except with winemaking. Technology and tradition come together well there.' He handed over a glass and they clinked them in a quiet cheers.

Theo didn't take his eyes from the screen. '*Phone Call from a Stranger* is underrated. Have you seen it?'

'I don't think so.'

'Worth a watch.'

They sat in silence for a while, slowly sipping the wine.

Theo scrutinised the glass. 'This yours?'

'I might be parochial, but I'm not going to make you drink my wine.'

'It's good, whoever made it.'

Oliver shrugged. 'Probably a burly, bearded man in Uruguay. It's a tannat. Reminds me of nothing we grow here. Perhaps that's why I like it.'

'Good to see you're still a sarcastic bastard,' Theo scoffed.

'And nice to see you're still a drifter.' Oliver swirled the wine, before taking a whiff. 'I have to ask. What brings you to wine country?'

Theo paused, then nodded as though he'd known the question was coming. The film finished and the credits started rolling on the screen. A spectacle. Oliver imagined himself clutching a bowler hat at the cinema, back in the fifties. He looked up and noticed then that Theo was ageing like him: a few grey hairs above the ears, similar lines around the eyes. He even trimmed his stubble the same way.

'It's time for a whisky, I think,' Theo said, standing. 'I can roll us a joint, if you'd like.'

'If it's your shout ...'

As Theo opened the door to the verandah, he called out, 'By the way, I put a few things out on the desk in the office.'

The reply, though good-natured, echoed with resignation: 'Make yourself at home.'

***

It was a typical Mudgee autumn: warm days, chilly nights, the kind where you sweated in a jumper but shivered in shorts. Oliver didn't usually smoke. The weed soothed him but at the same time made him edgy. Slowed everything down. He couldn't stop twitching his left leg. The whisky was peaty, and sitting on the verandah with his brother and smoking pot made him feel like a teenager again.

'What's that hole out near your shed? Are you planning on burying some bodies?'

Oliver laughed. 'Come for a walk and I'll show you.'

Crickets chittered in the cold as the brothers headed towards the hole. Oliver was still dressed in his boots from the wine show, but Theo loped through the grass sans shoes.

'Sorry it took so long to come around,' Theo said unexpectedly. 'I've been back for a while. Guess I was confused about a fair bit.'

'Hey,' Oliver said, 'don't worry about it.'

Don't worry about it? Jesus. Oliver knew he should be encouraging a more productive dialogue with Theo. Why didn't he want to open the door now that his brother had finally arrived? Would Theo's betrayal come to the fore before he was ready to properly tackle it with him? Oliver closed his eyes. Knew that he was retreating too far internally again. It was a habit he was honing instead of expunging.

'Nah, really,' his brother said after a while, expelling a torrent of smoke. 'It was pretty shitty of me not to get in touch at all. Thought about it a few times. It got so complicated I just didn't do anything.'

'Don't worry about it,' Oliver repeated.

He walked to the wine shed and flicked on a floodlight, and then joined Theo back at the edge of the trench. 'It's for a barrel of wine,' he explained, pointing down into the abyss. 'You bury it under the ground and the temperature stays consistent.'

'Does it make the wine better?' Theo asked.

'In a place like Mudgee, where you go from minus-five to forty degrees in a few months, I hope that it does.'

Theo only nodded.

A minute later, Oliver surprised himself by asking, 'Do you think about her much?'

'Mum?'

'Yeah.'

'All the time,' Theo said, emitting smoke through his nose. 'In the early morning, when I can't get back to sleep and everything is dark and cold and sombre. Know what I remembered yesterday?'

'What?'

'Coming home from school one day. She was crying, sitting on the piano stool. When I asked her what was wrong, she told me that Miles said to her she wasn't allowed to visit Nan without him. And do you know what I remember? The feeling. Like an elevator had fallen down my throat and into my stomach.'

'What did you say to her?' Oliver asked, almost urgently – suddenly feeling stupid when he realised everything was twenty years too late. 'Where was I?'

'Don't know ...' Theo paused. 'I remember telling her, "Just go." I was standing awkwardly in the door. Told her he's all talk and full of shit and that if she left we'd go with her.'

'What did she say to that?'

'Said it wasn't that easy.'

Oliver exhaled deeply. 'I wish …'

He didn't finish. The screech of tyres made its way across the valley. Kids doing burnouts. Probably racing. A dog, in the distance, barked in protest.

'Anyway,' Theo said, 'how settled are you here? Have you got a dog?'

'I'm settled. Have set myself up without any distractions. Can just make wine and do my thing. I must say, I love that your definition of settled means there's an animal.'

'Well,' Theo said. 'You won't own one if you don't plan on hanging around long.'

'The vineyard manager has a greyhound.'

'Is he the one who lives in that place up near the gate?'

'Yeah, that's Gabe.'

'Good bloke?'

'Yeah. He looks after nearly everything. I make the wine, he does the rest.'

'Married?'

'Now that his kind of marriage is legal, he might be one day.' Oliver paused. 'He's private. Don't tell him I told you that.'

Theo grinned. 'How about you? Got a partner or what?'

'Penny,' Oliver said. 'She owns the wine bar in town.'

'We'll have to check it out.'

'Sure.'

'Are you in love?'

Oliver scratched his fingers. His thumb ripped the corner of his middle fingernail; he noticed he'd drawn blood. 'Love's a big word.'

Theo was staring into his brother's eyes, waiting for Oliver to say something else.

'C'mon. Is she the one?'

'Maybe,' Oliver said. 'She doesn't know anything about Mum. The past.'

Theo grimaced slightly, before smiling. 'I'm sure a relationship built on omissions isn't the same as one built on lies.'

When Oliver didn't reply, Theo asked if he wanted another smoke. Oliver declined; he was already feeling tired.

'Hey, there's something I should show you.' From his jacket pocket, Theo pulled out a small piece of paper folded in half. 'Read it.'

He opened the letter, and Theo flashed a phone torch over the handwriting.

Theo. Come to Oliver's winery. Search for Four Dogs Missing. You'll find me there. We need to talk. Chase

'I'm guessing he's not here,' Theo said.

Oliver looked at his brother, then again at the letter. 'I've only seen him once since we were kids,' he said. 'And when we were young, he was basically a bully.'

'I thought it was a bit strange,' Theo said. 'He did the full one-eighty, apparently. Works in state politics.'

Oliver remembered Chase turning up at the vineyard in spring last year, completely out of the blue. He had barely changed since adolescence. Other than time having dyed the edges of his hairline grey, Chase looked scarily the same. He'd matured, though, that was for sure. Oliver remembered thinking that. And then after his visit he'd completely disappeared again, until a random and almost perfunctory kind of Christmas card had arrived in the mail.

'Hang on a minute. What's strange? Him getting in touch, or saying that he's here?'

'Both,' Theo said, raising his eyebrows. 'Hey, it's your favourite half-brother. Haven't seen you since I left home, haven't taken a speck of interest, but I'm showing up to one twin's place and writing the other a note.'

They walked back to the house and sat on the verandah. Theo began rolling himself another joint on the arm of the chair. 'You sure you don't want one?'

Oliver felt like he needed it. A letter from Chase? He couldn't help but wonder whether it was a fabrication, something Theo had invented as an excuse to visit. But there was something authentic about the letter. The handwriting, perhaps. It was familiar to him.

'Better not. I've got a lesson in the morning.'

Theo ran his tongue along the thin strip of the cigarette paper then picked a fleck of weed or tobacco from his lip. 'Piano?'

Oliver took a sip of whisky. 'How'd you know?'

'I went exploring.'

Oliver imagined Theo walking around the house, out into the yard, finding the barrels, wine bottles and the piano in the shed.

'You bought it back, didn't you?'

After their father was taken away, the family possessions had been sold off. A lady across the street purchased the piano for her granddaughter, an apparent prodigy. When Oliver approached her years later with enough money to reclaim it, she'd already sold it to someone else.

'Took me a while to track her down.'

'I thought Heather bought it?'

'She did. But her granddaughter flaked. She sold it to some hippie in Byron Bay.'

Oliver didn't want to tell Theo he'd had to pay over five grand to have it transported to Mudgee. Although the man had kept the piano inside his home beside the ocean, it stood against a wall that faced the elements, no open bottle of water inside. Oliver still twitched thinking of the damage time would have done.

'Oliver Wingfield, winemaker and piano saviour. Who's your teacher?'

'A Mudgee lady. She reminds me of Nan. Stern, no sense of humour.'

'Have you got your chops back?' Theo asked.

'Getting there.'

Oliver closed his eyes and remembered the scales he used to play, the speed and ferocity he'd force on himself. The metronome ticking diligently as he struggled to keep pace.

'Can I help with anything?' Theo said.

'What do you mean?'

'Like, around the vineyard. Pruning vines and shit.'

'It's coming into winter. Not much to do.'

Theo nodded. 'Yeah, I get it. I just didn't want to sit around the house being useless. You know, if you need me, I can help. Earn my board, start something new. I think it's time for a change.'

'Well. Thanks, mate,' Oliver said. 'I'll show you around tomorrow.'

'Sweet. That sounds good.'

Neither said anything for a while. Oliver wished he was better at keeping the conversation flowing. He wanted to ask if Theo had a partner, but suspected he already knew the answer. Theo owned nothing save for the belongings in his bag. He wouldn't have shown up otherwise.

Oliver knew Theo would have heard of his circumstances. Just shy of age twenty-eight, Oliver had purchased twenty hectares with old, decrepit vines. Some viticultural love and sensory technology, developed in the States, along with some daring had turned the vineyard into a success. The wines won awards. Cellared well.

Oliver Wingfield's odd behaviour – the way he shied away from the media – only amplified the demand.

Oliver was keen to rekindle his relationship with his brother. He wanted to ask Theo where he had been and discover the man he'd become in his absence. But he felt protective of what he'd built. It had taken a long time to wash away the past and to be comfortable in the life he'd constructed. There weren't too many people in Mudgee who knew who Oliver was, which was a blessing. Now, with his brother sitting beside him, he wondered whether the past would trickle back into his life. He wasn't sure how long Theo wanted to stay or what would transpire if he did.

Oliver said, 'That spliff knocked me around. I'm going to hit the hay.'

'Hey, Oli. Thanks for ... you know.'

Oliver stood up and the brothers shook hands, which then turned into an awkward embrace. 'I'll give you the grand tour in the morning. The spare bed's good to go.'

Theo was thinking of something else. 'Reckon we should go all Shakespearean and play a trick on your lady? Does she know you have a twin?'

'What? She will now,' Oliver said. 'You look younger than me. Less grey hair.'

'Piss off.'

'I better get you out of town quick smart with all that talk. You've always gotten me into trouble.'

Theo only took a deep drag of the joint and, as he exhaled, began to laugh.

***

'You're distracted.'

'What?' Oliver lifted his fingers from the keys and glanced sideways at Ida Munroe. She was standing next to him, leaning over his shoulder, fiddling with the metronome.

'Distracted,' she said, clearly pronouncing each syllable, as though berating a burdensome infant. Oliver caught a trace of coffee on her breath.

'S'pose I pay you handsomely for your candour.'

It was true, Oliver couldn't concentrate. He was supposed to be focused on the piano and all he could think of was his twin. Knowing Theo was back at the cottage made him feel edgy. And something about Theo in the flesh reminded him of his mother, and he couldn't stop thinking about her.

He looked at the polished keys of the piano as his fingers moved over them and wished he'd known the last piece she'd played on them. He could still remember the exact shape of her milky-white hands, the thinness of her fingers peppered with freckles. The ease with which she stretched them across the keys. Oliver wasn't sure he'd ever be good enough to learn whatever it was she'd last performed on this piano. His mother had become famous for her painting, not her piano playing. To Oliver, attempting anything like her work on canvas was simply sacrilege because Julia's art was sacrosanct. The piano felt more appropriate. Collaborative; like he was channelling something from the past.

When he woke up that morning, he'd left the bedroom to grab a glass of water and heard his brother snoring in the spare room. What did Theo know about him? Or, more pressingly, what did he know about Theo? Over the years, he'd tried to find him – on social media, the internet, via friends – but his efforts had yielded little other than disappointment. A trail of breadcrumbs leading nowhere. There was a Facebook profile in Theo's name that was so nondescript it was impossible to decide whether it was even him. Oliver typed his own name into Google and myriad results appeared, all about his winery. The top result was from *Gourmet Traveller Wine*. He couldn't remember reading the article, in print or online. He opened the webpage and scrolled down:

> It's pretty clear Wingfield and Aitken aren't interested in fame or recognition. For starters, there's no cellar door. You can't call the winery because they don't have a phone. Fax? Very funny. Email? Definitely not. The only way you can communicate with the winery is by post. Forget a marketing department, an outsourced public relations firm, a multi-layered distribution chain.

Towards the end, there was an interview woven into the piece. He remembered that, three or so years ago, Gabe had convinced him to invite some journalists for a tasting.

> 'We like to let the wine speak for itself,' Wingfield says to me quietly. 'It's always been a bit of an eclectic mix: a California-trained winemaker, a Spanish climate, some original Italian plantings. Super Tuscan-style wines with Mudgee terroir. Ultimately though, I just hope people enjoy the fruit and the wonders of fermentation as much as we do here.'
>
> And they do. Of the eight hundred or so cases sent out to their sole distributor, they don't take long to sell out, often claiming three to four times their original value in auctions or in bottle shops. Before Wingfield moved on to

talk to someone else, I had to ask about the name. 'Well, the property was for sale, and beside the sale sign was a board with "four dogs missing" sprayed on it. No one could ever tell me about the dogs or the person who wrote the sign. It was all a big mystery. I needed a name so I kept it.'

Before closing the window, Oliver looked at the photo used in the article. It was of him and Gabe, both holding wineglasses and having a conversation with someone off-camera. He knew that Theo would have read the article. If Theo had been back in Australia for two years as he'd revealed, why was he only coming to visit now? Why would Chase appear out of nowhere, writing to Theo when he hadn't even got in touch with Oliver?

Ida was clicking her fingers inches from Oliver's face.

'These polyrhythms. When I've gone you're going to sit yourself down with the metronome and focus on your timing. You're not getting there fast enough.'

'Nice change. I'm normally scolded for arriving too quickly.'

Ida moved towards the barn door. 'I tried to warn you the "Nocturnes" would plague your sense of perfectionism.'

'I'm nothing if not persistent.' Oliver stayed seated on the stool, flicking through the music.

'Each hand needs to play its share evenly, fluently, in time. At least, this must be the case before you are capable of true expression.'

Ida picked up her bag, signalling the lesson was over. Her grey hair was cut straight at her neck, a pair of crescent-shaped glasses leaving an indentation on the inside of her nose. Oliver had been told she was the best in the area. Serious, with an unknown past. He was too scared to ask; he had never seen her anywhere other than his shed. It suited them both well. Over the last three years, they'd debated old pianos and scales and composers and seldom indulged in anything personal.

'I saw your wine for sale in town,' Ida said, with a lofty gaze to the bottles lined up on the table. 'Far too dear.'

'They tell me that. Guessing you didn't partake?'

'My students don't pay me enough.'

Oliver nodded. 'I thought they didn't practise enough?'

'Both,' she said, a small hint of a smile on her lips. 'Before I go, three things. One, I don't barter. Even if one bottle of your wine is worth about three of my lessons. Two, if you avoid your scales again I'll know. And three, if you get too frustrated with Chopin, try some Debussy instead.'

Oliver cringed. 'Debussy is gross. Far too flowery for a country boy like me.'

He stood up and walked his teacher to the door.

'You're a strange man, Oliver. You know that, don't you?'

Didn't he know it. But he'd made peace with his strangeness, his desire for solitude, long ago. Oliver had constructed his life perfectly: if he was closer with Ida, he might have told her that he was worried Theo was going to upend it, bring everything crashing back down again.

3.

By the time Oliver arrived at Penny's duplex later that night, the temperature had dropped ten degrees. The cold took him by surprise; it was like stepping into a fridge, the kind of weather he hadn't expected until winter.

'Can I help you?' Penny said, a slight smile at the edge of her lips.

'Sorry to bother you. My car just broke down outside and I was looking for some shelter for the evening. Before the snow sets in.'

Penny nearly broke character. 'Sorry to say, but this hasn't been a bed and breakfast for many years.'

Oliver feigned surprise. He wasn't as good at this as Penny. It was something they'd done from the beginning. Play-acted when they arrived in each other's presence.

'Is there any chance I can convince you otherwise?' Oliver said. 'I brought along a bottle of Chateau Figeac, and I thought it might be nice to share it together?' He flashed her the bottle, fingers at the bottom, a sommelier proffering their pride.

'Premier Grand Cru?' Penny said, fully opening the door with one hand, glass of red for him in the other. She kissed him swiftly on the lips. 'Why didn't you say so?'

'I thought we could celebrate.' Oliver took the wineglass and Penny closed the door behind him, before she grabbed her own glass from the coffee table. 'I realised that sometime last week marked two years since we've been acting terribly together and sharing deliciously expensive booze.'

'That's too generous,' Penny said, taking the bottle and moving to the kitchen. 'Time certainly flies. How has your day been?'

'I had a lesson with Ida this morning and showed my brother around the vineyard this arvo. It's been … interesting.'

'I'm sure. I'm keen to hear everything about this estranged twin. Even more excited to meet him.'

'Maybe in a few months. If you're lucky. He's more of a recluse than me.'

'Impossible,' Penny mocked, moving to the sofa and sitting down. 'Will you be proud to know I managed to take the whole day off? On a Friday.'

'Incredibly.'

Oliver sat down next to Penny, who reclined and put her feet over his lap. 'It has been relaxing, although I've been worried about you.'

He looked quizzically at her. 'Why?'

'Well,' she said, taking a sip of wine. 'The twin brother you haven't seen for over a decade shows up out of nowhere. That'd rock anyone.'

'Yeah, well,' he said, 'it's been weird. He reckons Chase sent him a note asking to meet him here. I'm not sure what to make of the whole thing.'

Penny moved her feet and sat up slightly. 'Who's Chase?'

Oliver sighed. 'I've told you about him?'

Placing the wine on the coffee table, Penny stood up suddenly. 'No, you haven't really told me anything about your family. Other than an estranged twin.'

'There isn't that much to tell.'

'Right.'

She walked to the kitchen, where Oliver could see her leaning on the bench.

When they'd first met, something had clicked between them instantly, a feeling Oliver hadn't registered in previous relationships. He'd always been relatively independent, but he enjoyed spending time with Penny. They understood each other's need for intimacy and privacy. While he wanted to tell her everything about his family, he was worried if she found out the truth, she'd run a mile; he also knew if she found out from somebody else later, she wouldn't forgive him for the omission. He had mentioned once that the art adorning his living-room wall was painted by his mother. He was hoping, perhaps naively, that Penny had no clue as to their status or worth. So far, he'd managed to keep it that way.

'Chase is my older half-brother,' Oliver said, following her into the kitchen. 'I've seen him once since I was nine. He was a bad kid. He's got his life now and I've got mine.'

Penny approached him, nodding slowly. 'You can tell me these things. You know that, don't you? Please don't leave me in the dark.'

'I know. I honestly thought I'd mentioned him.' He kissed her on the cheek, tucking a wisp of her hair behind her ear. 'I'm sorry.'

They walked back out to the living room, where Oliver picked up a book from the coffee table. 'What's this weighty tome?'

'*Too Much Lip*. Nothing that would interest you.'

'Are you still eschewing books by straight white males?'

Penny smiled. 'Too right. I'm on the Indigenous train, at the moment.'

'Is it good?'

'It's good to read something that you can feel actually speaking to you, yeah.'

'Craig would be proud.'

'I don't think my father's read a book in his life.'

Oliver had met her dad, Craig, a handful of times. Reassured by his comforting smile, Oliver had warmed to him earlier and more easily than he had to Penny's mother. Katrina was a private schoolgirl from Balmain who, during her youth, had a penchant for bad boys. Craig, a rugby-league-playing Wiradjuri teenager from Dubbo, was the antithesis of the men Katrina had grown up with. Despite her parents' protests, Katrina had married him, ending up pregnant with Penny, followed by two boys. After the divorce – when the kids were older – she went back to university, before going on to practise law for a big firm somewhere near Martin Place.

'Craig's a good bloke, though,' Oliver said.

Penny grinned at the joke. One day, Craig had farewelled Oliver and Penny from his place with: *'I'll see you blokes later.' 'And you wonder why I grew up a tomboy,'* Penny had said as they drove away, the sun reflecting off her tanned and freckled cheeks, her grin and sass all the more beautiful in the afternoon light.

'I need to try harder. Read more. I haven't done much since I bought the wine bar.'

'It's a pretty busy gig.'

Penny looked down at the book she was flipping in her hands. 'You've got to be able to balance things, right?'

'Not always as easy as that.'

'As a woman running a business, some days "easy" has ditched the dictionary.'

'You're better at it than anyone I know, although—'

Penny grinned, interrupting him. 'Did I make it sound like you weren't already getting laid tonight? By all means, keep going.'

'I was going to say that you're the only wine-bar owner I know.'

'Intimately or at all?'

'Both.' Oliver laughed. 'I'm jesting, but not about you being the best in the business.'

The doorbell rang.

'I really must be,' Penny said, taking a long sip of wine. 'Because that's someone from my work. Delivering a pizza.'

He kissed her – again – on the lips. 'I think you're too good for me, and I'm hoping you'll never notice.'

***

'So,' Penny said halfway through dinner, 'when do I get to meet him?'

Oliver drained the last of his wine. Until now, he hadn't realised how warm the fireplace was. 'Whenever you'd like. Tomorrow. The day after tomorrow. I could bring him into the bar.'

Penny tossed her hair back and tied it into a ponytail. 'That'd be good. It might be hard to know who I'm talking to, though. Maybe message me what colour shirt you're wearing so I can spot the difference?'

'We look more alike as we've gotten older,' Oliver said. 'It surprised me. When I first walked out of the shed and saw him standing at the end of the driveway, I thought I was looking at myself. Like I'd gone troppo.'

'Well,' Penny said, 'already far too late for that.'

Oliver flicked her on the earlobe. 'It's good to get out of the house. It's been nice catching up with Theo, but I'm glad to be here.'

'I like that.'

'Me too.'

'How long is he staying?'

Oliver paused. A car's tyres skidded in the distance. 'I haven't been game enough to ask.'

***

Oliver lay on his back, spent with pleasure, and listened to Penny's exhalations. Moonlight leaked through a wedge of open blind. Instead of drifting off happily, he was disturbed to find himself feeling guilty for leaving Theo alone. He felt bad, but he'd needed to get away. Take things slowly. Catch up gradually.

An old wives' tale said you could feel what your twin was thinking, that you could sense their euphoria, or that you'd know if they were in trouble. Oliver thought of Theo a lot, that was true, but he could never actually *feel* his presence. He hadn't felt anything the years Theo was travelling, and nor had he felt anything during the years Theo didn't get in touch with him. Oliver wasn't spiritual or superstitious enough to believe it. He thought it was about as likely as masturbation sending you blind, giving you hairy palms.

***

The next morning, as Oliver drove into the vineyard, he spotted his neighbour's white Land Cruiser ute outside Gabe's cottage. Murray regarded Oliver and his biodynamic methods with a healthy dose of scepticism. The Vernons' label was everything Oliver despised in a winery: standard grapes, sprayed with pesticides and picked too late in the season. Hot with alcohol, one-dimensional, jammy sweet. *Cheap wine for tourists* was Oliver's diplomatic answer. Over the years, Gabe had tried to get Oliver and Murray to socialise, but their attitudes were too polarised for them to interract in harmony, even outside of work. As Oliver's car inched towards the gate, Gabe and Murray exited the house. He wound down the window.

'He's too young for you, Gabe. He'll only break your heart.' Oliver enjoyed riling Murray, who, despite his friendship with Gabe, was conservative at heart.

Murray donned an Akubra and opened his car door, turning to Oliver as he did so. 'I thought you might be the twin, but I've heard he isn't a cockhead.'

'He's worse than me,' Oliver quipped.

'Doubt it.' Murray climbed into his ute and kicked over the engine. Gabe tapped the tray in farewell as he walked to stand next to Oliver's open window. They watched Murray drive away, a trail of dust in his wake.

'What's the go?' Gabe said.

'With you and Murray?'

'Please. He's straighter than a honeymooner's dick.' Gabe quickly changed the subject. 'How long is Theo staying? I'm worried.'

Oliver took the car out of gear. 'You're always worried.'

'Maybe you should put him to work. From what you've told me, he'd be gone after a day.'

***

The front door was ajar.

'Theo?' Oliver called. No reply. He padded to the kitchen and ground some coffee beans, put filter paper in the machine and watched the liquid drip down into the jug. There was a blanket slung across the lounge and the television was still on. Theo had left it on standby, its brand name roving around the black screen like a fish confined to a tank. Oliver found the remote and switched it off. He wandered about, adjusted the cushions, folded the blanket and spent some time tidying the room. He was already keen to be alone in his house again.

While he waited for the coffee, he walked out to the shed to check on the wine and make sure everything was going right in the last ferment. He had tried to discuss the process with Theo yesterday. He told him about how they harvested the vines, how they decided the time to pick and plunge, what happened in the barrel, but even halfway through the explanation Oliver could feel his brother's attention waning.

He looked at the data on his laptop and noticed that Orson still hadn't made any updates, so he decided to give him a call. The phone began to ring, before eventually being diverted to a message bank. A recorded version of Orson told him, in his thick Californian accent, to leave his name and number and he'd get back to Oliver as soon as it was convenient.

'Mr Denver. It's your favourite winemaker from Australia. Call me when you get this.'

Something wasn't right. He walked inside again and poured himself some coffee.

'Theo, would you like a cuppa?' he called out. No reply. Theo might have gone to town. If he had, it would have been a long walk along the only road that led to Mudgee's centre. Oliver hadn't seen anyone walking on his way home, and the kombi was still sitting in the driveway.

The bathroom door was open, so Theo wasn't in the shower. Oliver could see the office desk was empty down the hallway. As he moved towards the spare room, he noticed a lone blot of blood on the wooden boards.

That was odd. Feeling somewhat uneasy, Oliver asked, 'You awake, mate?' as he slowly pushed open the door.

His cup fell to the floor with a crash. Theo lay on his side on the floor, a plash of vomit, of blood, dripping down his chin. The wooden boards were covered in tacky little pools of maroon. There was a piece of broken glass – from the whisky bottle – in Theo's hand, and his throat had been cut, a clean slice below his Adam's apple.

The wall was sullied with blood, and when he looked down, Oliver saw a hunk of Theo's hair curled around itself on the wooden floor. The mop bucket from the laundry was there, filled with cold water and what smelled like bleach.

Before Oliver even moved towards his brother, before he turned him onto his back and ripped Theo's shirt open, pumping his hands over his chest (it was identical to his own, even after so many years), he knew that Theo was gone. The blood had started to crust around Theo's neck. Attempting CPR was redundant, there was not a modicum of sense in doing so, but he persisted, desperately.

When Oliver finally stood and moved away from his brother's body, he saw Theo look at him one last time. *He just looked at me! He must be alive!* But Theo's head was scabbed and battered and his skin was veiny and paper white.

His eyes, still open, were charged with blood.

Dear Theo,

My name is Angie Proctor. To be perfectly frank, I'm not entirely sure you'll remember me. You gave me the impression you make a sport out of flirting with women who dine alone in wine bars. We met a few months ago in Sydney. I had just finished a long day at court and you were sitting beside me at Fix Wine. You told me sauvignon blanc from the Adelaide Hills was a 'yummy mummy' drink and that I should have something a little more 'complex'. I told you to fuck off and mind your own business. Despite insulting my palate, you somehow managed to pique my curiosity enough to ensure that I stayed for another glass, which then turned into another bottle, something I seldom do during the week. The latter part of the night is hazy, but I do remember briefly joining you in a small apartment somewhere close to the city. While I won't go into what transpired, I remember panicking about the time and leaving the room, suddenly. We didn't trade phone numbers or any further details, which is why this is being delivered to you as a letter. The only speck of luck I've had in tracking you down is that 'Theodore' and 'Wingfield' are both rare names. Maybe you walked straight out of a Tennessee Williams drama and into the wine bar?

Writing this has made me realise how much I like the romance of letters; not in the sense of 'love', but the measured and deliberate attempt to hold onto something a little antiquated or old-fashioned because of the satisfaction to be gained. Perhaps it's nostalgic, but I'm glad to be delivering my news like this rather than on social media.

Admittedly, I did try to find you on Facebook. It's safe to say that your online presence is best described as 'invisible', and I've flirted with the idea that you're potentially a figment of my imagination. Did I sleep with a handsome stranger one Thursday, or did I conjure you out of nowhere?

Some days, being a criminal barrister can have its advantages. For instance, if I need to track down someone who wishes to remain invisible, I have a surplus of excellent private investigators who are able to find someone like you or me before we've eaten breakfast. They gave me your address in Chippendale. Also a phone number, which I'm too scared to use.

Theo, I wanted to let you know that I'm pregnant. It's as tawdry typing this as I'm sure it is for you reading it. I'm not writing to you to seek an opinion, but I guess I do feel like canvassing the situation with you. After all, you did manage to convince me that riesling is probably a better accompaniment to a bad day than a sauvignon blanc. I may be in the final trimester by the time this letter reaches you, but I thought it's better late than never.

If, of course, you want absolutely nothing to do with me and wish to continue your plight of anonymity, I will disappear and you'll never hear from me again. If you'd like to write to me, you'll find my address on the back of this envelope.

Yours,

Angie

4.

As he waited in the interview room, Oliver wondered whether or not he was a suspect. Wondered if the police knew what had happened but hadn't told him what was going on. He could feel sweat spreading under his arms. Ever since he was a teenager, police stations had made him nervous.

Sergeant Mulaney had been the first policeman to arrive at the house after Oliver called triple zero. Oliver didn't know too many people in Mudgee, but he'd seen Mulaney plenty of times: in the newspaper, at wine events, Rocky's café. He was related to the mayor, somehow; was as entrenched in the community as the town clock.

'He was definitely murdered?' Oliver had asked, looking at the sergeant, trying to read whether he was holding something back. 'I just don't know who would do this ... But Theo wouldn't have cut his own throat, would he?'

'It's too early to talk about that yet, mate,' Sergeant Mulaney had said, agitatedly scratching his neck. His nose was splotchy pink.

'Let's wait until the plain clothes arrive. And we'll need a toxicology report.'

Gabe had stood there next to him, dumbfounded. Out the front of Oliver's house there were uniformed police officers, ambulance officers, a journalist from the *Mudgee Guardian* and random cars parked in the driveway.

It didn't make sense. From the bruises on Theo's body, it appeared as though he'd been in a fight. Plus, he looked sick. Poisoned?

After Oliver had been sitting in the interview room for half an hour, a detective arrived, a manila folder and notebook in her right hand and a bottle of water in her left. She smiled at Oliver and sat down opposite him, producing a small recorder. Then she leaned down and placed her water bottle on the floor next to her chair.

'My apologies for keeping you waiting. I'm also deeply sorry for your loss, Mr Wingfield.'

'Oliver,' he said.

'Right. My name is Detective Inspector Geraldine Everson. Before we have a quick chat, can I get you something to drink? A tea? Coffee? Water?'

'I'm okay.'

She nodded her head, as though she'd already known that would be his answer. Everson was dressed in jeans and a black leather jacket, and her blonde hair was pulled back into a bun. She was older than Oliver, but not by much.

'This is an electronically recorded interview between Detective Geraldine Everson and Oliver Wingfield.' She read the date and time and asked Oliver to spell his full name and state his date of birth.

'Oliver, apart from the people who have just spoken, is there anyone else in the room?'

'No.'

'Thank you,' she said. 'Now, I'm going to ask you a few questions in relation to the alleged murder of Theodore Wingfield. You do not have to say or do anything if you do not wish to, is that understood?'

It felt so surreal to hear it spoken aloud. *The alleged murder of Theodore Wingfield.*

'Yes.'

'Whatever you say or do will be electronically recorded and may be used in court. Do you understand that?'

'I do.'

'Do you agree to participate in an electronically recorded interview?'

'Yes.'

'Has any threat been made to you to make you take part in this interview?'

'No.'

'Has any promise or inducement been held out to you to make you take part in this interview?'

'Is all this really necessary?'

Everson smiled ruefully. 'I'm sorry, Oliver. Just the procedure. While our chat is informal, I just want to make sure everything I do is by the book and stored, should we need anything later. Does that make sense?'

Oliver nodded. 'Yeah.'

'Do you know what inducement means?'

'I do,' Oliver said.

'Has any inducement been held out for you to take part today, Oliver?'

'No.'

'As I said before, this is part of the investigation. I must tell you I am able to make you a copy of the electronic recording at the conclusion of this interview if that is something you would like. Is that understood?'

'Yes.' *For fuck's sake.*

For what felt like the first time in minutes, there was silence. Everson picked up the bottle of water from the floor and took a swig.

'From what I understand, Oliver, Theo Wingfield was your identical twin?'

'Yeah,' Oliver said quickly. 'Do you know what happened to him?'

Everson straightened. 'It appears he'd been in a fight. Someone tried to clean up some blood.'

'I don't think he was the kind to kill himself.'

Everson raised her eyebrows, surprised by the statement. 'Were you and Theo close?'

Oliver shrugged. 'Not really. We didn't hate each other, but this was the first time I'd seen Theo in over a decade.'

Everson pursed her lips. 'Obviously, you'd fallen out.'

'No,' Oliver said. 'He spent years and years overseas. I didn't hear from him.'

'Not at all?' Everson paused, holding eye contact for a long moment. 'I couldn't imagine not talking to my sister for a decade. Without a reason, of course.'

'Perhaps our relationship isn't as strong as the one you share with your sister.'

'So, you admit there were issues?'

'Nothing worth mentioning,' Oliver said. 'Twin-brother

stuff. We were close, then we weren't. There's no family to tie us together.'

Everson scribbled something in her pad. 'How long had Theo been staying with you?'

'He arrived on Thursday afternoon.'

'How long was he staying?'

Oliver put his hands in the air. 'I don't know. He didn't say.'

'Why was Theo visiting now?' Everson pressed.

Oliver shook his head. 'Your guess is as good as mine. He said that it was time to catch up. That he'd been back in Australia for a couple of years.'

'Did he mention what he'd been doing before his visit?'

'Not really,' Oliver said. 'I asked a couple of questions, but he always changed the subject. I didn't think much of it.'

'Okay.' Everson opened the manila folder and pulled out two large black-and-white photographs that had been printed on glossy paper. She gently placed them on the table, in a slow reveal. 'Do you recognise this man, this woman?'

The man in the photo had a beard, receding hairline and dark curls down to the shoulders. Maybe the beginning of a tattoo towards the base of his neck. The woman had dark hair pulled away from her face. Prominent cheekbones. Both photos were mugshots, dated years earlier.

'No.'

'Not familiar at all?'

Oliver shook his head, murmuring, 'Sorry.'

Everson slipped the photographs back into the folder.

'What do these people have to do with this?'

The detective exhaled. 'The man and woman in the photos are pretty heavily involved in the movement of illicit substances, art forgery, importation of fake wine.' She licked the very tips of her fingers and picked up another photo, where the man had been snapped walking alongside Oliver's twin brother. Fleetingly, Oliver thought he was looking at a photo of himself, taken somewhere he'd never been. A sleight of hand.

'So, Theo was involved with these people?'

'Maybe. We're wondering whether they had anything to do with his death.'

Oliver ran a hand through his hair. Theo dealing drugs? It was certainly plausible. Oliver didn't know anything about his brother anymore. It didn't feel right, but he didn't know enough to reject the theory.

'Do you think he was murdered because of his involvement?'

Everson shrugged her shoulders. 'I was hoping you could help me there.'

'I have no idea about any of this.'

'Oliver, sorry if this sounds offensive, you must forgive me ... but your brother's dead. There's really no point in trying to protect him anymore. If there's anything you can offer to help us, we can find out who killed him and—'

'He's never mentioned anything about drugs or hanging out with thugs.' Oliver blenched at the unintentional rhyme. 'Look, there's no reason I would withhold anything from you. He showed up on my doorstep and he didn't say why. He seemed lost. Said he was after a fresh start.'

Everson sighed. 'Did he mention anything about where he'd been, where he was going?'

'No,' Oliver said, stretching the word like a tired child. 'Only that he'd been back in Australia for a couple of years and was keen to get in touch.'

Oliver was reluctant to talk about the letter from Chase. Where was the letter? Had he taken it, or had he returned it to Theo? He didn't want to talk about his half-brother or his father with the police.

Everson frowned and looked at Oliver like he was hiding something. 'How did that make you feel?'

'What do you mean?'

Everson leaned back in her chair, threaded her fingers together behind her head and stretched. 'Knowing he'd been in Australia for two years and was only coming to see you now.'

Oliver shrugged. 'Yeah, it stung a little. If you knew Theo, though, you'd understand.'

'Where are your parents?'

'They passed away. Years ago.'

'Both?'

'Yeah. Both dead. We lived with our grandmother until we left school. She's dead, too.'

His father's voice, out of nowhere, reverberated in his head: *We're all dead in your eyes, Oliver. We didn't 'pass away'. Tell her we're dead. Don't fucken sugar-coat it.*

'My condolences,' Everson said, before taking another sip of water and writing something down. 'Just you and Theo?'

Oliver nodded. 'Just us.'

Everson was onto another train of thought. 'Do you have any enemies, Oliver?'

'Do I?' Everson nodded and Oliver exhaled. 'Am I popular in Mudgee? Definitely not. But I don't think I have any real enemies.'

'You don't think?'

'Well, no. I don't.'

'But not many friends?'

The truth of it was Oliver barely had any friends at all. Gabe, Clare, Orson, Penny, Rocky – who owned a café in town – and the rest, well, acquaintances at most.

'Why aren't you popular in Mudgee?'

Oliver looked up at the clock. He was thirsty and found himself craving a cigarette. His body was yearning for sleep, but his head was still spinning. 'I do things a little differently. With the wine.'

'Differently to other winemakers?'

'You could say that. I respect some people here, but there are a lot who … don't like what I do. Think that biodynamics are stupid, for one.'

'Like who?'

'Murray, my neighbour. His brother, Charlie. They make a lot of wine in town. They're old-schoolers, and are pretty popular, you know. We don't really have a whole lot in common.'

'Have you ever had a fight with them? Is there a reason either brother would visit you at home?'

'Wait,' Oliver said, sitting back. 'Are you implying that you think whoever killed Theo came for me?'

Everson bowed her head with a tight smile. 'I'm just asking questions, Oliver. I'm not implying anything.'

'Well,' Oliver said, 'the answer to that question is I don't much like Murray or Charlie, but I wouldn't pick a fight with them, and I don't think they'd pick a fight with me.'

'Even though you just won the local wine trophy and they didn't?'

Oliver snorted. 'The one with three nights' accommodation in Sawtell?'

The detective nodded.

'I don't think that's enough of a motive for a reboot of *Midsomer Murders*.'

Everson wrote a couple of extra lines in her notepad. 'You weren't home last night?'

'No. I was staying at my girlfriend's place in town.'

'Didn't go back home to visit at all?'

Oliver shook his head. Everson looked at her wrist, as if she was expecting to see a watch. It was bare. 'Can you just reply for the record for me please, Oliver. You didn't duck home to get a bottle of wine or anything? Late last night or early this morning?'

'No,' Oliver said. 'Penny can confirm that. Why do you keep asking?'

'Your colleague, Gabriel. He heard a car driving down to your place at a little after one this morning,' Everson said, stacking her papers and staring straight into Oliver's eyes. 'He didn't think anything of it. Thought it was you coming home.'

***

Gabe drove him away from the police station in silence. As they approached the vineyard's gate, Oliver said, 'You didn't tell me you heard a car last night.'

Gabe pulled up in front of his cottage, where Murray's Land Cruiser had been only a few hours earlier. 'It makes me sick, Oli. Knowing I heard whoever went down there. I looked, but I couldn't see who it was. I just assumed it was you or Penny.'

'I'm sorry,' Oliver said.

'Hey.' Gabe placed a firm hand on Oliver's shoulder. 'You have nothing to be sorry about.'

'It's a fucking mess. The detective thinks he's tied up in drugs. Art forgery. Something.'

Gabe shook his head. 'I think you're lucky.'

'What?' Oliver said, a little incredulously.

Gabe scrunched his eyes closed with regret. He switched off the ignition and the interior light flashed on. 'I didn't mean it like that. It's just ... shit. Imagine if they'd come to kill him and gotten the two of you confused? I can't stop thinking about that.'

The thought hadn't even occurred to Oliver. 'Maybe they meant to kill me. Got him, instead.'

'Don't be ridiculous,' his friend said sternly. 'As terrible as it sounds, Theo got involved with the wrong kind of people. Blind Freddy could tell you he was running from someone.'

Oliver didn't know what to feel. He sat in the passenger's seat and didn't say a word.

'It's messed up.'

'Gabe,' Oliver said, sounding harsher than he'd intended. 'My brother's dead. *That's* messed up.'

Gabe frowned. 'You're right. I'm going to go in and put the kettle on. Make us a cuppa.' He closed the car door gently, so that it shut sotto voce, and then he walked into the cottage.

Oliver went to get out, but found himself unable to move.

***

A few hours later, Oliver lay on Penny's bed and thought about his childhood properly for the first time in years.

Theo had always been the cooler twin. Oliver remembered, when they were sixteen, he had come home from a piano lesson to find Theo going down on a girl.

'Shit,' Oliver had said, opening the door to their bedroom and just as quickly half closing it, awkwardly. 'Sorry.'

Oliver didn't recognise her from school. She was naked. Funny that he remembered most her sage-painted nails. She smiled and curled around Theo, burying her head of mousy-blonde hair into his chest. She didn't seem to care that Oliver could see her without anything on.

'I'll watch some TV.'

'Hey, Oli,' Theo said, jumping up and putting on some briefs. 'Go for a walk on the beach or something for us, yeah?'

Oliver nodded, too awkward to argue. 'When are Mum and Dad coming home?'

His brother looked down at his watch. 'Not for another hour.' Theo closed the door, softly.

As Oliver walked on the sand, he wondered how long his mother had left to live. Wondered what news would come from the oncologist. He thought of how different life was going to be once she'd gone. Oliver had never lost anyone before, but he knew it was coming – a nascent storm on the horizon. Was it worse if you lost someone suddenly, or if their demise was so insidious that its impact spread everywhere, and everything receded away from you, slowly?

How could Theo be messing around with a girl?

When he walked in the door an hour later, Theo was sprawled on the lounge, shirtless, flicking through the channels on the television. His father was in the kitchen, straining pasta into a colander. He still remembered the steam wafting through the room.

'Where's Mum?'

Miles looked up, then shook the colander violently, water spilling out in uneven bursts. 'Playing the piano.'

'I've tried talking to her,' Theo said. 'She wants to be alone.'

Oliver walked down the hallway to the spare bedroom. He could hear her moving softly through Bach. When he opened the door, she stopped playing. Oliver sat beside her on the stool. Her bandana had slipped from her forehead. Oliver thought her hair had disappeared altogether, but he saw for the first time blotches of fluff. The room smelled of turpentine.

'I'm not giving up yet,' she told him and kissed his forehead. Then she played a couple of chords and broke into a wounded smile. 'If the world thinks I'm checking out without a fight, well, it doesn't know what's coming. You're the only one who believes I can do it.'

She grabbed his hand. In the silence, Oliver heard the metronome ticking.

***

Oliver awoke sometime in the dark, Theo in his dreams, the way he'd looked after he died. It was nearly six in the morning. He'd had too much wine and then spent the night longing for water. He'd tossed and turned and rolled around for half an hour before abandoning the bed.

'You all right?' Penny asked, as Oliver pulled on a dressing gown.

'Can't sleep. Just going to make some coffee.' When he bent down towards her, he noticed the sleep in her eyes. 'Like any?'

'Not yet,' she said, voice husky. 'I'm going to have a lie-in, if you're okay?'

'Of course,' Oliver said. He leaned in further and kissed her.

He was quiet as he ground the coffee beans. He brewed filter at home, but Penny had an espresso machine.

Once it was seven, he picked up his phone and called Clare. She was an early bird, bound to be awake. She answered after a few rings.

The line was crackly. 'Clare, it's Oliver.'

'I know, darling,' she said. Oliver could barely hear her voice. Then she brought the phone closer to her mouth. 'I heard about your brother. I knew you had one, but not that he'd come to Mudgee. I'm so sorry.'

'He was only visiting,' Oliver said. 'Hadn't seen him for years.'

'Still, fuck. What can I do?'

Oliver sat up straighter and took a sip of his coffee. 'How did you know?'

'Gabe called me,' she said. 'He's worried about you. I think Murray's in shock as well, by all reports.'

'Yeah,' Oliver said, 'all Murray would care about is how the murder will intrude on Mudgee's sterling and untarnished reputation.'

'I don't think so, Oli. You two pretend it's a pissing contest, but he cares about you.'

'He definitely doesn't.'

'Gabe looking after you?'

'Always. It's rattled all of us a bit. The cops think Theo was mixed up in drugs. Possibly got into a fight. Overdosed on something. Murdered. We really don't know.'

'Hopefully, you'll have some answers soon.'

'There's actually another reason I'm calling.'

Oliver heard a couple of dachshunds yap, the sound so piercing that for a moment he had to move the phone away from his ear.

'The boys say good morning.'

'I'm worried about Orson,' Oliver said. Since they'd first met, he'd observed that you had to stick to the script with Clare. She had been a friend of Orson's, and he had first met her when they'd all spent a vintage together in the Napa Valley. 'Have you heard from him?'

'Oh God, Orson. No, I can't say that I have. Why are you worried?'

Oliver stood up and started to make another coffee. 'He hasn't entered any data for a few days. Today is going to be the fifth day.'

'Actually,' Clare said, and then she said the word again and again, like its repetition held the answer to a question she'd failed to ask. 'I had noticed that, too. He might have gone away.'

'I thought the same, but he hasn't returned my call. You know what he's like, glued to his phone.'

'That's true.'

He heard Clare making tea: the sound of a kettle boiling and clicking over. A teaspoon tapping the side of a cup. The thud of the discarded spoon landing in the sink.

'I'm sure they're away or something. Look, I have Valerie's number. Why don't I give her a bell and we'll see where they are?'

'I think that's a good idea.'

'Now,' Clare said, sounding grave. 'I want you to look after yourself, please. I know how far inside your own head you can disappear.'

'I will.'

'I'm serious, Oliver. You call me. Anytime. Day or night, okay? I'm only in Orange. I'll lunge over the mountains if I have to.'

'Thank you.' The wieners started barking again. 'What's got their goat?'

'Oh, probably a couple of leaves that fell four streets away.'

'Keeping you safe.'

'Please, call anytime,' she repeated. 'Eat something. You've got a decent figure to maintain.'

'Behave yourself,' Oliver said, before hanging up the phone. It was something that Theo would have said.

For the first time, Oliver burst into tears.

5.

'Organising your twin's funeral is a perverse way of confronting your own mortality. On a Sunday, no less.'

Oliver sat with Penny at the kitchen table; he gave a feeble nod and squeezed her hand. He was onto his third cup of coffee.

'I just want the fucking thing to be over.'

He had no idea whom to invite, or where it should be held. His brother's driver's licence listed an address in Chippendale, but after some enquiries that morning he discovered Theo hadn't lived there for months. There was no cash in Theo's wallet and bugger-all possessions on him, other than clothes and a couple of books. Oliver was waiting to hear whether he'd even left a will. He thought it was more likely his brother had died intestate.

Oliver was the next of kin. That was obvious. There was no other immediate family left, other than Chase. He was worried about the funeral. Not only because he didn't want to see distant relatives – including Harold, the gallerist who'd launched his mother's art career, whom he'd actively avoided for many years

– but also because he knew Penny would want to come, and he couldn't risk her finding out about his father.

When they'd started dating, he'd flirted with the idea of telling Penny everything. But he'd avoided it at the beginning, and then after months together, it was too late to tell her the truth. The longer he avoided it, the more awkward it became. It was easier to say both his parents had died of cancer. And now he'd lied to the police, hoping that if he fibbed offhandedly enough, they wouldn't press things further; wouldn't discover facts Oliver would rather remain buried. He was surprised by how easily the lie had slipped off his tongue, how little guilt he'd felt sharing it with the police. It was a shield of armour, wasn't it? Would Penny want to be with him if she knew his father was rotting away behind bars for taking—

'Don't worry about it yet. You'll have to wait until you hear from the coroner.' Penny stood up and took their empty cups to the sink. 'I've taken the day off work. We can just watch movies and do nothing.'

'It's okay,' Oliver said. 'I don't think I'll be able to sit still. Too much going on in my head.'

I've already grieved for Theo, he realised. *He's been gone for fifteen years.*

'You're doing better than me,' Penny said, sitting back down. 'When Skye died, I didn't get out of bed for days.'

'How old were you?'

Penny had lived with Craig in Orange during high school. One night, at the vineyard, watching the sunset, she had told Oliver that she'd lost her childhood best friend to brain cancer.

'Seventeen. Fuck, it sucked. My first loss, right before my birthday. Before exams.'

A shitty time, Oliver thought. *A familiar time.*

A tear dwelled at the bottom rim of Penny's eye. 'Even though we kind of knew it was coming, it still stung. Everything happened faster than we thought, and ...'

Oliver squeezed her hand. Penny added, 'Sorry, that's not fair. You don't need to hear about this now.'

'No,' Oliver said. 'Opening up is healthy. I'm sorry I'm not as good at this. I'm trying.'

Penny's hand pressed against his cheek, a gesture of strength. *Remember this*, Oliver thought. *You're letting her in.*

Later, as he walked outside, a police car pulled up beside the kerb. It was Everson and Sergeant Mulaney. Everson exited the driver's side, but Mulaney stayed seated in the car.

'Thought you might be here,' Everson said by way of greeting.

'Any news?' Oliver asked, shielding his eyes from the sun with his hand.

Everson was wearing the same black leather jacket and a pair of Wayfarers on her nose. 'Waiting on some information to come through from the autopsy so we can get a firmer idea of the time of death.'

Oliver nodded. 'I'm trying to organise the funeral. Hard when you don't know who his friends were or where he lived.'

Everson snickered. 'There might be a few shady characters in attendance. Has anyone been in touch?'

'Who do you mean?' Oliver asked.

'Anyone. Theo's employer. No phone calls, no visits?'

Oliver shook his head. 'No visits. Are you sure he was involved with drugs? He has no money. Was driving a beaten-up kombi.'

Everson took a card from her pocket and passed it to Oliver.

'Ring me if anyone calls or shows up. The people Theo was involved with are … well, dangerous.'

'I figured.'

'Not the wine-and-cheese crowd.'

Oliver turned his back and moved towards his old Jaguar, his way of winding up the conversation. 'You'd be surprised, Detective. Australians are an eclectic bunch of bogans.'

'I remembered where I know you from,' Everson said, out of the blue.

Oliver looked back at her. 'I wasn't sure you *did* know me.'

Everson stepped towards him. 'Well, your wine. It was part of a heist a couple of years ago. Not sure you'd remember it on the news. I recall that a case of your wine is worth a pretty penny.'

Oliver nodded. He had heard about the heist, but didn't pay much attention to the media.

'Before you go. Did you leave Penny's on Friday evening? Anytime that night?'

'No,' Oliver said. 'I've told you that already.'

Everson pushed the sunglasses back to the bridge of her nose. 'Okay,' she said. 'Just checking.'

'Any answers on how he died?'

'Toxicology report will take a little while. We found something interesting in the glass of whisky on the bedside table.'

Oliver turned back around. 'There was a glass?' He guessed he'd only noticed the broken bottle. It was then he could see Everson weighing up whether or not to tell him.

'Filled with what farmers call "ten-eighty". Have you heard of it?'

'No.'

'Sodium fluoroacetate. A lethal type of dosage. Not the usual bait farmers can buy to kill foxes. Tasteless, odourless. Explains the vomiting and the blood.'

'He brought the whisky with him. I drank some as well.'

'No sickness?'

Oliver shook his head. 'So, whoever poisoned him did it after I'd left?'

Everson paused. '*If* someone poisoned him,' she said, climbing back into the car. 'I'll be in touch when we know more. You'll have to wait until the coroner releases the body before you can begin planning the funeral.' She raised an eyebrow and started to wind up the window. 'One thing you have to remember about the funeral,' Everson said, looking into Oliver's eyes. 'You can't have a wake in a town like Mudgee without a party pie.'

***

For the first time since Theo's death, Oliver sat down in front of the Bösendorfer. After rushing a couple of scales and a few chords, he started to play Brahms. Julia had conveyed the emotion better than he ever could. His grandmother was better again. Oliver hoped, with Ida's lessons, he'd reach a high enough level of competency to be able to convey the same kind of resonance. His fingers weren't as nimble, but he felt life just as intensely. He knew that much. And just like that, by absorbing the melody, he was back in his childhood home. Cramped next to his mother on the piano stool. He was eight, almost nine.

'Can you two come out and socialise with the rest of us, please?' His father had spoken softly to him from the door. Stressed 'please' as though it was a plea.

Chase was eating a toasted sandwich in the living room. Theo sat on the rug, laying out a deck of cards.

'Why do you play the piano all the time?' Chase asked Oliver, mouth filled with bread.

Oliver walked in and lay down beside Theo. His mother sat next to them on the ground; she watched for his reaction.

'I want to be a concert pianist one day.'

'Ha,' Chase said. 'That's fucking hard. And weird.'

'Chase,' his father snapped. He lit a cigarette and sat himself down on a lounge chair. 'Curb the language around the boys.'

'They already say it at school.'

Oliver struggled to remember his older brother's features. He remembered his mother, at the time, commenting that Chase had their father's eyes. His hair was short, shaved evenly across the skull. He would have been seventeen.

'Becoming a concert pianist is hard work,' his father said. He leaned back and took a drag of the cigarette. 'When I was your age, I wanted to be a professional golfer. I told my father that I wanted to be just like Jack Nicklaus—'

'Miles, don't,' his mother interjected.

'—and he said to me, "How are you going to do that?" And I told him that I'd practise every day, for hours, until I was good enough.'

'That's stupid, but, 'cause you're shit at golf.'

His father flipped Chase his middle finger. 'Language. I'm not shit at golf, but I'm not great at golf, either. I'll cut the story short. Basically, my dad told me that you can't polish a turd too much. You've got to have the talent first to be able to practise your way to fame.'

'I don't want to be famous,' Oliver replied, but as he said it he knew it was a lie. He was good at the piano, and he liked the attention people paid him whenever he sat down in front of the keys. He didn't have to talk, and he could say everything he ever wanted to without uttering a single word.

'Although, the artiste of the house seems to be doing all right with her talent. Selling some paintings. You may as well give it a go. But some of us have to work a bit harder for our money,' his father said.

'If looks could kill,' Chase said, 'you'd be in shit, Dad.'

His father's voice rang in his head: *You've got to be a bit of a freak to play that concert stuff. Have that crazy talent. You don't want to be a freak, mate.*

When Oliver released his first wine, people had called him a freak. He'd waited a few years and released his blends when they were ready. Put new juice in old barrels. Amphora. Co-fermented grapes some didn't think should pair together at all. Found in wine something that was utterly alien to his childhood and everyone he'd ever met. A new world, where no one knew anything about him, where no one knew anything about his family. It was a big risk – using his mother's inheritance to buy the vineyard. He'd worked with other winemakers in Australia, and with Orson overseas, but in the early days Oliver had polarised vignerons with his ideas. Some thought he was destined for greatness, while others believed he was just an overrated wanker. There wasn't much consensus in the middle.

To the old clique of Mudgee winemakers, the traditionalists of the earth, Oliver was a rogue, a renegade, a cowboy. Some respected him, but most were intimidated by what he could do with a bunch of grapes.

It's true, Oliver thought, playing the final notes. *You're not good enough to be a concert pianist.* But he'd found his calling with wine. And he would attempt to play the piano with love and feeling and clarity. Like his mother. After all, Julia hadn't lost her parents and her twin brother before she'd turned forty.

***

A voice roused Oliver from his thoughts: 'Why didn't you call me?'

Harold Keller stood, arms folded, in the doorway to the wine shed, his thick black glasses perched on the point of his nose. 'What the hell happened?'

Whenever Oliver stood near his mother's old gallerist, he smelled turpentine. It wasn't a hearty aroma like an open bottle pushed under his nose, but he caught a whiff in the distance; as though someone had inadvertently splashed some onto Harold's shirt and the old art dealer had simply walked away and let it dry. Perhaps over time it had seeped in with the linseed oil, finding its way into the cracks and lines and gashes of his fingers. Or it had become some kind of sensory memory for Oliver.

Oliver stood from the piano stool and moved closer to Harold. He should probably hug him, he thought, but he kept his distance instead. 'Don't know. Someone beat him up. Probably poisoned him. Slit his throat. The cops think he was involved in drugs. Forgery.'

Harold scoffed; the noise sounded like a horse exhaling. 'Theo couldn't organise a rock fight in a quarry. Drugs my buttocks.'

'I don't think it's a complete shock.' Oliver walked over to the table with the wine and cracked a bottle open. He found two glasses, dusty, and rinsed them off before pouring.

Harold took the wine and nodded his head, then changed the subject: 'How are you holding up?'

'Fine.'

'You make a sweet drop of wine, but you're a shithouse liar.'

Harold pulled over a chair, and Oliver sat back down on the piano stool.

'How'd you find out?'

Harold took a sip, before he licked the top of his teeth. 'It's been on the news, Oliver. Not sure if you get reception this far out, but it's not exactly a secret.'

'You didn't have to drive over here.'

'I drove to Rylstone for yum cha and thought it'd be rude not to call in.'

'What, Terrigal dumpling joints too grungy for the bourgeoisie?'

Harold snorted, then looked down at his glass. 'What am I drinking? It's interesting.'

'Barbera.'

Harold paused, considering his words. 'Oliver, your mother would want—'

'I know, Harold.'

'I'm just here to help, is what I'm saying.'

'I've got Gabe.'

Harold rolled his eyes and positioned his legs towards Oliver. 'I know, but family's family. It's not like we're both spoiled for choice.'

Miles's voice, again, was in his ear: *Don't let him think you've got no choice. You're not bound by blood. You know I never liked you and Theo calling him Uncle Harold. Hated it, in fact. Loathed it. Resented him. Abhorred the suave fucker.*

Harold's career had blossomed in Sydney before he set up shop on the Central Coast. He was well-travelled, his voice carrying both the Paddington pomp and the Tamworth twang. After spending his first eighteen years in the bush, Harold discovered he preferred paints and easels to clippers and a herd of sheep.

Growing up, Oliver remembered dinners where Harold had talked of his nascent years as an artist and auctioneer, retreating from his father's agricultural expectations. 'Art and commerce, oil and vinegar, it takes someone smart to emulsify them properly,' he'd declared.

After establishing a revered gallery in Bateau Bay, Harold was approached by Julia Crespo, a pianist who had pivoted to painting abstract vineyards and the ocean. *That bloke'd sell a painting to a blind man*, Miles had said. More than once. While he'd never trusted Harold, and told Julia to be careful in her financial dealings with him, he didn't complain when Julia's career skyrocketed and the money flowed in faster than any of them could have imagined.

'Oli? Did you hear me?'

He opened his eyes. 'Sorry. He arrived on Thursday afternoon, and he was dead by Saturday morning.'

'Had you seen him before then?'

Oliver shook his head. 'The last time I saw Theo was when I drove him to the airport, as he was leaving Australia. I tried getting in touch, but I guess he wasn't overly enthusiastic about finding me, either.'

'He came to my place last week.'

Oliver stood up suddenly. 'What?'

'He said he was coming here to see you. Didn't offer much else. I hadn't seen him for as long as you. Thought it was peculiar, him showing up out of the blue.'

Did he mention anything about Chase? Oliver wanted to ask, but instead said, 'Did he talk about drugs?'

Harold stood and signalled towards the door, and the two men walked outside. The sun was radiant, more than usual for autumn.

It was nice, Oliver thought, distractedly, after picking grapes through vintage, to stand outside without worrying about your skin blistering.

'I just can't see it,' Harold said. 'Selling drugs doesn't really seem Theo's forte. Smoking them, yes. Dealing them? Not so much.'

'What?' Oliver sounded as dazed as he felt.

Harold lowered his eyebrows and clasped Oliver's shoulder, stared hard into his eyes. 'Doesn't matter. Bury him here. In Mudgee. Scatter his ashes through the vines. He'd love that.'

Oliver looked across the driveway to the navy kombi van, gripped by a sudden sense of determination. 'If the detective doesn't find out who did this, I will.'

'I'm angry too. But don't—'

Without thinking, Oliver hurled the wineglass across the gravel. It hit the wine shed and shattered on impact. 'Someone came onto this property, slit Theo's throat and left him for dead, Harold.'

'Hey, hey,' Harold grunted, pulling Oliver into his chest. He smelled of cologne, sweat, wine, and something indiscernible and exclusive to men over sixty. 'They'll get the bastard.'

Oliver froze for a moment, took a couple of deep breaths and stepped away. 'Sorry, I'm still just processing it all.'

'Oliver, I'm livid too.'

'What happened to your hands?' Oliver frowned, noticing them for the first time.

Harold looked down before bringing them up to his eyes. 'Oh, nothing. Fixing some boards and staining the back deck. No one tells you your body becomes an apple when you're old.'

'What?'

'Your body bruises like one, I mean.'

A cloud shifted swiftly over the sun. The two men stood in silence.

'I'll be back in a couple of days,' Harold said, running a hand through his beard. 'I've got to drop off a few things in Orange now. Do you want to do dinner on Tuesday?'

'Sure,' Oliver said. 'I'll be here on Tuesday.'

They walked past the kombi to Harold's BMW. It looked incongruous in the middle of the gravel driveway, as though someone from the city had taken a wrong turn and abandoned the vehicle as they searched for help.

'We'll go to the police. Find out what's going on.'

'Yep.'

'Before I go,' Harold said, sliding his glasses onto his bald head and placing a pair of sunglasses over his eyes. 'Don't forget about the fox.'

'What?'

'The fox that taunted the farmer. The one that kept sneaking in and stealing the chickens. A new chook every night. Of course, the farmer caught on and hid out, ready to ambush—'

'Harold, I don't need a fable.'

'So,' Harold continued, 'when the fox got close, the farmer threaded some dry grass into its tail. And as the animal came back through the gate, chicken in his mouth, the farmer set the tail alight. The fox dropped the chicken, but then the bloody bastard bolted straight into the farmer's huge crop of wheat. And, well ...'

Oliver turned towards the house. 'Lucky I don't have any chickens.'

'Grieve, mate. Be sensible. I'll see you Tuesday.'

Oliver waved as Harold wheeled the car around, the crackly

chomp of tyres on gravel, and thought about Harold's hands; thought about how they looked like they'd been scratched and bruised from a fight.

Oliver peered into the spare-room window and couldn't help but wonder whether it had happened a few metres from where he found himself standing.

***

Later that afternoon, Gabe came down to the wine shed, his greyhound, Luna, on a lead. His gait was a little tired, and Oliver thought he was starting to look his sixty years.

'How would you feel about a companion tonight? I'm heading into the city.'

'Of course,' Oliver said, remembering. 'Your horse is running today.'

'Yeah,' Gabe said with a hopeful grin. 'Thoroughbred or donkey. We'll find out in a few hours.'

'No worries. Let Luna inside the house. She'll just sleep on the couch until I come in.'

Gabe waited a moment; didn't move. 'You sure? I can stay here. We can watch the race at the pub.'

'I'm fine. Penny will drop over after work.'

'All right,' Gabe said. 'Call me if you need anything.'

Gabe had owned horses for years and, from what Oliver could remember, joked about most of them becoming dog food. One mare had sold for a decent price after her racing career, but Oliver assumed the hobby was more of a break from the winery than anything else. Gabe and Murray were both a part of the same syndicates. They were involved locally but spent a lot of time travelling to Sydney meetings together. Oliver could think of nothing worse: betting on horses and hanging out with Murray at the same time.

Gabe was raised in Bathurst. His father worked as a butcher and a greyhound trainer, so the racing industry was part of his blood. Gabe had managed the marketing for some top boutique wineries in Australia and Europe, before trying his hand at his own winery in Beechworth. He had a bad run of flaky winemakers and two average vintages in a row, which forced him to close up, losing everything as a result. He admired Oliver's audacity, and after tasting his wine from the first vintage, offered to work for a low wage if he could live – rent free – in the neighbouring cottage on the vineyard. A year ago, as an act of good faith, and to ensure Gabe wouldn't be tempted to go anywhere else, Oliver had gifted him a twenty per cent stake in the winery.

Oliver watched them walk towards the house. The greyhound was no trouble: quiet, slept most of the day, was excitable when it was time to eat. He suspected he spoiled her more than Gabe did. Slipped some extra meat in the bowl. Let her up on the bed. Oliver had always maintained he was too busy, too commitment-phobic, for a dog, even though he enjoyed the company when it came.

After trying to taste the wine in the barrel and finding that his palate wouldn't cooperate, he joined Luna inside the cottage and lay down on the lounge. For half an hour, he kept thinking about putting a record on the turntable, only his eyes kept slipping closed. Finally, he fell into an exhausted sleep.

He drifted back into the police station in Mudgee. Instead of sitting with Everson, he was talking to Detective Hanson – the floral, citrusy notes of her perfume in the air.

'It's not easy, Oliver, but you're being brave. If he's guilty, he needs to be locked up. I know how hard that must be for you.'

He was in front of Everson now.

'I've already testified against my father. I'm not telling you about Theo. He's not like my dad.'

Everson smirked. 'Maybe you're both more like him than you think.'

'Don't,' Oliver said, feeling his temper flare. He wanted to grab something, anything, to squeeze, to subdue his anger. But there was nothing.

Everson was gone.

Oliver could only hear the metronome ticking somewhere, too fast, and the sound of someone beating on the door. Then, a familiar smell.

He opened his eyes, felt Luna lick his mouth. He pushed her away, and when he sat up he realised it was almost dark and he was coated in sweat.

***

Penny called to tell him there were people everywhere. There was some kind of event in town and the bar was teeming with tourists. His girlfriend's bar was one of the few places in town where Oliver felt comfortable. While Penny mostly featured local wineries, she'd also cherrypicked some excellent examples from around Australia and the rest of the world. She loved wine like no one else he knew: emailed winemakers in the Rhône, Bordeaux, Uruguay. Stayed up talking about biodynamics and how different clones of pinot were taking off well in particular places. She'd told Oliver she had been both proud and deflated to be the only Aboriginal sommelier in her class.

'It's good to be busy, but I hate having a late shift on a Sunday.'

'Busy is good,' Oliver said. 'Keep opening those expensive bottles. You can always come out later.'

Penny sounded doubtful. 'You sure?'

'Of course. The greyhound and I are watching *MasterChef*. We're learning how to poach hapuka.'

'Well,' Penny said, 'sounds like you're sorted.'

Oliver took a swig of beer. 'Now go and sweet-talk someone into buying a bottle from that weird Four Dogs Missing winery.'

'Ha,' Penny said. 'It would help if you were here to convince them.'

'I'm a terrible salesman.'

Since Oliver had found Theo's body, he'd tried to spend as little time in the house as possible. There was a loneliness now that he hadn't felt before. He wasn't a superstitious person. Didn't believe in ghosts or spirits. Didn't think there was any reason he should have to move – to leave his home. But he did believe in energy. The cycles of the moon.

He wasn't sure what to do with the spare room now; he knew he could never really use it for anything again.

The phone rang. His landline, a nineties yellowy-cream model with a cord, which, despite the odds, still worked well. Barely anyone had the number; it was the phone Oliver had used before Penny finally pressured him into purchasing a mobile – a cheap flip phone, barely capable of basic tasks outside of calling and texting, but it had probably saved their relationship more than once.

'Hello?'

No one spoke. Oliver said the word again. He wondered whether the delay was a telemarketer calling from overseas, trying to sell him something superfluous. Then he heard the faintest hum, someone breathing, the sound of a metronome. A familiar beat.

'I'm hanging up now,' Oliver said, before gently placing the receiver down. He strode to the wine shed, almost jogging, and when he pulled open the door and got to the piano, he found the metronome moving. He stopped it and listened, but the shed was quiet. Luna trotted around his feet, exploring the barrels, sniffing for mice.

'Who's here? Come out.'

But no one did.

A little after ten, halfway through his fifth beer, the phone rang again.

'Who are you? Get off my property!'

'Darling, calm down. It's me,' Clare said, her voice cutting through more clearly sans the barking of dogs.

'Sorry,' Oliver murmured. 'Someone's been pranking this number. Did you hear from Valerie?'

'You, my friend, have sharp instincts,' Clare replied gravely.

'What do you mean?'

'About Orson and his data. He probably didn't answer your call because he'd been taken to hospital.'

'Fuck,' Oliver said. 'Is he all right?'

There was a pause one rarely heard when speaking to Clare. 'Sadly not,' she said eventually, her voice strained. 'Valerie said he passed away this morning.'

6.

Penny arrived a shade shy of midnight.

'It's rather late,' Oliver said, opening the door, struggling to maintain their lighthearted ritual. 'We weren't expecting any visitors.'

'Hello there. I think I might be lost,' Penny said, leaning on the wall and removing her boots.

'Lost?'

'I know it's late and cold, but I was told there was a chef out this way poaching some hapuka.'

'Ah, I see. Your intel's correct, but I'm afraid I have unfortunate news.'

Penny bent under Oliver's arm at the door and moseyed into the kitchen. 'All of it? Gone?'

'Afraid so. Although, I'm told there's some kind of bespoke aperitif waiting for you in the fridge.'

Penny took a plastic container – last night's leftovers – which Oliver had waiting on the bench, and placed it in the microwave. 'Is that so?'

'Mysteriously cloudy. Bottle brewed. Preservative free. Lovely golden hue.'

Penny opened the fridge, grinned and proceeded to crack the top off a stubby. 'Jesus, and you tried to tell me earlier you're a shithouse salesman?' She stood beside him at the bench.

'I am.'

She swigged the beer. 'You made a stubby of Coopers sound like vintage Heidsieck.'

'That's my problem,' Oliver said. 'I'm all over-promise and under-deliver.'

'Sometimes. But not always,' Penny said, smiling, as the microwave beeped three times.

The dog – snoring on the lounge – didn't stir as they sat down.

'I'm hoping the proverb about bad things happening in threes is a load of shit,' Oliver said, realising he sounded suddenly morose.

Penny blew on the steaming contents of her fork. 'What happened?'

'You know how I told you I was worried about Orson?'

'Yeah, about him not entering any data?'

'Clare called. He had a heart attack. Died in hospital this morning.'

A month ago, Orson turned sixty-two. He was sprightly for his age: fit enough, moderate drinker, didn't smoke. Looked after himself. Jogged almost every morning. It was likely the diagnosis was right, but Oliver couldn't shake the feeling that there was something more going on. Orson hadn't mentioned anything was amiss. After everything that had happened, Oliver wanted to talk to Valerie. As irrational and far-fetched as it sounded, part of his intuition said there might be a connection between the deaths of Orson and his twin brother.

'Holy fucking shit,' Penny said, dropping her food container onto the table and moving in for a hug. 'I'm sorry. We only posted the wines recently as well.'

Oliver had forgotten that they had sent Orson some small, not-yet-released samples, alongside some other good bottles from the area. Most years, Orson would send over wines from Napa: some from his cellar, others he'd enjoyed recently, wines he wanted to discuss with Oliver. Samples from his barrels and amphora. That was perhaps the best part of his tutelage with Orson all of those years ago – the excitement of trying something out of the barrel, something still in the throes of maturation.

'True,' Oliver said. 'I'd forgotten.'

'Can I make you a cup of tea?'

'Nah, it's late. Bed sounds good.'

'Do you want to talk about Orson?' Penny asked. Oliver tried to maintain eye contact with her but had to pull away. 'It's a big deal. Two losses in a week.'

'Not tonight. Maybe tomorrow.' When Penny only nodded, he added, 'Is that okay?'

'Sure,' Penny said, but the way she replied made Oliver think it wasn't. He hated the voices creeping into his head: *You'll jest and play-act with me, but you won't open up about anything important. Why is that, Oliver?*

A few minutes later, after watching Penny add her empty bottle to the line on the bench, Oliver said: 'I need to go and see Clare in Orange. Sort out the tech company stuff now that Orson's gone. Get away from the vineyard as well. You're welcome to come.'

Penny stood and moved in for a second hug. Her hair smelled like shampoo and obscure kitchen spices he couldn't discern.

'Sure,' she said. 'Are you just planning what happens with the company?'

'I suppose. There was a directors' agreement we all signed when we started out. We'll have a valuation, or something like that, and then Clare and I will buy the shares from Orson. Well, from his trustee. I don't know, it's a bit much to think about right now.'

'Too complicated to think about after midnight.'

'A pain in the proverbial,' Oliver said. 'I'm just keen to get away.'

Penny stayed in his arms, leaning up for a kiss. 'I've always wanted to travel with my own personal chef.'

Oliver grinned. Despite everything that had happened, he felt like he would drop off to sleep as soon as his head hit the pillow.

Luna jumped from the lounge and languidly stretched in front of them. She moved towards the bedroom but stopped halfway to look back at the pair. After a moment, she emitted a long and overly dramatic wail.

'Hope you don't mind sharing the bed,' Oliver said.

***

Oliver slept poorly, continually dreaming about Harold's hands, the story about the fox, and the fact that Everson had mentioned poison that killed vermin only hours before Harold had arrived at the vineyard.

He left his bed early and rode his bike into town. It was cold, with a residue of frost flecked across the grass. Mudgee was pretty as it dipped its toes into winter. He regretted not wearing a warmer jacket.

He sat inside his favourite café and ordered a black coffee. Rocky, whom Oliver had known for years, roasted his own beans, and they were the best in town. The roaster-cum-barista added a splash of banter with every order. Oliver remembered he'd posted a sign beside the coffee machine when they'd reopened after the first COVID lockdown: *Please maintain at least the length of Rocky's penis (1.5 metres) between each other, or we'll have to close again.*

Oliver found the newspaper, but after a while noticed he was reading it without digesting the words. So, he folded the paper in half and left it beside him.

'Another one?' Rocky said, clutching Oliver's empty cup in one hand, a precarious stack of plates in the other.

'I'll have a piccolo this time.'

'Can't keep up with you, mate.'

'Trying not to be predictable.'

'You're doing a good job. Would you like some breakfast?'

Oliver moved his head to and fro, thinking. 'I'm not that hungry.'

'Sandwich? Bit of cake? You're wasting away there. Made a honey-and-fig baklava this morning.'

'Toasted sandwich sounds good,' Oliver said. 'Not in the mood for fancy. How about some tasty cheese between a couple of slices of Wonder White?'

'Fuck me, there's a bakery down the road that serves that shit.'

'Awful coffee, but.'

'Yeah, yeah. I've got a leg ham and gouda.'

'Perfect,' Oliver said.

Halfway through the sandwich, Oliver's phone began buzzing on the table. He had to look twice to make sure he wasn't hallucinating. Orson's name appeared on the screen.

'Hello?'

'Oliver, it's Valerie. I only just saw your missed call.'

He ran a hand over his stubble and pulled the phone close to

79

his mouth so he wouldn't have to talk too loudly. 'It's okay, Clare called me last night. I don't know what to say …'

'We all loved him,' she said.

'I saw that he hadn't entered any data and knew something was off.'

'I guessed you and Clare would notice first. We thought he might hold on there for a while.'

'What happened?'

'Oh,' Valerie said, not seeming to have registered his question, 'Clare told me about your brother. I'm sorry, Oliver, to have that happen in the same week. If there is a God, he's a goddamn bastard for testing us like this.'

You can say that again, Oliver thought, but he said nothing.

'It all happened so fast,' Valerie said, back on track. 'He had a coughing fit, didn't feel well. We thought he was having a heart attack and took him to emergency. He died the next day.'

'Jesus. He was healthy. I know he's not a spring chicken anymore, but he isn't a dinosaur.'

'You do what I still do,' Valerie said, the sound of a smile in her voice. 'Refer to him in the present tense.'

'Sorry,' he murmured.

'Don't be. It's nice.' She took a big breath and began speaking quickly. It was hard for Oliver to keep up with the speed of her words, the cadence of her accent. 'I was going to call you. I thought you might be able to help me understand. Before he started sputtering and having chest pains, he'd been drinking.'

'A lot?'

'No,' she said. 'He had the occasional big night, but whenever he did tastings or any events, he'd always spit the wine.'

'I know,' Oliver said. He could picture the exact look on Orson's face as he theatrically directed the liquid into a spittoon, or onto the grass if he was outside. According to Gabe, there was a photograph on his Facebook profile of Orson doing exactly that.

'But the night it all happened, he was drinking. You know how much he loved your wine. He was drinking the samples you sent over.'

Oliver felt his skin prickle, a line of goosebumps erupting over his arms. 'Did you try any?'

'I wish I could have,' Valerie said. 'I can't drink at the moment. I'm on this awful blood-pressure medication. The stress of this isn't helping either, I can tell you that.'

'So, you think something was wrong with the wine?' Oliver said at last.

'What? Of course not. I just wanted to tell you it was the last thing that he drank before he died. He would have wanted you to know that.'

Oliver was sure it was supposed to sound thoughtful, but there was a frisson of spite in her voice. He looked down: his foot was shaking under the table. 'Have you heard anything more about the autopsy?'

'Not yet,' Valerie said. 'The doctors are keeping things close to their chest. They won't tell me what they suspect happened – they're waiting for the results.'

'Of course,' Oliver said, his mind elsewhere. 'Look, keep me posted on what they tell you?'

She picked up the tension in his voice. 'Is everything all right there?'

'Just in shock.'

'You and me both. I'll call you soon,' she said, before hanging up.

Oliver felt as though he'd walked through a messy spiderweb, threads everywhere; strands and non sequiturs he couldn't see let alone attempt to understand.

Before he walked out, he gazed up into the corner of the room and spied a small security camera.

'Hey, Rocky,' he said, pointing. 'Do you think you could help me put up one of those?'

***

'How would you blend it, then?'

He was thinking about the summers, the two vintages, he'd spent in California. Oliver remembered grabbing a wineglass from Orson's hand, swirling and sniffing it before taking a small sip. He'd gone over to the table and splashed three different decanters of red wine into one glass.

'Slightly more merlot. I don't think you should be scared of it. Other winemakers around here grow it at lower altitudes and pick it too late, but this one is particularly spritzy with smooth tannins. It has cedar and tobacco flavours and isn't too fruit-stewed on the palate. If you have the merlot blended at fifteen to twenty per cent, you lose the coarse edge of the cabernet. A touch of petit verdot to finish,' he said, handing the glass to Orson, 'and that's how I'd blend it.'

Orson smiled as he swirled and smelled the glass. He took a sip, inhaling air loudly through the thin circle formed by his lips before swallowing the wine.

'This is good,' he said, pointing the empty glass towards Oliver, 'but it's not what I love most about the blend. It's the fact that you know I'm self-conscious about the merlot. And I think you're right that it can take a larger portion in this release.'

Oliver smiled. Sometimes he liked to imagine that Orson was his father, and that Miles hadn't ever lived. In his reimagining, Oliver had been conceived in California and moved to Sydney with his mother when he was an infant, returning to the Napa Valley as an adult to meet his father for the first time.

'I'm going to go with my blend because it's what I came up with. But only with half of the fruit. The rest will be made into your blend, and you can call it what you want. I'd prefer you blended more merlot so that we can begin introducing people to it, slowly. I want people to know that we can produce it seriously, and that we're able to blend it well.'

Oliver nodded. 'Sounds good.'

He looked across and saw Orson studying his face. 'You're not used to receiving compliments, are you?'

'No,' Oliver said, blushing. 'I guess not.'

'You're a promising young winemaker. You know that I don't let anyone study with me every vintage, don't you?'

'I'm grateful. Honest.'

Orson paused for a moment. 'No winemakers in the family?'

Oliver shook his head. 'I'm not sure they ever even drank wine.'

Orson picked up a decanter and poured a glass for himself and another for Oliver. 'Mine neither. Most scholarship winners, like yourself, don't come from a wine background. There's an innate desire to make something of yourself. There's no fancy family estate for people like us to rely on if things go awry. Anything less than perfection won't do.'

He would always remember Orson that day in California: talking about wine, purity, perfectionism. The mountains and the sun, the way the light lit up the rows of vines like waves ready to break. His mentor's grey hair slicked back and the coarseness of his hands. They'd raised a toast with their glasses and sipped.

Oliver still recalled the excitement he'd felt when he'd called Orson to tell him that he was moving to Mudgee.

'I thought you were looking for a little vineyard in the Barossa? Or somewhere in Victoria?'

'Too expensive. The good plots are taken. I don't know why there aren't hipsters here experimenting. Maybe they're scared of the weather. I had a wine with a friend in Sydney last week and the potential blew my mind. It's an interesting climate, Ors. Warm. Well, hot days but cool nights. Altitude ranging from four hundred metres to eleven-hundred metres. Some crazy good soil.'

'Have you found a vineyard?'

'Oh, yeah. Some of the gnarliest vines in the area. Some old vine cabernet. There's barbera here. Some of the original plantings in Australia. They came out on the plane from Italy, back in the days before there were beagles at the airport.'

'What condition?'

'Rough. But we can get to work with them.'

Oliver could sense Orson's excitement on the other end of the line. 'We can experiment with the software in that particular climate and with those grapes. Very different to what I have here.'

Oliver found he couldn't stop smiling.

'If you buy it, let me know. I'll book a plane ticket.'

'You might want to,' Oliver said. 'They accepted my ludicrously low offer on the place this morning.'

He'd never told Orson that his father was in jail or even that his mother had been a revered artist. He never mentioned that even though his family weren't winemakers, he'd inherited enough money from his mother's estate to purchase his own vineyard without having to take a loan.

Now Oliver wished he'd told him everything. About his family, his past, the fact that he'd often dreamed that Orson was his father.

But it was too late for wishing now.

***

Mid-morning Monday, the first thing Oliver did when he arrived back at the wine shed was check the data. Not just his own, which was up to date, but also the inputs from Clare. When he logged into the program, he saw that she'd already added the numbers for that morning. Relief washed over him. He wasn't sure whether he was paranoid – he had barely been sleeping – but he felt there was something going on with the program. Orson's death seemed strange; he could tell even Valerie suspected not all the evidence was pointing towards a heart attack. If Orson's death wasn't natural, and if someone had killed Theo by mistake, thinking he was Oliver, did it mean Clare was next?

Oliver wasn't sure why anyone would target their trio. They owned a company that invested in vineyard technology. Collectively, they shared results and made good wine. The company was worth a lot of money, yes, and it was certainly arguable that their wine scored higher and sold better than their immediate competitors, but that alone wasn't grounds for murder.

Oliver stood outside the shed. He loved the end of autumn, the amber leaves and the smell of the vineyard, cold and earthy and fresh after a brief downpour. He wended his way up the incline, through the vines towards the top of the hill. Inhaled chimney smoke. Either his own or the Vernons' next door; perhaps a melange of both. A mob of kangaroos hopped and bounced among the vines. *Don't pat them*, he remembered his father saying once. *They're a feral animal. Untamed. Nasty. Best shot and eaten before*

85

they fuck up your bonnet. A breeze from the west quivered the gum branches and Oliver felt its coldness creep across his arms.

Days ago, before Theo had arrived and everything changed irrevocably, Oliver had toyed with the idea of spending more time in the city, of making friends and drinking late in bars, of visiting galleries and riding ferries. But he couldn't do it. The rush hour, the traffic, the Sydney smells. Stress that somehow reminded him of his boyhood. Whenever he needed to be creative, to think about what he should do next with his grapes, he'd walk along the driveway and through the vines, up the hill, all the way to the top, where he could look across to town.

Eventually, he walked towards the house and whistled for Luna. She wasn't particularly obedient, and was more of a cat than a dog in some respects. Putting her on the lead, he led her to Gabe's garage. When he entered, he noticed that Gabe's car wasn't there; he hadn't returned from the race meeting in the city. Oliver went to check the messages on his mobile, to see if Gabe had tried to call, but remembered he'd left his phone at the house. He found the spare key above the garage doorframe and let himself into Gabe's cottage.

The house smelled of coconut, incense and dried herbs. No one was home. The place was immaculate. Luna trotted in, jumped up onto the leather lounge and looked at him as if to say, *What now?*

Oliver padded along the corridor and checked the office. There was nothing amiss. Laptop closed on the desk. Papers neatly arranged to the side. He flicked through them, discovering nothing unusual: bills to pay for equipment, invoices Gabe had sent to others. There was a photo framed above the desk of Gabe and his sister, the one Oliver had met a handful of times; plus, some family photographs, typically staged, almost an obligatory display in case anyone who was pictured stumbled across them.

Oliver wasn't sure what he was searching for. Everything seemed in place and he felt guilty for thinking there could be a clue about the poison. He wasn't sure why he even felt compelled to look. Still, he opened the drawers, half-heartedly pawing through the contents. The bedroom was clean; no clothes on the floor. Nothing out of place. He heard Luna jump from the lounge and run to the garage door. Then she started to scratch the doorframe. He glanced through the front window to see if Gabe was driving in. He couldn't see a car, only a shower of dust.

Rushing to the toilet, he sat down on the lid and closed the door. He heard Gabe enter the house and say something to the dog. After a moment, Oliver stood up and flushed the toilet.

'Hey,' he called out, going to the vanity to wash his hands.

'Oli, are you in there?'

Oliver walked out and stood in front of Gabe, who was placing his bag on the floor next to the kitchen bench.

'I literally just brought Luna back and realised nature was calling in a big way.'

'Oh God,' Gabe groaned. 'Steer clear of that part of the house, you're saying?'

'For a little while,' Oliver said. 'Might be wise.'

Gabe was busily unpacking his bags and placing items he'd purchased onto the bench.

'How'd the horse go?'

'You know what,' Gabe said, hands in the air, 'he actually ran pretty well. It's only his third start and he finished a close second. The trainer was happy. We made some money for jam from the bets.'

'That's good. They take a little while to come into their own, right?'

'Mostly,' Gabe said, looking Oliver up and down. 'Every horse is different. I've got high hopes for this one. The vet bought a fifty per cent share. That should tell you enough.'

Oliver nodded. Gabe asked if he wanted a cup of tea, but Oliver had already moved to the window. There was a car coming up the driveway. Everson.

'Who is it?' Gabe asked.

'Police. Again.' He walked outside and watched as the black car pulled in beside the cottage.

'You're practically off the grid,' Everson said from an open window. She wasn't getting out of the car.

'I'd be lying if I said you were the first person to tell me that. My little flip phone's up at the house. I think the battery's dead.'

'I need you at the station. Got something I want you to see.'

'Today?'

'Right now. I'm not giving you a choice.'

'Okay,' Oliver said. 'I'll meet you there soon.'

'No,' Everson countered, a thumb pointing to the passenger's seat. 'I'll save you the petrol. That green car looks too pretty to venture out in the mud.'

***

Gabe followed them. Everson said she didn't mind if he sat in. They waited in the same room Oliver had been interviewed in the day Theo was killed. Everson didn't take as long to enter this time, armed with a laptop instead of a manila folder.

'As you know, my days consist of trying to find out what happened to your brother.'

'Have you got something?' Oliver asked.

'Well,' Everson said, 'you tell me.'

She opened the computer. There was a video already paused on the screen. She hit the spacebar aggressively with her thumb and the video kicked to life. The image was in colour, but he could tell it was dark. There was a time stamp in the bottom right corner: 01:09:45. The camera was pointing to a dimly lit street, the same road that led from Penny's terrace to Four Dogs Missing. Oliver tried to work out exactly where the camera was; he knew the area, but couldn't pinpoint the location.

'Is this it?' Gabe said, evidently bored with the footage.

'Just wait,' Everson said, pointing to the screen.

After another thirty seconds or so, a car entered the frame and made its way down the road towards Oliver's property. Without Everson having to rewind and slow the footage, he knew it was his green Jaguar. His 1969 bottle-green, restored Jaguar E-type.

'That was my car.'

'Well,' Everson said, pausing the video. 'Don't know too many others around like it.'

'What time is it?' Gabe asked.

'Ten past one,' Everson said. 'So, let me ask you this question one more time, Oliver. And if you want a lawyer present, now might be the time to get one. Did you leave Penny's at all that night and go back to your house?'

Oliver scratched his ear. The room was warm. He didn't know what to say.

'Are you sure it's mine?' he said finally.

'I'm sure,' Everson said. 'If you slow it down and pause it you can make out the licence plate. Registered to one Oliver James Wingfield.'

'Can you see who's driving?' Gabe asked.

'No,' Everson said, frowning. 'Sadly, the camera isn't in the right position for us to see who's inside.'

'I didn't leave Penny's apartment. She'll vouch for me.'

'Did Penny leave at any time?'

'What are you saying?' Gabe directed at Everson, followed by a little laugh. 'That *Penny* had something to do with this?'

'I'm as confused as you are, Mr Aitken,' Everson said, staring at Gabe. Then she turned to Oliver. 'The way I see it, there's a car leaving town and heading towards your place at a time you said you were somewhere else.'

'Does the car return?' Oliver asked. 'Can you see who's driving when it heads the other way?'

'That's the thing,' Everson said. 'We've got a clear vision of you driving to Penny's apartment at five in the afternoon. Then we've got footage of your car going in the other direction at one in the morning. And that's it. The car doesn't return. The next time we see it on camera is at eight-fifteen am.'

'But it would have had to come back so that I could drive home in the morning.'

'That's right,' Everson said. 'This isn't the only way you could have returned to Penny's. There are other routes to avoid the camera.'

'I had no idea this security camera even existed until now,' Oliver said. His neck was itchy, but he was wary about scratching it in case it made him look guilty. 'Why would I drive a different way?'

'Well,' Everson said. 'That's why you're here. I was hoping you'd tell me.'

'I didn't leave Penny's at any time that night,' Oliver said, starting to sense the anger in his voice. 'I can guarantee you the person driving that car isn't me.'

'Who else could it be?'

'I don't know. Someone making it look like I drove home at one in the morning.'

Gabe folded his arms and stared at Everson. 'You said these people Theodore was tangled up with are dangerous. Perhaps they had the motive and means to do something like this?'

'It doesn't make sense,' Oliver said, unable to take his eyes from the screen.

'There are plenty of possibilities. I'm more interested in facts. The fact is your car is driving at a time you said you were asleep. That makes me wonder whether I can trust you.'

'Clearly, someone's murdered Theo and they're trying to frame Oliver,' Gabe stated in frustration.

'Wait,' Oliver said. 'Have you spoken to Harold Keller yet?'

Everson pulled a strand of her hair behind her ear. 'You've never mentioned a Harold to me before.' He assumed that Everson was writing his name into her notepad. 'Why would I have spoken to him?'

'He came to the vineyard yesterday and told me that Theo had been to see him last week.'

'Why?'

'I don't know,' Oliver said as the internal heating clicked over and began humming. 'He just said he'd seen Theo a week before he died. I've never known Harold to rock up unannounced before. He said that he'd heard about Theo and wanted to call in.'

'What?' Gabe said. 'You didn't tell me Harold was here.'

'Who *is* Harold?' Everson asked.

'He's an old art dealer. Family friend of Oliver's. Would sell water to a drowning man, but I really couldn't see him murdering—'

'His hands,' Oliver interrupted. 'He had scratches and gashes on his hands, like he'd been in a fight.'

'Well,' Everson said. 'How old is this Harold?'

Oliver looked at Gabe, who shrugged his shoulders. 'Retirement age?'

'Interesting,' Everson said, before she snapped shut the computer screen. 'Not trying to send me on a wild goose chase in the wrong direction?'

'Why would I do that?'

'To hide something from me.'

Oliver wondered if Everson had already spoken to Harold. Crossed him off her list? It was like she wasn't even interested in entertaining the possibility.

'I'm in the process of getting a warrant, Oliver. You can expect to see me soon. Unless I can follow you back now? Let me have a look around.'

'No,' Oliver said, standing up. 'I think I'll get a lawyer. Dust the furniture, put on the kettle. That kind of thing.'

There was an earthquake under his feet, in his mind. Thousands of tiny fissures spreading through the paddocks, away from the winery, leading everywhere and nowhere at once.

Dear Angie,

You're not only a great barrister, but a decent detective. Congratulations on finding me. I'm a little insulted you'd think I would ever forget you. An intriguing woman sitting alone at the bar. There was something about you. 'Haughty' was in yesterday's crossword, so let's roll with that. In a good way. I'll have you know I was hoping to get your number, but you'd bolted before I could even chase you down the hallway to ask.

Do you think it's a little odd that you can be with someone for years and never entertain pregnancy, but spend all of a few minutes with someone else and then find a little letter waiting in the mailbox?

I'm glad you got in touch, as I was hoping to talk to you more. I like what you do with words. But as I said, you left before I had the chance.

I don't do the social media thing. I liked your little love letter about letters, so let's keep writing to each other.

Something different, hey?

Peace,

Theo

7.

Oliver needed to shower. He took a whiff under his arm; he'd get away with waiting until he got home from dinner with Gabe. He sat on the lounge chair and exhaled. The house was quiet. Closing his eyes, he tried to think who the hell could have driven his car, in the middle of the night, without him knowing. No one else had a key. Surely, he would have heard someone trying to steal it outside? Or he would have heard someone come in to Penny's to grab the key. There was a spare inside the cottage, but he'd locked it up when he'd left, and it wasn't missing.

Who wanted to make Oliver look guilty? There were people in town with whom he didn't see eye to eye, that was for sure, but no one despised him enough to *kill* his brother and somehow attempt to frame him. He barely spoke to anyone. The only people he shared colourful banter with were Murray and Charlie, and he wasn't sure either of them would break in and drive the Jaguar. Thinking about the whole ordeal made him feel dirty; like someone had been sleeping in his sheets, had dipped their muddy feet in his freshly drawn bath.

Oliver walked to the computer and typed into Google the name of the poison Everson had told him about. *Sodium fluoroacetate.* He looked over the formula: *FCH_2CO_2Na*. Symptoms: *nausea, vomiting … cardiac anomalies. Toxic.*

Oliver's heart began to hammer harder with every new paragraph. If the poison could lead to heart failure, it could have caused Orson to die. Did he need any further evidence that someone had slipped poison into the wine he'd sent to Orson? The question wasn't how, but why. And who.

Although the internet speed was excruciatingly slow, he found himself reading through article after article; a rabbit hole he couldn't seem to stop himself from going down.

As he racked his brain for a connection, he clutched the house phone and called Clare.

'I heard from Valerie,' he told her without preamble when she picked up.

'Me too. She's still waiting to learn what happened.'

'It's going to be weird without him.'

'You're not wrong,' Clare said. 'Hard for us with the equipment. From a technical perspective, I mean.'

'Hey,' Oliver said, closing the door to the verandah and checking to make sure he was alone. 'Do you remember that conference we went to last year?'

'The Australian Wine Industry Tech one?'

'That's it,' Oliver said, feeling the adrenaline pump through him.

'What about it?'

He paused, unsure how to bring it up. He remembered the conference well. Afterwards he, Clare and Orson had retreated to their hotel. They'd had a nap in the afternoon, before having dinner in the restaurant downstairs. They'd imbibed a couple of bottles between them and finished the night perched by the fire in the hotel's courtyard.

'Do you remember after we had dinner, we sat around drinking outside for a while?'

'I suppose,' Clare said. 'Although I'd be lying if I said I could recall every boozy dinner I've had in the last twelve months.'

'Right,' Oliver said. 'Remember we saw that government minister walking to his hotel room? The balcony above the courtyard?'

'Oh. I remember. The cute one from the conference. Yes, he was smoking and walking hand in hand with his press secretary. His male press secretary.'

'Even though he's married,' Oliver said. 'With kids.'

'That doesn't seem to stop anyone these days. Maybe they're non-monogamous.'

'The state's Minister for Industry and Trade being a swinger? Doubt it.'

'Valid point,' Clare said with a cough. 'Dare I ask, what does the issue of parliamentary monogamy, or lack thereof, have to do with Orson?'

Oliver sighed. He knew how outrageous he was about to sound, but it had started to niggle at him during the online search. 'I was trying to think why someone would want me dead. Would want Orson dead.'

'Orson died of a heart attack, Oliver.'

'They haven't confirmed it yet. Valerie told me that Orson was drinking our wine samples – you know, the ones we'd recently sent him – just before he had the heart attack. And you know the police told me that Theo was poisoned. I just researched the poison found in Theo's drink. It induces a heart attack and vomiting.'

'What?' Clare barked. 'Slow down, hold up. What are you saying?'

'I'm trying to understand what the hell's going on. Someone poisoned Theo, and now Orson is dead, and if he had a heart attack after drinking *our* wine, then it's possible that he was poisoned too.'

'But why would anyone want to poison Orson?'

'The same question as why would someone kill Theo in my house and then try to pin it on me.'

'Okay, you're moving far too fast for an old lady like me. This is why they invented Valium.'

Oliver was pacing around the kitchen. He pulled the cord of the phone with him as far as it would go, feeling as though he was making some kind of progress.

'Clare, the police have a video of my car leaving Penny's place and heading back to the house the night Theo was murdered. It wasn't me. I think maybe someone was supposed to kill me, or they wanted to make it look like I killed my brother.'

The line was silent for a moment. 'Why would anyone want to do that?'

'I have no idea,' Oliver said. 'It's weird. I don't have a good feeling about it, let's just say that.'

'You're upset, darling. You've lost your brother and one of your best friends in the same week. That's going to be tough on anyone.'

'It could be somehow related to this minister.'

Clare laughed. 'I'm sorry, I shouldn't, but that's too funny.'

'What's funny?'

'A man poisoning two people because a few drunk winemakers saw a minister holding hands and having a sneaky pash with his secretary?'

Oliver sat down at the computer and started typing a name

into Google. 'Is it ridiculous, though? John Geraghty is no longer just the Minister for Industry and Trade. Next month, he's the candidate for premier.'

'Oliver, you know I love you. But take some time out. Think about this.' Clare dropped her voice. 'I don't think there's anything there.'

'Yeah,' Oliver said. 'Maybe you're right. I'm just trying to think of something.' He remembered Harold's hands. 'You know, Theo visited Harold in Terrigal before he came here.'

'Harold?' Clare said. 'The gallerist you grew up with?'

'Yeah.' Clare was one of the only people he'd spoken to about his childhood. He had been tipsy and acquiescent one night, too many bottles of wine down, and let most of it leak. 'He dropped by yesterday. I don't think he's telling me everything he knows.'

'Well,' Clare said. 'Maybe you should talk to him again. I think that theory holds more gravitas than our politician friend.'

'I threw that bone to the detective. Penny and I are going to come and see you soon to go through everything. Until then, be safe. You call me if you see anything weird. And watch what you drink.'

Clare sighed. 'I'm looking forward to seeing you. Please, try not to worry too much?'

'Never do.'

When the call ended, Oliver sat at his computer and typed 'John Geraghty' into Google then pressed 'enter'. It was the man he'd locked eyes with that night. The one who had presented him with his award at the wine show. It was an arbitrary train of thought, but he'd file it away in the back of his head. There were answers out there, he just needed to start putting the pieces together. Harold was returning the next night, and he would work out how to catch him off guard. He knew something, Oliver was certain of it, and he wasn't going to let Harold leave without sharing it.

***

'Your vineyard manager, what's his name?'

'Gabe,' Oliver said to Rocky, who was balancing right near the crest of his ladder.

'Isn't he pretty tech savvy?'

Oliver watched as Rocky positioned the small camera on one of the top shelves, wedging it between a couple of bottles of dusty wine. It was noticeable if you looked hard enough, but he was sure no one would have any idea the camera was there.

'He's all right,' Oliver said. 'But I don't want anyone to know it's here. I'd rather you do it.'

'Not stealing from you, is he?' Rocky asked as he made his way down. Once there, he nabbed Oliver's laptop and began fiddling.

'No. Definitely not. I'd just prefer to keep things … covert.'

'Fair point,' Rocky said, pushing the computer back to Oliver. The screen was clear and there was a monochrome image of the two men talking, the ladder in the corner of the frame. You could see the piano clearly behind them. 'Do you want one in the other room with the barrels, or just in this part of the shed?'

'Here's fine,' Oliver said, checking out the footage that appeared on the screen. 'Wow, it's pretty sharp.'

'Yeah, it should work all right. Might have a few delays and drop out occasionally, depending on the signal. Oh, forgot to tell you,' Rocky went on, opening the bottle of beer Oliver passed him. 'Your brother was in the café on the weekend. Before, you know …'

Oliver swallowed his first sip of ale. 'Theo was at the café?'

Rocky squinted his eyes, concentrating. 'Yeah, on Thursday. He was the last customer we had. He was reading a book and writing something down.'

'It was definitely him?'

'Well, I thought it was you. Sarah told me you weren't as chatty as usual. And that you'd ordered a soy latte. I was cleaning the kitchen when he came in.'

'Jesus, soy milk. Should have raised the alarm.'

'I remembered you telling me ages ago you had a twin. Guessed that was him.'

'Only had one doppelgänger. As far as I know.'

'Sorry to hear, mate.'

Oliver nodded politely. It was maybe the first time he'd really been taken aback by someone acknowledging Theo's passing. 'Still need to get the funeral together. Haven't heard from the coroner.'

'Grisly business. Drugs, they reckon?'

'Apparently so. Not sure yet.'

Rocky took a long swill of beer. 'This is good. Different. What is it?'

'Something I make during vintage. A cleansing ale for when it's warm. It's nice to have a relaxing beer after a big day.'

Rocky laughed. 'So, you're already busy but you make a beer as well?'

'Yeah,' Oliver said, finishing the remainder of his bottle. He was nervous and had drunk it in three sips. 'A lot of pale ales on the market have the same annoying hops. This one is better.'

Rocky patted Oliver on the shoulder. 'You're different, mate.'

'What do I owe you?' Oliver asked. 'For your help.'

'Nothing.' Rocky flicked his hand. 'My pleasure.'

Oliver walked over to the wine shelves, grabbed the neck of a bottle and wiped away the dust. 'This is supposed to be good, but I've heard the winemaker's a bit of a nutter.'

'Ha,' Rocky said with a wide grin. 'All the best ones are.'

***

'You're drinking too much again,' Gabe said. He was sitting beside Oliver at the bar; they had just shared a lamb shoulder smothered in anchovy paste and sprinkled with mint, and Penny was opening a second bottle of red. In a strange upheaval of order, Oliver was electing to be away from the winery as often as possible.

'I'm not sure I even care at the moment,' Oliver replied. Penny poured a small sip for him, then offered one to Gabe, who initially waved his hand in protest before deciding to taste.

'That's really good. You can definitely get a feel for the grenache in there,' Gabe said, planting his nose deep into the glass.

'It's one of my favourites at the moment,' Penny said, topping them up. The inky hue comforted Oliver somehow. 'Why are the police bothering with a warrant? What do they think they'll find?'

'They think I've got something to do with it,' Oliver said. 'They've got the video footage of my car travelling down the main road at one in the morning. They even asked if you could've been driving.'

'Right.' Penny shook her head, baffled. 'It's really weird. I definitely didn't hear you get out of bed.'

'I barely slept, but still I didn't hear my car start outside. I would have woken up.'

The phone rang and Penny left to answer.

Gabe swirled the wine, took a small sip and turned back to Oliver. 'I'm sorry. But you did say to tell you if you were drinking too much. After how paranoid you got last time.'

Last time, Oliver thought. He'd been drinking heavily. Smoking too much weed. Something he'd given up until Theo arrived. Had it been five years since Gemma had left him? Five years since the waves of malaise had oscillated so intensely he could barely leave the house? His first romantic heartbreak had occurred well into his thirties. It had felt so banal – so untimely – at that age, but Oliver guessed that it always came for you, whether you were ready or not.

'Thanks, mate,' Oliver said.

'We'll get through it. Just a couple of hurdles.'

'You hated Orson.'

Gabe chortled. 'I didn't hate him. He was just full of himself. Homophobic.'

'I never saw that side of him.'

'That's such a fucking straight-man thing to say. Your business partners are eccentric, but they're smart and they make good wine. I'll give them that.'

'Smarter than I am.'

'You know I'll excuse excessive drinking, but I won't allow shameless self-deprecation.'

Oliver sighed. Penny walked past, a bottle in one hand and three glasses in the other. They both loved wine equally, but the thought of doing Penny's job made Oliver twitch.

Gabe finished his grenache and silently signalled for more.

'And you said I was drinking too much.'

'Yeah, well someone has to keep up with you. This is delicious, by the way,' Gabe said, as Penny poured. Once she had moved to another table, he added, 'Why didn't you tell me about Harold? What do you mean about his hands being all scratched up?'

'He said he'd done it when he was staining the back deck in Terrigal. But I just don't trust him. I'm lucky if he makes a phone call these days, let alone arrive on my doorstep unannounced.'

Before Oliver continued, he felt something behind him. Could sense someone's presence.

'Mind if I pull up a seat?' It was Murray Vernon.

'What do you want?'

Murray laughed, long and slow. 'Gabe, mate. What are you doing working with this rude prick?'

'Muz,' Gabe said, 'you smell like a brewery. Might be time to call a—'

'Fuck that,' Murray said, moving closer to Oliver. He could detect beer and garlic on Murray's breath. Chimney smoke and sweat. 'Just came to talk to our mutual friend here. Although, he never seems to give me a warm welcome.'

The vintage before last had been, in Oliver's words, an unmitigated disaster. It had rained for what felt like years. Buckets from the sky. Dirt roads had deteriorated into mud baths. No one's fruit was in good shape. Some winemakers, like Oliver, elected not to make much at all; small parcels to blend with older vintages, whites that became botrytis. Murray and Charlie had decided their fruit was mostly unaffected by the maelstrom. The Vernons' particular geographical position afforded them the privilege of a sheltered location that others in the area didn't enjoy. They told the media everything was fine and dandy with their fruit. Spruiked their wine and the fuck-awful vintage to anyone who'd listen.

'I don't have anything to say to you,' Oliver told him.

Murray sniggered slightly and rolled his head back, so far gone he was struggling to maintain control of his limbs. 'Only to the media, eh? About how shit our wine is.'

'What? One day I'm a recluse, the next I'm pillorying your wine to the media?'

'Penny,' Gabe said, leaning over the bar. 'I think our friend here needs a taxi. Would you mind calling us—'

'There's poison, they say. In the whisky.'

'Who's they?'

'Oliver, Gabe,' Murray slurred, circling his finger in front of both men. 'Shit look for our town. This poison and the murder. Mudgee's been through enough. I think it's time you boys packed up and ...' He drew a thumb, pointed to the door and whistled.

Oliver dropped the volume of his voice. 'My brother's dead, Murray. I thought out of anyone you'd be sympathetic to that.'

'Didn't know before now you even had a brother. You're not that open with things, are ya?'

Gabe stood up and walked across the bar to Penny, who was on the phone. A few diners had turned their attention to Murray and Oliver.

'Plus,' he said, his breath hot and heavy, 'I know your dirty little secret.'

'You're making a dick of yourself.'

He leaned closer to Oliver's ear, whispering. 'Does Penny know your old man killed your mum?'

Oliver didn't even look up. He felt spit lash his lobe. Grabbing Murray by the collar, he hauled him across the restaurant and pinned his neck to the wall.

'If you say anything like that ever again, I'll kill you.'

Murray made a sound – Oliver couldn't tell whether it was laced with fear or hubris – but before he could speak, he took a swing; grazed Oliver above the eye. Gabe moved in and ushered Murray to the door.

'Oh, you're more like him than you think,' he said. And then he said it again, before Gabe slammed the door closed.

Everyone in the bar sat in silence, the only sound coming from the speakers as one song faded into another.

***

The last of the red wine, the altercation, had left Oliver giddy.

'I didn't start that,' he said as the taxi left the vineyard. 'He was as pissed as a fucking parrot.'

'Yeah,' Gabe said, brushing something from his leather jacket. 'But you finished it. What are you doing roughing him up? In Penny's bar, of all places.'

'He knows.'

Gabe looked concerned. 'About your dirty little secret? Being more like him than you think?'

'He said to me, "Does Penny know your father killed your mum?"'

Gabe's let his head fall back. Exhaled. Gazed up to the sky. 'Oli, you should have told her from the start.'

Oliver vigorously shook his head. 'I don't want anyone knowing.'

'We are mates. But I didn't tell him, if that's what you're about to suggest.'

Oliver didn't respond. Instead, he watched Luna scratching at the window, murmuring a dictum of disapproval.

'Murray fucking Vernon. How would he know?'

'I have no idea.'

Gabe opened the door and Luna launched straight for Oliver's feet. He suspected Gabe had told Murray. Probably let it slip after too many wines in the corporate box at Royal Randwick. But what could he do? Gabe would never admit he'd divulged anything.

'I'd be locking that door, if I was you.'

'Why?' Gabe said, leaning down and scratching Luna's stomach.

'I think there's someone creeping around the shed. They keep pranking me on the landline.'

Gabe raised his eyebrows. 'Really? Right. Thanks for the tip.'

'I need to be the one thanking you. For helping out with Murray. I don't want to cause tension or trouble in paradise.'

'I did it as much for my sanity as yours.'

'Well,' Oliver said, beginning the stagger back to his cottage, 'that's why I pay you the big bucks.'

'Just for the record …'

When Oliver turned around, he could see Gabe illuminated in front of the porch light.

'You're far less like him than you think.'

***

Oliver opened a bottle of port and poured himself three fingers. Throwing a redundant log onto the dying fire, he sat on the lounge with a blanket. He was going to turn on the television, but he was too groggy and enervated to find the remote control. He was missing Luna. He'd have to adopt a dog; that would be a good distraction.

Eventually, he stood up and poured himself more wine, then got the fire going again. Went to the record player and put on the Sharon Van Etten LP he'd bought the week before. As he was about to sit back down, he heard a thump. It sounded as though it was coming from the roof. He waited, poised in an absurd half-crouch, but didn't hear anything more. He again went to sit down but heard another noise that was quickly followed by the sound of footsteps. Oliver walked to the verandah door, suddenly nervous, and clicked on the light.

You're more like him than you think.

He looked outside but couldn't see anything unusual. The cold was vicious. If someone had come to kill him, they wouldn't be skulking out there for too long.

If someone killed me now, would I die a good man?

Oliver walked back and sat on the lounge, eventually succumbing to fatigue and lying down. The record kept playing, echoing through the empty house.

He wondered how Theo could be tied up with drugs and crime rings after everything that had happened with their father. Oliver had been the one who went to the police first, he knew that. Theo was more scared of what would happen if their father wasn't found guilty – what he would do to them.

'There's blood in the boot,' Oliver had said to Theo. They could hear Miles crush an empty beer can in the living room before he expelled a large burp. The sound of laughter from a sitcom.

'So? It could be from something else.'

'You know it's not.'

Theo sighed. 'I know, but what if there isn't enough evidence to convict? You know what his temper's like. He'll throttle us if we send him to the police.'

'Fuck him,' Oliver said, unsure where the courage was coming from. 'Mum wouldn't run away now. Not without saying goodbye.'

'I get it.'

'But you don't want to do anything about it?'

'I'm scared, Oli. I don't know what he'll do.'

Oliver closed his eyes. 'I'll do it. You can stay here. But we can't let him get away with it.'

Oliver heard Miles stand from the chair and walk into the kitchen. Moments later, they heard the sound of a can being cracked open.

They both paused to make sure Miles was still enraptured with the television. They heard him let out a little giggle. Was he watching *Seinfeld*?

'He's a controlling arsehole with a temper, but I don't think he'd kill her,' Theo said.

'We need to make sure. I can't live with myself thinking I didn't do something about it.'

'Do you think he suspects anything?'

'Don't think so. We need to move, before he does something with the car. Cleans it or whatever.' As Oliver finished the sentence, Miles let out a trickle of little laughs.

'It makes me sick,' Theo said, 'that he's laughing right now.'

'I can't even go out there,' Oliver said.

While Miles watched television and Theo left the house, Oliver walked into his bedroom and closed the door. He strode over to his bed and lay down and screamed silently into the pillow, before beginning to sob, as soundlessly as he could, as intensely as he ever had before. Days later, his father would briefly be in custody for the murder of his mother, and for beating Harold to a pulp. The twins' grandmother would whisk them away. Change their names. Anything to protect them from their father. Not only because of what he'd done, but because of what he could do next.

Julia's body had been dumped in the ocean, before washing up within twenty kilometres of the family home.

***

There were noises outside, interrupting his thoughts. Oliver was sure someone was there, but he was too drunk to worry. *They can come for me*, he thought. Let them come. He wasn't like his father.

'I'm in here, you fuckers!' he yelled, before breaking into a fit of laughter at his own outburst.

He was alone. He was warm, and for the moment, that was all that mattered.

Dear Theo,

Your reply arrived today, quicker than some return an email. It's always exciting to receive something with a handwritten address in the pile of letters. Better than the envelopes with multiple plastic windows; the ones that tend to bear bad news.

You're right, people do perceive me as haughty. I suppose it's part of the trade. You don't want someone defending your livelihood if they're shaking their notes or repeatedly clearing their throat with uncertainty. I'm glad to hear that you do crosswords. I've done them since I was a kid, although admittedly I'm terrible at anything cryptic. Perhaps that's why I was attracted to you; being the straight shooter that you are.

If I asked for child support I'd be inviting you into my life, as well as the life of my future child. Do I want you in my life, Theo? I don't know the answer to that question. We've met, all in all, for a couple of hours. Opening up a dialogue is good, but to put you at ease, I'm not going to ask you for child support. You might be someone who hoards weird figurines, someone who doesn't wash their hands after they take a shit. I don't know you well enough to make a decision.

Furthermore, I have decided I won't be keeping the baby. While having children is something I've pondered for many years, I'm not sure the timing is right. I'm not sure that I'm ready. For a while, at the beginning, I thought that I would have the baby. On the train, I watched people walk past with prams. I watched mothers carry newborn babies on their shoulders. At the supermarket, I noticed men walking with their kids, dour-faced, looking for any kind of reprieve from the whining. Have you noticed how many fucking children there are in the world? I thought I was ready, but I'm not, Theo. It might sound selfish to you, but I'm not ready to give up everything I've built to walk around the supermarket, eyes sleep sapped, wondering what I've done with my life.

I've resisted the urgings from family for so long – to settle down, find an appropriate suitor with whom I will have children so my mother can be called 'Nanna'. I know for a fact that even those like me, who have maintained a staunch opposition to such a lifestyle, sometimes wonder whether it all might not be so bad, after all. But an hour later, I'm back to sharing feminist memes on Facebook and ranting on a news website about our country's dismal attempts at staving off climate change. I like drinking at a wine bar quite late after a hard day at court, my brain feeling as flat as batter. I can hear your protestations: raising a child and doing those things aren't mutually exclusive. I know that. I'm just getting my head around it.

I'm not sure if I'm ready to change my life so drastically. I'm not sure I'd be a good mother. I'm not sure the world needs another child. I'm not sure how I'll deal with the guilt of having it done, even though I've been programmed otherwise.

What would you do, Theo? If you found out you were carrying a stranger's child?

Yours,

Angie

8.

When Oliver woke up on the lounge, opening his eyes, someone was tapping his forehead with a bottle of wine.

'Good afternoon. Or good morning, whatever you'd prefer.'

It was Harold. Was it midday already? The light floating across the room was vivid.

'I knocked,' he said, 'but you were out of it.'

Oliver was dreaming that thugs had broken into his cottage. They'd made a mess, turned the furniture upside down, spilled coffee beans everywhere searching for money Theo had left behind; had tied Oliver up and thrown him in the back of a truck. Taken him to a warehouse in the city. Some of the same people in the picture with Theo. The mugshots.

Harold moved to the kitchen and placed the wine and a glass jar of something on the bench, the echo of his boots reverberating through the cottage. Oliver sat up and smudged his eyes with his palm.

'Big night?' Harold asked.

'Wasn't little,' Oliver said, eyeing the coffee table – there was a tipple of port still in the glass. 'Weren't you coming for dinner?'

Harold was dressed in dark jeans, a chartreuse button-up and a leather jacket. He stood in front of Julia's three paintings. 'I need to be back on the coast but thought we could cook lunch. I brought some lemons I preserved from last year. Been hankering for a good roast chook and I want to try out an Ottolenghi recipe.'

Oliver stood next to Harold, who was gazing at the paintings. Landscapes – more seascapes, really. One of a vineyard beside the ocean and the others of the land and the sea and the clouds. Somewhere on the Margaret River, where Julia had grown up. Wide strokes with thick oils. Close up, the paint was so glossy it appeared as though it hadn't finished drying. When Oliver stood back, everything morphed into something less abstract.

'Ah, don't we miss her.'

You miss the money.

No, that wasn't fair. Harold had always loved Julia. He'd encouraged her when others hadn't been as supportive. Miles was not an emboldening character. Oliver and Theo were too young to fully understand the gravitas of the art and the talent their mother possessed. Harold had fought hard for Julia when most others had found her style too risky to pursue.

'I miss her every day,' Oliver said eventually.

Harold appeared old. He was ageing ordinarily enough, but Oliver knew that when you only caught up with someone once every blue moon you noticed the wrinkles, the receding hairline, the extra paunch, that little bit more. Whenever Oliver thought of Harold, he remembered him the way he was when Oliver was a kid: a jet-black beard and the same thick glasses; someone always immaculately dressed. And now he was stooped slightly further forward, the little hair he had left had gone grey, beard white, voice gravellier and more guttural.

Over the years, Oliver had imagined Theo overseas, his appearance the same as the day he left – resembling someone who was perpetually twenty-two. Which was stupid, considering he stared at himself in the mirror every day and knew he'd left that juncture of life long ago. *Why would your twin cease ageing while you continued looking so much older?* It was a ludicrous supposition, but the mind was less rational than most of us considered. Oliver believed that.

He peered at Harold, who was deeply engrossed in Julia's art. *Did you peter out bit by bit*, Oliver nearly asked him, *or did you just change overnight?* This sudden shift from middle aged to fully bald? A slow coastal erosion or an unanticipated earthquake?

Under normal circumstances, he would have made a joke about it. Teased Harold about his grey hairs and extra chins. But instead, he stayed silent.

Harold broke the stillness by walking over to the coffee table and picking up a novel.

'Book, book,' he said. 'The sound a chicken makes. Don't know about you, young man, but I'm fucking starving.'

***

Heavy black clouds teetered in the distance, opaque over the mountains.

Harold clutched the Jesus handle of the ute. 'I didn't know it was going to storm today. It was clear when I left Orange. I should have grabbed some shopping on the way in.'

'They were predicting rain,' Oliver said, avoiding potholes as they drove towards town. It looked nasty; broodier than it usually did at this time of the year. 'Better get you fed and out of here before you're washed in.'

'The Beemer loathes this road when it's dry,' Harold said. 'Wouldn't like to be cruising around here while it's bucketing down.'

There was a small stretch of dirt and gravel between the tarred road and the vineyard that was fraught with holes and rocks. Uneven and imperfect. Oliver loved that it deterred tourists, although taking the Jaguar out for a drive along here wasn't always easy.

'Imagine it,' Harold said. 'You and me, stuck at the vineyard together for a couple of days.'

'Gabe's got a canoe. I'd paddle you out.'

'I'd love some time among the vines. A few days to relax.'

They passed a wombat, dead on its side. Oliver thought it appeared ready to leap away at any moment and mosey back into the trees.

'Harold,' Oliver said, 'I've known you for nearly thirty years and I don't think you've taken a proper holiday once.'

'I like a good working holiday. There'd be some bumbling artist I could sign up out here.'

He wanted to ask Harold about Theo. Why his twin brother had been to see him before arriving in Mudgee. *Why have you been here twice in a couple of days, when I've barely seen you for years?*

He opened his mouth to ask the question, but when he looked at Harold – gazing out at the countryside, watching a flock of sheep shuffling through the grass – he decided he'd wait until they were eating lunch.

He would bring it up once Harold had finished a couple of

glasses of wine. When he was becoming more relaxed, biddable, open to questions.

***

Harold tended to the chicken with precision. He stuffed it with stale sourdough crumbs and herbs he'd picked from Oliver's garden, then basted it with preserved lemon juice and stock. He even massaged morsels of salted butter under the skin. And once he'd placed it in the oven, he returned multiple times to watch it crisp under the element until it was done.

'I wish we had more time,' Harold said as they were eating.

'In life?'

'For the chook. You're supposed to let it almost go bad.'

'What are you talking about?'

'You're meant to warm up the meat before you cook it, make sure it's at room temperature so it cooks evenly. It makes the protein tenderer. If you put the chicken into the oven when it's too cold, the outside crisps up but the inside stays raw. So the outside is overcooked before the inside is even halfway where it needs to be.'

'It was fine,' Oliver said, rolling his eyes slightly.

Harold moaned as he chewed. The meat was good, but Oliver wondered whether it was for show. Part of his act. Always looking to plug the silence with something. Oliver had read somewhere that some men would rather zap themselves than spend time alone with their thoughts. Harold was one of those people. While Oliver kept himself busy, he'd learned to love the peace of the winery and the freedom to work at his own pace. It helped the past remain buried; kept it from rising too often to the surface.

'You're not eating much,' he said, pointing to Oliver's plate.

'I don't have a huge appetite at the moment.'

'You can talk to me. You know that.'

'Not much to say.'

'Let's go back to the day Theo arrived.'

'I'd rather not.'

'Why?' Harold was cutting up pieces of his chicken, as though preparing to feed a child. 'We both know you can't ignore it forever. It's not healthy, mate.'

'Righto,' Oliver said. 'Let's do it, then. Someone poisoned Theo, Harold. They beat him up. Bruised his ribs. Cut his throat with broken glass from a bottle of whisky. Or maybe he was so sick from the poison he cut his own throat to escape the pain. There was blood everywhere, skin scabbed, a bucket of bleach beside his dead body and specks of blood splashed up the wall. Is that what you want to hear?'

Harold leaned in. 'You need to talk about it. Let it out. It's no good festering inside—'

'I know you were here,' Oliver said, leaning back into his chair. 'The day he died.'

He was taking a punt by playing it this way. He didn't know whether Harold had been at the vineyard, but he wanted Harold to think that he knew more than he did, and it paid off when he saw the telltale sign that Harold was about to lie. The art dealer closed his eyes before shaking his head, feigning a look of indignation.

'What shit are you dribbling? I came here to see you, Oliver—'

'Stop lying. You were—'

'I didn't fucking kill him!' Harold said, straightening his jacket with a lugubrious movement. 'But I was going to talk to him.' Visibly rattled, dour, he grabbed his wine and tipped back the rest of the glass in one gulp. 'Whether he died or not, I was coming to visit on Sunday. Theo took something of mine.'

'You were here the day—'

'I visited you, yes. Two days ago.'

'So, the whole caring-about-me thing was just an act?'

'Stop talking fucking rubbish.'

'Well, what did Theo take?'

'Paintings,' Harold said. 'He took two of Julia's canvases. Unfinished ones. I thought he must have been visiting last week to … catch up. But he came for the unfinished pieces. I know she was your mother, Oliver, but they're mine. And I need them back.'

***

Oliver and Harold searched the kombi van. Behind and under the seats, in the back, lifted up the floor – they found nothing. They trawled the wine shed, Harold with the urgency of a setter on the scent. After a fruitless search, the rain began thrashing the shed's tin roof so loudly Harold could barely hear Oliver yell that there was no point looking any further.

'Why didn't you ever tell me about them?'

'What's there to tell,' Harold said half-heartedly. 'Your mother had so many unfinished pieces. You have the ones you wanted. You know I have to manage the estate. If Theo wanted them, he should have asked me. Not just pilfer them like a pickpocket in Prague.'

'How did you let him leave with them?'

'I didn't. He must have come back. I don't know how he took them, but they're gone.'

'How do you know it was Theo?' Oliver challenged.

Harold tilted his head and tittered. 'Don't they say a coincidence will always be a coincidence until its significance is realised?'

'I'm not sure it has been yet. I can't find them and neither can you.'

119

'He took them, Oliver.'

'Why does it matter so much if they're unfinished and not really worth anything?'

'Everything is worth something. You know that. Everything has its place, has its order. You don't just nab something you believe belongs to you.'

A few minutes after the BMW left the driveway, Oliver began hunting through the house. He turned on the lamps. It was quiet, the place peaceful, nothing ominous. He opened the spare-room door, its hinges groaning in protest. He gazed at the bed, stripped of its sheets, and the chest of drawers. The room was basically empty. Who had cleaned it? He certainly hadn't. The police? Maybe Gabe had helped – organised it without him knowing. It was something he'd never thought to ask.

Theo definitely hadn't mentioned anything about stashing paintings here. He hadn't had the chance. Oliver was sure if his brother hadn't been murdered that he would have told him about why he'd taken them from Harold.

Unfinished pieces? Oliver had never questioned any of the arrangements from his mother's art or her estate. He'd decided to let it be, and he was wondering now whether that had been a reckless oversight. He was realising that he should have heeded the warnings from Miles about Harold a little more genuinely.

Where were the paintings? Maybe someone Theo knew had seen him take them and had stalked him. The predator had waited until the prey was asleep in bed before it pounced. Theo, despite his proclivity for trouble, wasn't stupid. He was lucid when he'd showed up at the end of the driveway. He liked a drink and a joint, but that was nothing unusual. He didn't think Theo would leave two paintings, worth more than a block of land in Mudgee, in a navy kombi van. They were probably safe, somewhere else, a place known to no one other than Theo. Maybe he hadn't taken any of the paintings at all, and Harold was trying to throw Oliver off the scent?

Oliver remembered the bedroom they'd shared as kids. Where the two of them had hidden things. Theo had stolen a copy of their father's *Penthouse* magazine. They had a desk with a large black leather chair, which had a zip at the bottom where Theo had stashed the magazine. Oliver remembered they both took turns in sharing it, looking at the naked women, the sex. Maybe they were twelve? They had studied the pages like the contents were closer in style to a comic book than pornography. It was more educational and entertaining than it was erotic. Oliver remembered they also hid anything they wanted to keep private underneath the drawers of their bedroom cupboard.

A thought hit Oliver, suddenly. He'd slept beside Theo for the first fifteen years of his life, had loved and hated him for the next fifteen years, and then thought he would likely not see him again. How had he allowed them to drift so far apart? They'd lost their closeness, their bond, but Theo showing up on his doorstep was a sign that he had been ready to rekindle one.

He needed to find the paintings. Walking over to the chest in the spare room, he opened the drawers. They were empty inside. He pulled the bottom one off the track and looked underneath. There was nothing but clean carpet.

Oliver walked around the house. There were no drawers you could pull out in the living room or the kitchen. He checked the ones in his walk-in robe but found nothing. He went to the office and tried the chest of drawers, which he quickly realised were being used as a filing cabinet. He pulled out the bottom drawer and there they were. Two rectangles wrapped in butcher's paper, right at the back. He pulled them towards him and then placed them atop the desk. Ripping off the paper, he peered at the colours beneath, feeling both relief and dread course through him all at once.

Oliver had the two canvases in his hand and was about to leave the cottage when the phone started. Before he went to answer it, he ran to the office, opened the laptop and kicked the camera to life. He could see the piano, the cellar, which seemed empty. After a moment, he saw someone appear in the corner of the frame. Although they looked familiar, he couldn't tell who it was. He almost thought it was Chase, but he couldn't be sure. The man didn't have a phone to his ear. Oliver finally picked up the landline, expecting to hear the metronome, only to realise that he'd missed the call. He waited a moment, but the phone didn't ring again. When he refreshed the camera, the man was gone.

Keeping the light on, he walked to his car as fast as his legs would carry him.

***

Oliver kept glancing at the paintings on the passenger's seat as though they might suddenly dissipate if he wasn't careful.

On the outskirts of town, a car turned around and put its siren on. Oliver cursed, flicked his blinker and reached behind the passenger's seat in the ute, sliding the paintings as far back as they'd go.

When he saw the door open in the rear-view mirror, the car's interior light came on and Oliver noted that Sergeant Mulaney was in the driver's seat and another uniform was in the passenger's seat.

After a few moments, Mulaney approached. 'In a hurry, are we?' he said, surveying the scene.

'I wasn't speeding.'

Mulaney leaned down, staring into Oliver's eyes. 'Heard about your little squabble last night.'

'Huh?' Oliver said, growing anxious. 'What are you talking about?'

A couple of cars with bright-white lights whizzed past.

'You play it like that, then,' Mulaney said, raising his eyebrows. 'You're lucky I haven't arrested you both for assault. You know that?'

Oliver nodded, a schoolboy scolded.

'What does he know?' Mulaney demanded.

'Thought you had your finger on the pulse. Knew things.'

'If the Vernons are in any way involved, you need to tell us. Keeping this to yourself isn't going to do you any favours, Wingfield.'

'Maybe. My lawyer told me I shouldn't talk to you anymore.' It was a lie; Oliver still hadn't spoken to one.

'Don't do anything stupid.' Mulaney peered inside the car, his eyes quickly scanning the interior. His entire nose was pink, swollen like a pimple ready to pop. 'There's no reason I need to search the car, is there? Not in possession of any illegal substances or weapons?'

Oliver felt his heartbeat quicken. He was glad Mulaney's finger wasn't on his wrist or he might feel the speed of Oliver's pulse. How nervous he was. First, the stranger in his cellar, and now this. He could explain the paintings, but he was paranoid any connection to a canvas might raise an alarm, imply a connection with Theo's file.

'Go ahead,' Oliver said, pointing a thumb to the back.

The sergeant squinted his eyes, checking behind Oliver's head towards the rear of the vehicle. Oliver could tell, without the sergeant having to say anything, that Mulaney believed him to be innocent. Idiotic, reclusive, antisocial, perverse. A pain in the backside, but not guilty of murder.

'You know what. I've been living in Mudgee for twenty-two, nearly twenty-three years. And we've had plenty of drug busts, assaults and accidental deaths. But this feels cold and calculated, your brother dead like that. I want to get to the bottom of this before anyone else or anything else falls down here. Does that make sense to you?'

Mulaney paused, staring deeply into Oliver's eyes. To intimidate him, or to see if he was listening?

'You need to work with us. Do you understand that?'

Oliver smiled at Mulaney and said that yes, he understood. After the sedan had pulled out and driven away, Oliver reached down and touched part of the canvas, to make sure both paintings were still there. He watched a couple of sets of lights approach from the rear-vision mirror and move towards town.

Eventually, he put the car into gear and merged into the traffic.

***

It was dark and raining when Oliver reached Penny's, the wind scourging the gums and the hedges, the coldness so stark he felt it must be coming from snow.

The first thing Penny said when she opened the door was, 'I know it's been a shit week, but can you leave the punch-ups out of the bar?'

'I didn't start it,' Oliver said. 'You know he's an arsehole.' He pecked Penny's cheek, giving her a brief hug.

'I know,' she said. 'He knows better than that. To come into a bar that legless.'

They moved to the kitchen table, where there was an open magazine and a steaming cup of green tea. 'I was pissed off, but more so because I didn't hear from you. You should have called me.'

'I passed out,' Oliver said. 'And then Harold came the next day.'

'That name sounds familiar.'

'You know how I've told you my mum painted?'

'And played the piano?'

'Yeah. Well, Harold was her manager. He exhibited her works. I haven't seen him for years.'

'Oh,' Penny said, blowing on the steaming liquid. 'Was he closer with Theo?'

'Apparently, Theo visited before he came here. And there's something I need to show you.'

He walked back outside, grabbed the paintings from behind the seat and set them up on the dining table. Both were unfinished – some paint splotches on each canvas, pencil marks and lines. Newspaper and ripped paper were blotted to the canvas, a rough layer of gesso applied to both.

'They were stashed under a drawer in the office. Theo stole them from Harold. It seems that Mum painted them before she passed.'

Penny's fingers drifted to the canvas. 'Do you mind if I touch them?'

'Go for it.' Oliver did the same. Closing his eyes, he traced the coarseness of the canvas. He was hoping it would make him feel something profound – seeing a piece of his mother's artwork for the first time – but there was no smell, nothing fresh, just dried paints and the paper's curling, dehydrated edges.

'Can I keep them here?' Oliver asked. 'I want to find out why

Harold is so protective of them. I wouldn't be surprised if he decides to search for them again at the vineyard.'

'Of course,' Penny said, and Oliver took them to the office. As he placed them down, he noticed for the first time the small black writing in the bottom right corner of the paintings. One said, *Oliver 18th* and the other *Theo 18th*.

'Was she making these for your birthday?'

Oliver breathed in through his nose. 'I suppose so.' It gave him a sense of comfort, knowing Julia was painting them something. 'It's great she was starting them. Really sad, though, that we didn't get to see the finished product.'

Penny hugged him and offered him a wine, but when he didn't reply immediately, she took a bottle of gin and poured them each a good couple of nips, adding ice to each glass and topping it with tonic water. They sat down. The fireplace was toasty, painting the walls a warm amber.

'Tell me about the art,' Penny said.

'Mum was a good painter. You've seen her works, on my wall.'

'What was her name?'

'Julia Wingfield,' Oliver said, taking a sip of gin to quell the unease he felt at giving her a false name. 'She was talented, but obviously not every artist's success continues when they die.'

'Do you think Theo took them because they were meant for you?'

'Perhaps Harold hasn't passed them down like he was meant to. It might have been in Mum's will and he's ignoring her wishes. I guess it's a possibility.'

'But if they're not worth much, why bother holding on to them?'

It was a good question, but he couldn't really tell her the truth. That any work of his mother's – finished or otherwise – would be worth a small fortune. Which was what made the fact that Harold had never mentioned them before so suspicious.

'Although Theo was smart, he could be erratic as well. But I just don't think he would have stolen them for no reason. There must be more to it.'

'Smart but erratic sounds a little like someone else I know.'

After the gin, Penny reheated a duck pasta left over from the bar. Oliver hadn't realised – until he was halfway through the meal – how hungry the ordeal had left him.

'That really hit the spot. Thank you.'

Penny stood up, took their empty bowls and rinsed them in the sink. Oliver followed her into the kitchen as steam wafted through the room.

'It's funny how you can know so much about someone, but still so little.' Penny's words weren't heartening; they almost sounded like an allegation.

'Yeah,' Oliver said, hoping to avoid an argument.

'Do you think whoever killed Theo was connected to the paintings? Connected to Harold? But when they killed him they didn't find what they were looking for?'

'I have no idea,' Oliver said. 'I really don't know why Harold or anyone would kill Theo for a couple of unfinished paint blobs on canvas. He would have given them up.' Or would he have fought to keep them? Oliver couldn't be sure of anything at this stage.

'These people in the photos that detective showed you. They were involved in art heists. Maybe Theo was doing something for them?'

'Maybe, but I can't find any other clues. I've looked for any kind of hint, but there's nothing. Other than the fact that Harold wants them back. But Harold's an old gallerist. He'd stress about a parking fine. I don't think he's telling me everything, but I don't think he or this group the police mentioned killed Theo.'

'Then who did?'

Oliver wasn't sure how he was going to tell her about his theory. Clare had basically insinuated that he was crazy, and while Gabe had been intrigued, he'd quickly rebuffed him and hadn't brought it up again.

'Do you remember when I went to the wine conference last year with Clare?' he began. 'Orson flew down for it as well.'

'You actually leaving town? Of course I remember.'

'Well, the three of us were having a drink in the hotel courtyard. Then we saw a politician holding hands and flirting with his secretary. He looked shocked, annoyed, when he knew we'd seen something.'

Penny rolled her eyes. 'Barely page-three bullshit, by the sounds.'

'His secretary was a man. And John Geraghty has a wife and children,' Oliver said. 'I have a bad feeling about him. The way he glared at me. A few months later Theo winds up dead, and I'm thinking maybe it should have been me. And it seems likely that Orson was poisoned and now I'm really worried about Clare.'

'Wait,' Penny said, sitting up straighter and moving away from him. 'You honestly think he'd have you killed? To keep you quiet?'

'I don't know. It's possible, isn't it? I've got nothing else. Other than Harold.'

Penny breathed in through her nose; she exhaled a sound that was a blend of a sigh and a groan. 'It's all fucked up, that's what it is.'

Oliver felt himself burr up. 'So, you think that my theory is fucked?'

'I didn't mean that. I said this whole thing's fucked.' Penny waved her arm in the air, emphatically.

'I don't know. The cops think I might have something to do with it. If Orson was poisoned and Theo's dead, it's not looking good for me. And Harold wants his precious paintings back.'

'Are you going to give them to him?'

'I honestly don't know yet,' Oliver said. 'I just want all of this to be over. I just want to be checking on my barrels and tending to my old vines. I want Theo's funeral done with and to be able to move on in peace. I've never left the bloody vineyard so much since I've owned it.'

'I don't think you have anything to worry about with Clare. Maybe Theo got in too deep and Orson had a heart attack? I think you just need to cooperate with the police and it'll all be over soon.'

'Yeah, if no one kills me first,' Oliver said, standing up. 'I really think there's some link here, something bigger going on, and it's pissing me off that no one's taking me seriously.'

'I didn't say I wasn't taking it seriously.' Penny went to say something else, but stopped.

'You didn't have to,' Oliver murmured. 'If it's not Geraghty, then who? Why would Harold be framing me? And who could have driven my car from your place to my cottage the night Theo died without either of us hearing a thing? If Harold didn't kill Theo, the only other person could be me.'

Penny sat up abruptly, letting go of the cushion she'd had pressed to her belly. 'But you didn't!'

He pointed to his car parked on the street, feeling his frustration mounting. 'I know! But they've got video footage of the car leaving this terrace and driving to the winery. How the hell did that happen?'

There was a long, heavy pause.

'Oliver, what was Murray talking about at the bar?'

He felt a prickle of panic. 'What do you mean?'

Looking up, he noticed Penny was the picture of frustration. 'I heard what he said to you. About your "dirty little secret".'

'I honestly don't know—' he began, but she cut him off.

'*Honestly*, I think you do.'

'No, Penny. He was drunk. Ranting, being a dickhead.'

'And yet he seems to know something about you that I don't. Why is that, Oliver?'

Gabe's voice came to him: *Oli, you should have told her from the beginning.*

'Don't you get it?' Oliver said indignantly. 'I don't *want* to talk about it. I moved to Mudgee for the sole reason that I don't have to fucking talk about it.'

'Yeah,' Penny sneered. 'You've made that pretty clear.'

'Just ...' *Come on*, Oliver thought. *Use your words.* 'All we do is pretend, Penny. Drink wine and talk shit. And now you want to suddenly act like you care about me and everything that's happened in my past?'

Penny pulled back. 'You think everything between us is just an act?'

Wrong words.

'I didn't mean it like that.'

'Oh, it definitely sounded that way to me. You've had a big day,' she said. 'I think it's time you go home and sleep it off.'

He leaned towards her. 'Penny—'

She jerked away from him and stood abruptly. 'I'm going to bed now,' she interrupted. 'Before I say something that I shouldn't.'

'I'm sorr—'

'See yourself out.'

Oliver closed his eyes, expecting to hear the door slam, but the sound never came. He found his keys on the bench and made sure the door was latched as he closed it behind him.

9.

Oliver rose early, dread moving through him with the force of a hangover. He walked past the vines and the falling leaves to the creek, where he stood and watched the sunrise materialise behind wispy clouds. He fixed a wind sensor in the vineyard and was relieved to see Clare had already added her inputs. After half an hour, feeling more human, he ambled back to the house and stood under a hot shower until his skin was pink and wrinkled.

In his room, he packed an overnight bag with a change of clothes, toothbrush and a bottle of wine. Suddenly drowsy, he sat down on the bed and, after setting his phone alarm as a precaution, rested his head on the pillow. The next thing he knew, he was jerking awake, propelled out of a dream, still draped in a towel, to the sound of a thump. A persistent knocking.

Putting on pants and a shirt, he walked out of the bedroom, but there was no one standing at the glass-paned door. As Oliver stepped outside the cottage, he noticed Ida's car parked beside the navy van. She'd already walked to the wine shed, had let herself in and was tinkling on the piano.

'You forgot I was coming, didn't you?' she said, smiling at him, playing three increasing chords in quick succession, each movement made with a kind of dexterous precision. He realised then, observing the look on her face, that she had no idea what had happened to Theo.

'Ida. I'm sorry. I forgot to call you.'

'Impudent to cancel now. Didn't your mother teach you that's no way to treat a lady?'

'The murder,' Oliver said, without really thinking. 'You didn't hear about ...'

Ida stood from the seat, walked over and set her hand on Oliver's arm. 'I seldom leave the house and I barely listen to the wireless these days. You'll have to take it from the top.'

They walked outside. Oliver told her about staying the night at Penny's and coming home to find his brother dead, throat slit with blood everywhere.

'Oh, Oliver. Oliver, Oliver, Oliver, I'm so sorry.'

'Thank you,' he said. They were both too awkward to instigate a hug.

'I wish, I – I honestly had no idea.'

'I should have called. To cancel.'

'You have more pressing things on your plate. It was strange, actually. It's not like you to forget a lesson. I knew if you put me off today, something was wrong.'

'Pardon?'

'Well, I came out here early on Monday evening. After six, as scheduled. But you weren't here. When I knocked on the door, there was a man inside.'

'A man?'

'Yes. Not Gabriel. Someone I'd never met. He didn't introduce himself. He said that you'd gone out for dinner and that you'd give me a "buzz".'

'Ida. There was a man inside the cottage?'

She stopped, swivelling towards Oliver. 'Well, yes. I assumed that he was staying with you. He seemed to be in command of the ship.'

'Hold on, what did he look like?'

She gripped her bottom lip between her thumb and finger, like a student poring over a maths problem. 'Oldish. My mother might have said fanciable. Thick dark glasses, not much fluff on top. Debonair. Noticeably so for a man in Mudgee.'

Oliver sighed and said, 'Sounds like you met Harold. He's been poking around, looking for something he lost.'

***

Rocky was frothing milk, his apron coated in coffee grounds, when Oliver walked into the café. The room was empty save for a young couple at the back, obviously tourists, hands together on the table. It was almost closing time.

'I'll take one of your best double piccolos,' Oliver said. 'To go.'

'You know a piccolo should always be a double ristretto? And I don't do weak shit. Also, I didn't see you as the fighting type.'

Oliver had forgotten the bruising around his eye. He offered only a fake punch as a way of explanation.

'Did you find who was snooping around your cellar?'

'I wish,' Oliver said, taking the coffee from Rocky.

'Food?'

Oliver perused the contents of the small display fridge. 'Got any banana bread?'

'Toasted?'

'Yeah. Throw some butter on it.'

Rocky smiled. 'It comes with a little walnut crumble and our espresso butter.'

'Christ,' Oliver said. 'Actually, don't worry about toasting it. I need to hit the road because I slept through my alarm.'

Rocky peered up at the clock. 'Fuck me, I think I'm going to throw in the towel and become a winemaker. You hiring?'

***

Oliver played Rachmaninoff. When he got bored of listening to that – he'd heard it so many times – he found an old Pixies CD in the console and let the car swallow it from his fingers. Penny was on his mind. He knew that he should call her – message her, at least – but he wasn't sure what to say. He would eventually apologise, but he needed more time.

Oliver knew his lies were reaching their expiry, but he couldn't tell her everything now. How long until she googled Harold's gallery and perused his clients and the estates he managed? There'd be something online about his mother. Penny would keep clicking and she'd find it. Fucking Theo. Fucking Harold. Everything had been going so well. Oliver needed to sort out what had happened. He wanted to get everything together before he turned into a blathering mess on the phone. Talk to Clare; he hoped she had spoken to Valerie.

When he arrived in Orange he checked into an old hotel, all of its character reserved for the exterior of the building. Oliver assumed the interior would be quaint with a heritage vibe – small chandeliers, old door handles with large keyholes, string cord light switches – but instead the place had been renovated years before, with a brief to keep it simple and modern. It was awkwardly incongruous. Oliver thought about staying with Clare, but preferred being able to leave if he was feeling tired or uncomfortable. In case he had the sudden urge to be alone.

The receptionist smiled at him as he entered the hotel. 'Welcome back.'

She was in her forties, blondish hair with brown tips that swayed at her shoulders. Smile full of teeth.

'Thank you. Here I was thinking it was my first time.'

'The other week,' she said. 'You and a lady.'

Oliver studied the foyer. It was clean and basic, with tourist brochures strewn over the counter. 'I haven't been to Orange in years.'

The woman was perplexed. 'I must be mixing you up with someone else. Do you have a reservation?'

'Not yet,' Oliver said. 'Just a night if you have one available.'

'No problem.' The receptionist typed slowly, careful not to dislodge her acrylic nails.

'Sounds like I've got a doppelgänger,' Oliver said. 'Might have been separated at birth.'

The woman only smiled weakly. *She thinks I'm being a prick,* Oliver thought. He wanted to tell her it was most likely his twin brother who had checked in with a woman. The same twin brother he'd found dead, in his cottage, a week later.

***

Oliver walked upstairs to his room and sat down on the firm bed. Bounced twice. What the hell had Theo been doing in Orange? Surely the receptionist would have searched the previous registration and discovered their last names matched as soon as he'd left the room. She'd checked his licence, possibly for that purpose. A woman? Did Theo have someone special in his life? He closed his eyes, wishing he'd asked his brother more questions.

He tried to relax, but his imagination wouldn't let him sit still. Deciding to walk downstairs, he found a small waiting room with a computer for guests. Opening Google, he searched 'Harold Keller and Julia'. Of course there were articles. No photos. They'd worked together in a time before the internet was ubiquitous. There was an article that mentioned Julia's art and her murder, but having to click a few pages to get there, Oliver wondered whether it was as obvious as he'd thought. He then simply searched 'Harold and Julia' and was glad to find nothing of relevance.

What the hell had Harold been doing snooping in his house when he was supposed to be in Orange? He'd obviously been looking for the paintings. But to let himself in when he knew Oliver was away? There was now more than one reason to ensure he locked the doors and windows each time he left.

Oliver googled John Geraghty. Deep down, he knew it was a silly theory that he needed to abandon. He read a couple of paragraphs of an article relating to parliamentary privilege before he was bored. There was nothing really that piqued his interest, nothing else slightly scandalous. He opened a photograph of Geraghty and looked into the man's eyes. Was he capable of subterfuge? Double murder? Unlikely. Oliver could barely even convince himself anymore; he knew he was using his memory of Geraghty as a scapegoat. Trying to deny any other possibilities from being real, possibilities that would sting.

After half an hour, Oliver went back to his room and grabbed his car keys. He was keen to walk among the vines with Clare and check on her grapes. Her vineyard was perched beside a mountain, and the chardonnay was a textbook-perfect example of the variety. He loved Clare's chardonnay as much as he did similar wines from Chablis.

Clare was more of a social winemaker than Oliver. She owned a cellar door, ran a wine-tasting club, and displayed the basics like a website with a phone number and an email address. The property had an elaborate brick front gate that reminded Oliver more of a wealthy thoroughbred stable than a winery.

By the time he arrived, the cellar door had turned its blackboard to reveal 'CLOSED'. He pulled the Jag into one of the parking spaces and walked up to the glass and peered inside. The room was modern, clean, empty. Hanging wineglasses, a spittoon in the centre of the room. After a moment, Oliver heard footsteps on gravel, followed by a cacophony of barking. Two sausage dogs blowing his cover.

He crouched down and tried to pat them, the attempt futile.

'Don't worry,' Clare said, walking towards him. 'You're not getting special treatment. They're like this with everyone.'

'You'd think they'd be more social after all of these years,' Oliver said, looking at the brown dachshund near his feet, which was still barking, its once tan nose now speckled with grey and white.

'You'd think so,' Clare said. 'They're nothing if not consistent.'

He moved in and kissed Clare on the cheek, giving her a hug.

'I thought Penny was coming,' she said, taking a band from her hair and letting it fall across her shoulders. It was jet black, the odd bit of white visible at the roots. 'She wasn't the one who gave you the black eye?'

'Sadly not,' Oliver said, grazing it with his thumb. 'She had to work. Festival in town or something.'

'Fair enough.' Clare walked towards the house, the dachshunds trotting determinedly behind her. 'There's always some kind of tourist event these days.'

'I wouldn't know,' Oliver said. 'I don't really do the tourist thing.'

'Maybe you should. Take Penny on a holiday. You both deserve it.'

'I guess. I need to get everything sorted with Theo first.'

Clare grabbed a jacket and they walked across the vineyard, catching up on everything that had changed in their lives over the preceding days. Then, the weather. Droughts, fires, floods; news from the unpredictable part of the earth they found themselves living in. The wine they'd been drinking. Clare hadn't heard from Valerie again. Oliver didn't bring up his theory about John Geraghty, nor did he mention anything about the paintings, and Clare didn't touch the subject.

'So, what happened to your face?'

'Let's save that one for dinner.'

'If you insist.'

Kicking the gravel with his feet, he asked, 'Have you spoken to a lawyer about the business?'

Clare sighed and looked towards the mountains. Everything was green and amber and gold. The wind stirred the trees and leaves fell in front of their feet. The sound of birds darting between trees, frolicking before sunset, permeated the atmosphere.

'Only briefly. He said it's not going to be complicated. Orson set up the initial plan to be quite simple. We just buy out whatever his share is worth and go from there. I think his brother already requested a valuation.'

'Thought he would have. Let me know when you need me to sign something.'

'Of course,' Clare said, waving her hand, a movement that said *later*. 'I've made some gnocchi for dinner. Picked a pumpkin out of the garden earlier. Want to help me cook?'

'You have a good memory.'

'Why's that?'

'I remember telling you one of the best pairings in the world was your chardonnay with gnocchi.'

'I've got a couple of vintages for us to try.'

'Jesus, what are the cops like here? I might get a bit tipsy.'

'You'll be fine,' Clare said. 'You're welcome to stay the night.'

'I might have to. I'm sure it's more of a criminal offence to leave your wine unfinished.'

***

It began to rain, gentle and diligent. Oliver cut the pumpkin into chunks, bathing the tray in olive oil and spices, before sliding it into the oven. Clare was cutting the log of gnocchi into pieces akin to small pillows. She tossed them through flour, a spray of snow across the bench, and marked each one fastidiously with a fork. There was a pot of water boiling on the stove. Steam everywhere. Clare didn't bother with things like rangehoods or bathroom fans.

When the pumpkin was cooked, she removed it from the oven. And after the gnocchi floated to the top of the salty water, she spooned the pasta into a spitting pan of butter, folded the pumpkin through and topped it with crisp sage leaves. At the table, she showered his bowl with shavings from a crusty wedge of pecorino.

'Not going to lie,' Oliver said, taking a sip of wine. 'This is probably the most relaxed I've felt for a long time.'

'That was indeed the plan.' Clare tipped her bowl back, basting the last potato dumplings with the sauce. 'Getting out of town always helps. So, are you going to tell me what happened to your eye?'

'Murray Vernon happened.'

'What?'

'He came into Penny's bar asking for trouble. Told me and Gabe that Mudgee has been through enough without a murder and poisoned wine. He was acting all high and mighty, like he owns the town.'

Clare put her wine down onto the table. 'Fucking hell, Oli. That's awful. The last thing you need.'

'Yeah. Well.'

'You don't think they have something to do with Theo's death, do you? They're renegades, those Vernon boys, but I don't see them as the killing types.'

'I doubt it,' Oliver said. 'But I don't know anymore. I can't seem to put anything together. The police don't really have much, other than trying to pin it on me.'

'It's hard to imagine,' Clare said, off on a tangent. 'Your identical twin looking so much like you but being so different. Chalk and cheese.'

'I hate that saying.'

'Riesling and pinot grigio?'

'That's worse.'

Clare took a sip of wine. 'I'm out of idioms.'

'I don't know. We're alike in some respects. Theo was more outgoing than I am, but he still kept things close to his chest. He didn't even slightly imply what he was involved in – this art business, or taking the paintings from Harold.'

'Hold on. He took paintings from Harold?'

'Yep. And Harold's been snooping around my cottage looking for them. I have a feeling that he's embroiled in this somehow. Actually, more than a feeling. I know he is, I just don't know *how* he fits in.'

'There's got to be more you can find out,' Clare said, before forcefully holding up her hand. 'But don't. Let the police do the work. They'll find it. They're smarter than you think.'

'Maybe,' said Oliver. 'I don't know.'

He took the empty bowls to the sink and slid them into a bath of suds. Clare was taking the cork out of another bottle, and Oliver walked out of the kitchen as it popped.

'I shouldn't,' he said. 'Big day tomorrow. Big drive.'

'One more glass. I'll seal it up. The punters won't know their luck in the cellar door in the morning.'

'I might have to call in before I leave,' he teased. 'Be a pest. Ask the staff some technical questions.'

'They're well trained.'

'What percentage of new oak does the wine see? Which clone? What kind of soil? How high is the vineyard above sea level?'

'They'd have a good stab at those if they don't know already,' Clare said. 'Believe it or not, there are some real wine wankers out there you have to cater for. And the trade, of course.'

'You've reminded me why I don't have a cellar door.'

'Jesus, imagine you talking to people without being a prick. I think Gabe would manage, but not you.'

'He's talked about it. But he believes our cloistered style of marketing works best.'

'Each to their own. It's a lot harder doing the cellar door without Max.'

Clare and her late husband had purchased the vineyard together more than twenty years ago. He wasn't a winemaker – had nothing to do with that part of the business – but he had been instrumental in spruiking the brand, running the cellar door and doing things behind the scenes that were integral to the operation.

'Has it gotten easier?'

'No,' Clare said, smiling. 'Not easier. Different. Sometimes, it feels like a completely new place.'

Oliver hadn't met Max. He'd died around the time Oliver purchased Four Dogs Missing.

'How did Max pass?'

Clare swirled the wine in her glass. She was adept at it, like a professional wine writer showing off to a group at a tasting. 'Heart attack. What you'd call your stock-standard myocardial infarction. He would have hated that it was so banal.'

Sometimes, Oliver forgot that both Clare and Max had been doctors before becoming winemakers.

'The same as Orson?'

Clare frowned. 'Can't be certain as I haven't seen his death certificate. Max presented with the same symptoms, though. Chest pain, nausea, vomiting, sweatiness. We called an ambulance, and the ECG showed ventricular tachycardia. With the chest pain preceding, I knew it must have been a massive heart attack. Max would have known it'd kill him before he died. Despite being a general practitioner for most of his life, he liked a cigarette and cigar with the best of them. He wasn't always a picture of good health.'

'Orson was pretty healthy. Do you think it's the same thing?'

'It's hard to say. I didn't assess him or see any of the results. Sadly, it's not uncommon for any man – or woman, in fact – of that age to have a heart attack, Oli. There could have been previous problems he hadn't disclosed. Patients can lie just like anyone, even though it might negatively affect their health. It's interesting, though. When you brought up the poisoning, I did a bit of research.'

'Of course you did.' He'd expected nothing less from someone as methodical as Clare.

'There are many poisons aside from sodium fluoroacetate that are tasteless and odourless that cause arrhythmias, as well as ECG changes that mimic a heart attack. And a fast arrhythmia can cause chest pain. So, I'm not going to call you crazy because it's possible that someone could have poisoned Orson. I spoke to Valerie and told her to seek a detailed autopsy and obtain a toxicology report. I'm not sure how long they take over there, but it will be the only way to know for certain.'

They talked through another glass of wine. Oliver felt relaxed enough not to bring up Harold or the Vernons again. Maybe Clare and Penny were right: Theo was the one responsible for his own demise. Maybe Orson's ticker had stopped racing. After all, someone of his age and profession was probably a prime candidate for a heart attack. A clear toxicology report would certainly quell Oliver's anxiety, though.

'I forgot to tell you,' Oliver said. 'When I checked in at the hotel today, the receptionist mentioned that I'd been there before with a woman.'

'What do you mean?'

'It was definitely like Theo had been there with someone.'

Clare nodded, a little addled, tapping her fingernails on the tabletop. After a moment she stood up, the chair groaning on the bare boards. She looked suddenly fretful. 'Let's go outside, darling. There's something I need to tell you.'

The dachshunds followed them. The dappled dog sniffed

around the wet garden, while the old boy cocked his leg and pissed on a verandah post. The rain left a cold breeze in its wake. Oliver shivered, pining for a cigarette.

'I didn't take too much notice,' Clare said, 'but one of the girls who works in the cellar door said that you were here.'

'What do you mean?'

'A few weeks ago. I was visiting my sister for the night. Amanda only told me the other day that you came to the cellar door.'

'What for?'

'She said you tasted the wine, engaged in conversation, and that you were with a woman.'

Oliver paused. 'So, you think it was Theo?'

'I thought she must have been confusing you with someone else. I just didn't really think too much of it. And when I found out Theo had been murdered, I wondered, but I wasn't sure telling you he may have been here would have helped at all.'

Oliver nodded. 'What do you think he was doing?'

'You can come here if you're heading to Mudgee. Maybe he stopped in. It's just enough of a coincidence to mention, now that someone else in town also thought you'd been here.'

Oliver walked over to a wrought-iron table and sat down on one of the chairs, pulling his jacket around him. Clare had picked up one of the dogs and was holding it in her arms.

'Did he mention he stopped in here? Did he have a partner?' she asked.

Oliver sighed, rubbing his stubble. 'He didn't say. It's what I'm most guilty of, you know. I assumed we'd have more time. That he'd tell me about his life – open up the longer he stayed. I didn't want to jump straight into the specifics. Didn't want him to feel like I was interrogating him. When we were younger, he always accused me of belittling him, of making him feel like the dumb one. So, I didn't ask for that reason. Stupid, isn't it?'

'You're not a psychic, my dear. You weren't to know someone was going to arrive and poison him and slit his throat.'

'They did a good job,' Oliver said. 'There was blood everywhere. I'll never be able to unsee it.'

'I'm sorry.' Clare moved towards him and grabbed his hand in hers. Her nails were painted a glossy crimson. 'I'm glad you're talking about it.'

'One positive. Despite the fact that he'd been murdered, he looked at peace. So often he wasn't quite comfortable, drifting from place to place, trying to discover something. He was discontented. But when I found him, it was as though he'd accepted something. It was as though he was looking right at me. It's hard to explain.'

Clare didn't speak, just squeezed his hand in sympathy. 'I'll help you find his friends. The girl he was with. We'll give him a proper funeral,' she offered.

'It's okay, you don't have to—'

'Shut up. That's what friends are for. Now, would you like a nightcap or do you need to find a pillow?'

Oliver checked his watch. It was nearly nine. If he had a whisky, he'd get drunk and emotional with Clare. He remembered the wine he'd packed in the suitcase, which was still in the hotel room. If he needed help sleeping, he'd have a tipple there.

'I think I need a pillow, if that's all right.'

'Of course it is. You look like you've run a marathon. The spare bed's ready to go.'

'No, it's okay,' Oliver said. 'I've only had a couple of wines. I've paid for the hotel room, so I may as well use it.'

Clare placed the dog on the ground and pulled Oliver into an embrace. She smelled faintly of French oak and freshly laundered clothes.

Oliver walked inside, found his keys and said goodbye to the dogs, who ignored him and instead loped for cover behind their culinary benefactor. As he opened the car door, it began to sprinkle. 'I'll see you for a coffee in the morning,' he told her. 'Behave yourself.'

'No fun in that,' Clare said as Oliver closed the car door and kicked over the ignition.

Dear Angie,

I like how you use words. You remind me of someone I knew in London. We get on well, although she always disliked anything popular and used to get into an argument at the drop of a hat. Seemed to love it. Must be a lawyer thing? I'd much prefer to fade into the surroundings.

I will admit your letter hit me pretty hard. I guess I never thought it would actually happen to me. You know – getting someone pregnant. By accident. My mother's not even alive to scold me for omitting a condom.

I know I don't have any say in the matter, but I think it's good you're still working out what you want to do. Whatever you decide will be the right decision. I guess it has to be. We seem to tell ourselves it is. We choose the lives we want for ourselves – someone said that to me once and it just stuck. We think there are forces out there that make decisions for us, but we send every message, make every call, decide where to eat every dinner. We choose the lives we want for ourselves. Even if it's not the life we think we deserve. Somehow, we seem to stay. Or we leave ...

Sadly, there are no weird figurines at my house. I should probably tell you a little more about me. As you know, I live in Chippendale, but I don't spend a whole lot of time here. I'm pretty close to the city still, I guess. As we talked about a couple of months ago, I work for a courier company and bartend at night-time. I basically drive packages around through the day (sometimes over a couple of days) and shake a jigger over my shoulder at night. I worked in a lot of bars overseas, so I suppose it's kind of my profession.

I haven't always lived in Sydney. At different stages I have lived in London, Milan, Bruges, Singapore, Phuket, San Francisco and the

Napa Valley. As a kid I grew up in a small town near Sydney, but we moved to the Central Coast when I was in primary school.

Random fact. Not sure I mentioned it when we met, but I'm actually an identical twin. My brother's name is Oliver and he's a winemaker. He's always been the more successful sibling. We were close once, but I moved overseas and I haven't made any effort since I've been back. I feel guilty about it every day, but I guess he hasn't tried too hard to find me, either.

Last things: I really like old Hollywood films and I have an impressive collection of cocktail bitters. More appropriate than figurines, I hope. I've begun writing a diary. Putting together some stories. Memories. An attempt at catharsis, maybe?

Once you have the baby (or don't have the baby), you should come to my place and I'll make you a cocktail. I promise I won't judge your choice. I like writing to you, but I'd also love to see you one day. If you'd like that.

Peace,

Theo

10.

Oliver left Clare's vineyard through the palatial-looking gate and veered left onto the road that went all the way into town. He drove into the hotel's parking lot and realised, as he patted his pocket, that he'd left his phone on Clare's table. He checked between the seats, in the cup holder, but no dice.

Shit. He wondered briefly whether he could wait until the morning, but he wasn't sure when he might need it. The truth was, he felt safer waking up with it by his side because it doubled as his alarm.

Walking upstairs, he entered the room. Spotted a fake bunch of globe artichokes in a glass vase and decided it would do. After rinsing the vase in the sink, he opened the bottle he'd brought with him and quickly decanted the wine. He then swirled the liquid around the vase and left it to open up.

Oliver struggled out of his jeans, which were definitely feeling too tight after the bowl of buttery pasta. He took a shower and changed into a tracksuit. Pouring himself a small taste of the wine, he decided it needed a bit longer to open up – it would be perfect when he returned.

Back into the car, heading off along the main road. There was another way that would get him there at a similar time, but he didn't want to think too hard about the route he was taking. Apart from one car in the distance, the road was quiet, cold. Gum branches flapped in the breeze, intensifying his anxiety. The grass on the roadside was long after the rain, and Oliver kept checking it fastidiously for roos. About one hundred metres from Clare's driveway, the sedan in the distance put on its blinker and turned into the winery.

Oliver touched the brakes, but then decided to keep driving slowly to avoid suspicion. He looked at the car's clock: nine-fifty-four pm. Driving past the gate, he watched as the sedan crept towards the cellar door, where he had parked a few hours earlier.

He turned his car into another of Clare's driveways, a hundred metres or so away. There was a gate – this one a touch more spartan – with a padlock and a chain alongside a 'NO TRESPASSING' sign. It was the road that some of the viticulturists and labourers used to access the westerly vineyards.

Who would be visiting Clare now? Oliver had asked about her life; she hadn't volunteered anything unorthodox, hadn't mentioned any love interests. Maybe he should turn around and go home? He really had no intention of interrupting Clare in the throes of passion. Another thing he'd never be able to unsee.

Sighing, he switched off the ignition and decided he might as well check out what was going on, see who was inside. Even if the visitor had turned up at Clare's on a romantic whim, Oliver would still have time to say hello and grab his phone before anything intimate began. Clare wasn't a teenager anymore. Surely, she and whoever was with her couldn't light the fire that quickly in the cold.

Closing the car door, he was halfway towards the gate when he realised he'd left his lights on. Oliver walked back to the Jag, flicked off the lights and locked the doors. Then he leaped over the gate and jogged alongside the vines, through some shiraz plantings, until he could see the house. The lights were still on in the kitchen. As he moved closer, he could see the sedan not far from where he was. He couldn't read the numberplate. It was an older model, maybe from the late nineties. It was probably red once. A rough life and years of weather had helped paint it pink.

He stepped up onto the balcony. One of the dogs was barking, the other yelping.

A man's voice, a baritone.

Oliver walked towards the door. Pulling his fingers into a fist, he knocked twice. A couple of seconds passed and he heard the sound of a gunshot. It was immediately followed by another. Muffled, as if they'd been fired through a silencer. The *pew* of the blast reverberated through Oliver's ears. A sound he'd heard hundreds of times in films, but never in real life. The dogs began to howl.

Fuck.

He felt the muscles in his stomach tighten. As he crept to the end of the balcony, but just before he'd turned the corner, a man dressed in black-and-grey tracksuit pants and a hoodie ran out the door. Oliver didn't see his face. Had the man seen him? He didn't have time to decide.

Once Oliver turned the corner, he galloped across the grass towards the vines, into the dark, as fast as his legs would take him.

He sprinted until he reached the fence of the neighbouring property. As he doubled over, trying to catch his breath, he scolded himself for being so unfit. The man obviously hadn't chased him, for if he had Oliver was certain he would have been shot dead. Inhaling a couple of deep breaths, he stared at the lights in the distance. He couldn't hear anything. The vineyard was quiet; no birds, cicadas, crickets. Just the crunch of grass and fallen leaves at his feet. He heard the exhaust of the faded red car, could hear it moving through its gears as it sped away.

Was the shooter going to come after Oliver now? Was he waiting back at the house? Oliver didn't think so. Whoever had fired the gun was halfway to town and not returning.

Heading reluctantly towards the house, he dreaded what he was going to see. Two shots. Surely Clare was …? He'd run away before he even knew if she was dead or alive.

Coward.

No, there wasn't much of a choice between fight or flight. There was no fight he could have attempted unarmed, he told himself. There might have been two dead winemakers. He'd flown so he could fight for Clare now. *Please be alive*, he begged silently, starting a slow jog, gaining momentum. *Please let me save you.*

The dogs were no longer barking. They greeted him outside, desperate for attention. If the intruder had shot Clare, why not the two wieners? At least he'd spared the dogs.

Taking a deep breath, he walked into the house. And found Clare sprawled on the kitchen floor. No movement. He went to look again, but scrunched his eyes closed instead. Needed a minute to compose himself. This was the second time in a week he'd seen tacky pools of blood, some of which the dogs had stepped in, unwittingly painting the kitchen tiles. When he opened his eyes, there were two bullet wounds: one through the temple, another in the sternum. The heater was still going. Oliver found the remote and turned it off. He knew it was already too late to worry about touching things, with his fingerprints already peppered throughout the house.

Doing his best not to throw up, he walked to where they'd eaten dinner and found his phone sitting where he'd left it – beside an ornamental bowl in the middle of the dining table. He began to call triple zero, but stalled on the final digit. Let his fingers hover over the buttons. He backspaced and called a different number, instead.

Gabe answered after a couple of rings. 'Are you bored in Orange?'

'Someone's coming after us.' Oliver was still out of breath as he walked out of the kitchen and closed the balcony door behind him.

'What?'

'Someone just shot Clare.'

'Whoa, whoa, slow down.'

'Someone was here. They shot her, Gabe. I had to run—'

'Where are you right now?'

'I just, um—' Oliver had to stop and take a couple of breaths. He could feel himself on the cusp of a panic attack. He started the slow jog towards the car, needing to stay active, to keep his mind moving. 'I came back to get my phone. Left it on the table after dinner. Someone was here. I heard them shoot her, Gabe. A fucking professional.'

'Have you called an ambulance? The police?'

'No. She's gone, mate.'

'The cops? You need to call the police, Oli. Right now.'

'I can't.'

Oliver arrived at the car, unlocked it and jumped in. There was no one around him. The road was dark, the stars gold and raw and almost offensively bright.

'What the hell do you mean?'

'They'll think I killed her,' he cried. 'They'll try to pin it on me. They're already trying to pin Theo on me. Whoever shot Clare knew I was at her place. They waited until I was gone and then they swooped in. I'm going to kill the—'

'Take a deep breath. Where are you now?'

'I'm going to get my shit from the hotel. Maybe they're waiting for me there? I don't know, I'll see if it looks safe. I'll come tonight. Can I stay with you?'

'You don't even need to ask,' Gabe said. 'I saw Penny this morning. She's gone to Sydney to see her mother.'

'Yeah, right.' Oliver wondered if she'd told Gabe about their quarrel. 'Look, I'm worried. I shouldn't be the one to get locked up over these murders. You know I wouldn't kill them, don't you?'

'Calm down, Oli. If Clare's dead there's not much more we can do.' Gabe made a choking sound. 'Shit, I can't believe I just said that. You need to keep safe and look after yourself. Maybe stay at the hotel tonight. I'm not sure it's a good idea for you to drive.'

'No, I won't be able to sleep.'

'Well,' Gabe sighed. 'Get your stuff. Drive slowly. Come back here and we'll sort it out, all right?'

'Okay,' Oliver said, and when Gabe didn't reply, he said it again.

No one was waiting at the hotel. There were three other cars in the parking lot that Oliver remembered seeing earlier. No sign of the faded sedan. He walked up the stairs to his room, put his ear to the door and made sure there were no noises on the other side. After a minute, he moved inside and scoured the room.

Empty.

Hastily packing his bag, he did a final sweep, making sure he'd left nothing behind. He poured the wine out of the decanter and back into the bottle, put the lid back on and placed it in his bag, leaving the stained vase in the sink. Then he tossed the key onto the bed.

Two hours later, he pulled into Four Dogs Missing. Gabe flicked on the light and came outside in a striped dressing gown, Luna by his side.

'Jesus, I said slow. You shouldn't be here for another half an hour.'

Oliver walked up and hugged Gabe, letting out what sounded like a single sob. 'I'm all right,' he said, standing up straight, composing himself.

'Come in. I'll open a bottle.'

'I've got one in my bag. I decanted it earlier.'

'Of course you did,' Gabe said, peering into the night.

Once Oliver walked in, Gabe turned off the light, closed the door and clicked the deadlock.

***

Oliver was numb. He sipped the wine slowly, unable to relish it as he usually would. He kept imagining flies falling into the liquid, drowning, dead on their backs, and couldn't touch his glass again. Gabe sat across from him, stroking Luna's fur, the dog snoring on the chair beside him. Oliver was jealous of the ease with which the dog could fall asleep. Gabe looked defeated, as though words had evaded him.

'I don't understand,' Gabe said finally.

Oliver nodded. 'Makes two of us. Surely, Harold doesn't have something to do with this?'

'Harold? What happened at your dinner?'

'He came to my place early. Ida saw him snooping around the

house when we were at Penny's bar on Monday night. Theo stole two of Mum's paintings from him.'

'*What?*'

'They're unfinished, and he wants them back.'

'I've never quite trusted that man either,' Gabe said, concern swamping his features. 'He's suave, but … I don't know, Oli.' He stood up. 'You need to tell that detective everything. Maybe go into some kind of witness protection.'

'Nah,' Oliver said, his voice raspy with tiredness. 'I've got to do this alone, mate. My gut is telling me that Harold knows something that's going to solve this mess.'

Gabe walked to the kitchen and when he returned, he brought back a bottle of Lagavulin. 'Tip this down. You need to sleep. You're not going to be useful to anyone with insomniac theories and bloodshot eyes.'

They both took a large swig.

'Could it be related to the business?' Gabe asked.

'What do you mean?'

Gabe took another gulp from the bottle and winced. 'I don't know. A competitor. At the moment, nothing's out of the question.'

'Yeah, well.'

'You're the Howard Hughes of the Australian wine world. Don't go chasing people.'

'Can you at least compare me with a less creepy recluse? I'd prefer to be the Emily Dickinson of the Australian wine world.'

Gabe was too tired to jest, and Oliver felt ashamed of making a joke. But the whisky was waking him up, pumping more adrenaline into his body, rather than calming him down.

'Just let the police do their job,' Gabe said. 'You'll make things worse.'

'I can't sit back and wait. I'm not going to let someone set me up for this.'

After a moment, Gabe said softly, 'I need to call the police in the morning, you know that.'

'Don't, Gabe.'

'They'll trace our calls. Where are you going to go? What are you going to do?'

'I'm going to confront Harold. I think he killed Theo.'

'You go, Oli, but the police need to know. I'll let you leave in the morning and then I'm going to tell them. We can't both go to jail.'

'I think he's behind all of this,' Oliver said, focused only on his theory. 'I just don't know why he'd kill Clare and Orson.'

'Let's talk about it tomorrow. It's getting late.'

Oliver glanced at the clock above the fireplace. He picked up the bottle of whisky and studied the label, before placing it back down onto the coffee table.

Gabe found him a blanket, said goodnight and let the fire smoulder to embers.

Lying there, studying Gabe's ceiling, Oliver felt more alone than he'd ever remembered feeling before. He really was on his own. When he'd first moved to Mudgee, it had felt like a permanent vacation. The smell of chimney smoke everywhere. Sipping red wine by the fire. It was the best kind of wine holiday, one that refused to end.

But now it had.

In the morning, as soon as it was light, he would get in his car and drive to Terrigal. Straight to Harold's house by the beach. He'd acquire a gun, a small one, something that he could use to scare Harold, something he could use as leverage to coax him into admitting that he'd killed his twin brother. For what, a couple of incomplete prints? He was involved in something too deep for Oliver to fathom. Absurd scenarios roiled through his mind, plans he knew were no longer beyond him. If he found out who had hurt Theo and Orson and Clare, he didn't know what he'd do. The last week had changed everything. Did he even want to make wine anymore? He wasn't sure. He thought about calling Penny, but it was nearly two am, so he sent her a message, instead.

Everything's fucked. I'm sorry I didn't tell you about my family. Or my past. I've never really dealt with it well. If you give me a chance, I'll explain it all. I miss you. Je suis désolé, mon amour.

Eventually, listening to the wind and the spitting embers, Oliver's imagination dissolved and he lost his thoughts to sleep and fell into a deep dream.

***

Oliver was seventeen. One afternoon, when Theo was out and his parents weren't home, he took the keys to the Barina. Immediately after entering, he needed to throw out some empty bottles from the passenger's seat; there were pill packets and fast-food wrappers scattered across the floor. Winding down the window, he let the sea breeze move through the mildewed scent of the old hatchback. Oliver jolted out of the driveway and stalled at the bent 'give way' sign at the end of the street. It was the first time he'd driven a manual car on the road; his palms were clammy as he tried to kick the car into gear.

He cruised along the esplanade slowly, perusing the shops and the cars and the people dotted along the pavement. It was late winter, which meant there were barely any tourists in Terrigal. After fifteen minutes, he spotted her. Rosie was sitting alone outside the corner store at the end of the street. He idled beside the gutter and before he turned off the car, before he thought of something witty to say, Rosie had already slipped into the passenger's seat beside him.

'Can I smoke in here?' she asked, a cigarette clasped between two fingers.

Bit late to ask now, he thought. 'Yeah, won't be the first time.'

Oliver drove. The sun pierced the windscreen and he pulled down the visor, his hands sticking to the wheel with sweat. They passed the school, continuing to drive up the hill, towards the trees and the park. He passed Miles, standing on the side of the road. His hands were cuffed together and he was dressed in a green tracksuit.

'Where are we going?'

'Dunno,' Oliver said, too scared to peer in the rear-view mirror. The radio didn't work and the silence lingered like a bad smell. He eventually glanced back, but Miles was gone. 'Do you want me to drop you home?'

'Pretty sure you don't want to drive me all the way to the city,' she said, but he couldn't remember where she was from. Sydney? Melbourne?

'You don't like the coast?'

She paused a moment, and said, 'It's complicated.'

'Always is.' Oliver glanced at her legs; the cigarette smoke was a kind of offence against the purity of her school uniform.

He flashed then to an image of her on the beach, her body in a bikini and her skin wet and slippery as the waves crashed and pummelled her to the shore. He wanted to dive into the water, clip her damp hair behind her ears and feel her skin pressed to his own.

Then he saw Orson walking along the shore. He closed his eyes, opening them again and focusing instead on Rosie beside of him.

'Can I ask you something?' she said.

'Yeah.'

'Nah, never mind.'

'You can tell me,' Oliver said.

Rosie sat, adamant, shaking her head. 'It's nothing.'

'It's obviously something,' he pressed.

Her posture straightened as she pouted, and he noticed then the freckles dotted around her nose.

'Do you think I'm a bad person?' she asked, tossing the cigarette from the open window.

'What?'

'A slut?'

Oliver looked to the road ahead, running straight, nowhere to turn. A question so blunt was out of character for Rosie, wasn't it? He tightened his grip on the wheel and spoke in short bursts.

'No. Definitely not. Who cares about that stuff.'

She scoffed. 'Whatever. Doesn't matter.'

'It obviously does, if it's worrying you this much.'

'Do you think life would be easier if I was more like other people?'

'I don't. Well ...' Oliver said softly.

'It's true. People think I'm easy. That's why you pulled over today and picked me up, isn't it? So you could take me someplace and nail me in the back seat?'

Oliver flashed to a picture of her on the beach, the car parked in the darkness down the end of some dirt road, violently rocking to and fro, nothing moving between them but the auburn drape of her hair.

'What? Fuck no.'

'So,' she said, vexed, 'you wouldn't want to?'

'Are you sure you're okay?'

She exhaled and faced the road ahead, her eyes closed and her throat moving up and down with regret. She'd bunched up onto the seat, cocooned herself into her legs. Oliver saw Clare approach the passenger's window, an empty black hole through her temple, her fingers dripping with blood. *Don't look, Rosie!* he nearly shouted. Instead he closed his eyes, willing her away.

'Sorry. I just hate it here,' Rosie said.

'No need to apologise.'

'Do you ever just think one day you'll wake up and not a single person in the world will believe a word you've said?'

'What?'

'They won't be able to tolerate your shit anymore.'

'I don't understand,' Oliver said. 'Why wouldn't people like you?'

Rosie wasn't listening. 'Even if the person isn't worth it, you still worry, don't you? Why do we care so much? My mum is old and smart, but she still spends so much time fretting about the littlest things.'

Clare was trying to open the car door, but Rosie didn't hear the sound of the handle rocking up and down.

Oliver quickly drove her in the direction of the shop. The car halted and she opened the door and stepped once more into the heat of the day.

'Are you going to the party on the weekend?' she asked him, leaning half her body in, a bead of sweat slipping down her forehead.

'Yeah,' Oliver said. 'I guess I'll see you there.'

'Bring me a bottle of wine. Something sweet?'

Day blended into night in seconds. Oliver continued driving, finding himself on Rosie's street. It was months later, a memory flooding in. He turned around at the end of the cul-de-sac and crawled by her house again, just to be certain. To make sure it wasn't Theo's ute parked in her driveway at two in the morning. He drove past again and again, but the image remained the same.

What was his twin brother's ute *doing* in Rosie's driveway? When Theo knew that Oliver loved—

11.

Dawn.

The dreams were getting worse. Occurring more often. Some of the images were more akin to a memory, while others were peppered with fantasy. They all took place in the heated mood of adolescence Oliver could only conjure in his subconscious.

He crept to the toilet, pissed and washed his hands. Gabe's door was closed, but he could hear percussive snores coming from the room. Kicking on his boots, Oliver lurched back to his cottage. A vehement breeze was throwing leaves and broken branches along the driveway, dancing together near his feet.

The cottage felt the same as he'd last left it. No one had ransacked it while searching for paintings, drugs or God knows what. Oliver showered fleetingly and dressed, shivering in the cold. Then he brushed away wine from his teeth and lips and considered making a coffee, but in the end decided to grab his keys and jog to his car parked at Gabe's so he could drive into town.

Once on the road, he gazed across to the hills, flecked with gums and pines, and realised how peaceful the countryside was.

How starkly different to the world inside his head.

'You know you can't do this to me,' Rocky said, sounding legitimately concerned when Oliver turned up at the café.

'What?'

'Come in this early when it isn't vintage. I'm going to be off-kilter all day now.'

'I need a favour,' Oliver said.

Rocky raised his eyebrows. 'You mean something more than a cup of joe?'

'Yeah,' Oliver said. His phone vibrated in his pocket: Penny. 'Hold that thought,' he told Rocky. 'I'll be back.'

Walking out of the café onto the street, he answered the call. The town was quiet, people still snoozing alarms. Miners in their Land Cruisers were hooning to work.

'Hey.'

'Are you all right?'

'I just wanted to apologise …'

'Oli, your texts last night were worrying.'

'Texts?'

'As in plural.'

Oliver pulled the phone from his ear, but couldn't navigate his device well enough to read what he'd written without hanging up on Penny.

He breathed out heavily. 'Yeah, it's not good.'

'Did something happen yesterday?'

'Someone shot Clare.'

Penny was silent. Then, sharply: 'What?'

'As in, shot dead. I'd just driven up to her place. I heard them do it.'

'Jesus Christ. Where are you now? Why didn't you call me?'

Oliver couldn't recall Penny ever sounding so disturbed. 'I'm back in Mudgee,' he said, 'but I'm driving to the Central Coast.'

'Why?'

'I'm going to pay Harold Keller a visit.'

There was a pause, then Penny said, 'Is that a good idea? What did that detective say?'

'I haven't spoken to her about it,' Oliver said. He was going to keep it at that. He knew Penny wouldn't approve of him withholding information from the police. He just needed time to get Harold to confess, before they linked Clare's death to him, to Theo, to Orson across the ocean. He'd have it all worked out for Everson. Present it on a platter.

Penny's voice had a rare frisson of fear about it. 'Oli, don't go all crazy vigilante on me. Let the police handle this. They'll lock him up if he's guilty.'

'They're not doing anything about it,' he argued.

'Give them time.'

'I won't do anything stupid, I just need to talk to him.'

'Can you please just leave it?' she begged. 'I can't believe someone killed Clare.'

'I can't just leave this. Not when they're hellbent on trying to pin everything on me.'

'Oli ...'

'I'm just going to talk to him,' Oliver said, hand in his jacket pocket. The breeze was picking up. 'Look, I've gotta go, but I'll call you. Are you staying with your mother tonight?'

'I don't know yet,' Penny said. 'I might need to come in to work. I'm avoiding Mudgee a little at the moment, though. The whole place is creeping me out.'

'I know.'

'Please, just ... be careful. We need to talk when you get home.'

Oliver paused, waiting for her to say something more, but she didn't. 'Are you breaking up with me?'

He heard her sigh. 'I don't think I can do this anymore. I feel like I'm wearing this blindfold. And you know, it's tight. Pressed hard into my skull. Not knowing when—'

'Please,' Oliver cut her off. 'I need one more chance. We'll talk when I get home.'

'Will we?'

'I'll tell you everything I should have told you already. That's a promise.'

'I don't know,' Penny replied. 'I don't want to kick you while you're down, but you need to acknowledge this hasn't exactly been a walk in the park for me. Running a bar is stressful enough in itself.'

Oliver inhaled, scrunching his eyes closed. 'I know.'

'I'll call *you*. When I'm in Mudgee.'

'Pen ...'

He nearly said he loved her, but she ended the call before he could form the words.

Rocky already had a coffee waiting on the counter when Oliver walked into the café. There was no one else sitting down, only an ambulance officer lingering for a takeaway. When he'd gone, Oliver stood up and sipped his coffee next to the machine.

'About that favour,' Rocky said as Oliver finished his piccolo, nodding for another. 'Why do I have a feeling it's going to be something illegal?'

'Because you're a smart man.'

'I don't deal anymore, mate, if that's what ...'

Oliver bristled. 'What? No. Not as smart as I thought you were. Um, you're still part of that pistol club, aren't you?'

Rocky checked the door, ensuring they were alone. 'I can't give you a gun, mate. They're locked up. If they connect it to me we're both fucked. Like seriously fucked. Prison time.'

'I won't get caught.'

'Says everyone who's ever been caught,' Rocky scoffed.

'Don't even load it,' Oliver reasoned. 'There's someone I need to scare. I reckon he's the one that killed my brother.'

'Jesus, Oliver. I know you're a little bit sheltered, enjoy your own company and all that shit, but there's this government service that's been around for a while. They call themselves the police force.'

'Can't, mate. Long story.'

'I really wish I could help you.'

Oliver paused. 'Then help me.'

Rocky closed his eyes, pushed his hands through his hair.

'I'll give you a case of the southern block cabernet,' Oliver added. 'Two cases. I don't care. A case every year for the rest of my life.'

Rocky exhaled. 'You're lucky I love your wine. I've got this little Luger that belonged to my old man. It's not technically registered ...'

'Perfect,' Oliver said. 'I'll have it back in a day or two.'

Rocky frowned, uncertain. 'I don't know.'

'Where is it?'

Rocky glared at Oliver like he was daft. 'Yeah, it's just here behind the juicer. Hold on.'

'At home?' Oliver asked, ignoring the sarcasm.

'Yes, at home. Fuck me,' Rocky said. 'When do you need it?'

'Now. I'm going to Terrigal. Don't tell the cops that if they come in here searching for me.'

'Yes, I'll be sure to tell them I gave my unregistered pistol to a rogue winemaker heading to the coast to intimidate someone.'

'Can we go and get it now?' he begged.

'Alira doesn't start her shift till seven-thirty. You'll have to hold your horses, cowboy.'

'Okay. May as well have some breakfast.'

'Good idea,' Rocky said. 'And no arguing, I'm putting through a full English. You look like shite.'

'Done.'

'And, Oliver,' Rocky said, scribbling something illegibly on a pad. 'Don't get yourself killed. I want at least one bloody case of wine for the trouble.'

***

The Luger looked like something straight from the Schutzstaffel. Oliver twitched as he thought of its history. He wondered whether he'd be able to elicit a proper confession without bullets. He didn't really have a plan, but he wasn't too concerned; all he cared about was getting Harold to confess. If Oliver appeared sleep-addled and potentially murderous, then all the better for his cause. He wanted nothing more than to scare the shit out of the man. If he didn't succeed in that, the whole thing would have been in vain.

Oliver sped towards the coast, heart pumping. While he had maintained a decent bill of health most of his life, he felt as though he was close to being sent to the emergency ward. There was pain, a light tug, somewhere in his chest. Maybe the beans and bacon. Or more likely the grief and tension of the past few days. He wondered, driving along, what there was to live for. The wine?

Penny? His friendships? Three of the best ones snatched away from him, cruelly and prematurely. Maybe a heart attack would do him—

No. He still had a reason to continue, he didn't need to convince himself of that. He owed it to his friends, his brother, to find out the truth. He could feel it inside of him, beneath the fear and anxiety. The adrenaline was pushing him further, but his mind was making him work for any kind of clarity.

He passed a police car. He was driving across a bridge on the outskirts of the Blue Mountains. It would be too awkward for the sedan to turn around and follow him, so instead the driver raised a finger in admonishment. Looking down at the dash, he realised he was travelling well in excess of the speed limit. He tapped his foot to the brake, checking the rear-view mirror; the police car didn't turn around in pursuit. A small speckle of luck.

He stopped at a café in Lawson and ordered a coffee. Stared at his antediluvian flip phone and, perhaps for the first time, wished he had something smarter to do some poking around on. He was feeling nervous, sick, the dreams still lingering. Rushing to the closest public toilet, he hurriedly opened the door and banished his breakfast in three sharp hurls.

Dear Theo,

A few men in the past have offered to buy me a cocktail, but I think you may be the first to extend the offer to the preparation as well as the purchase. What kind of cocktail do you think would suit my soccer-mum palate? I tend to go for a gin martini after a rough day – with an olive – or a negroni if it's been a better one. I've temporarily forgotten what it's called, but I also enjoy the Italian one with some kind of bitter spirit and prosecco. Refreshing in the summer.

Yes, a bitters collection, albeit arguably eccentric, is far better than dolls or figurines. I dislike superhero franchises and comic books, so the fact that you didn't mention those is promising.

Today has been a tough day. I'm writing this without a glass of wine or gin by my side. Therefore, yes, that means I'm still pregnant. And yes, I know, the window of time to make a decision is closing in. I can tell you with almost certainty that I won't be keeping the child. But I don't want to talk about that today. I'm working quite a high-profile murder case at the moment, one that's been brewing up in the media for some time. Let's just say this particular judge isn't on my side. It's okay, I wouldn't piss on him if he was on fire. It just makes the job tougher than it should be. It's fun to be able to vent anonymously, in a letter that no one else will read. No email trail. No fear of my phone being tapped because of shady clients. No proof for a potential disbarment. It's a pleasant feeling.

A twin? Two identical-looking Theodores scolding legal professionals for their choice of vino?

Tell me more.

Speaking of more, where do you propose we have that drink?

Yours,

Angie

172

12.

Oliver parked a couple of doors down from Harold's house. His street was behind the Terrigal esplanade, a few hundred metres up the hill. The place was private, built around the ocean views. Oliver hadn't visited for years, but he'd been here at least twice over the last decade.

The house spanned a few different levels, with steps separating living areas. He noticed the garage was closed. There was no hint to help ascertain whether Harold was home.

Winding down the car window, he let the breeze move through the Jaguar. He'd only been on the road for four hours, give or take a few minutes. He'd left a chilly morning and arrived in a balmy afternoon, as though he'd boarded a plane, landing suddenly in an antipodean land.

A lady, pushing a pram, walked by. A couple of joggers laughed and whacked each other's arms as they cantered down the hill towards the esplanade. Oliver realised then, sitting in the car, feeling like some kind of failed detective, that he should have taken Gabe's ute; as soon as Harold walked onto the street, or veered into his driveway, he'd more than likely spot the Jag and know that Oliver was there.

Opening his phone, he fumbled around and eventually found the icon that was used to record conversations. He was going to make Harold admit that he was somehow tangled up in all of this. That his art-dealer friends, the corrupt ones, were complicit. That they knew about or had instigated the murders – not just of his twin brother, but potentially Clare as well. There was a plethora of missing puzzle pieces, but Oliver knew, as he sat contemplating Harold's house, that he'd find a couple buried inside the beachside mansion somewhere. Stuffed and sewn up in the fabric of an old chair. He wasn't sure how he'd find them, or what he'd have to do to get Harold to reveal them, but he was going to give it a crack.

A family walked into view. Two men and a young girl with a grey, curly-haired labradoodle. Oliver couldn't help but wonder whether that could have been – should have been – him and Penny. What if Miles hadn't killed Julia and dictated everything for the rest of them?

Perhaps Julia would have recovered after her chemotherapy. She would have left Miles, and Theo would have come back to Australia sooner. They could have all congregated on the Central Coast for Christmas, popping corks from champagne early in the morning, Penny stirring and scrambling eggs in the pan, the kids and the dogs scurrying around the kitchen and onto the deck, overlooking the ocean, the blue skies, the clouds, picture perfect, primed for painting, Julia erecting the easel and—

No, Oliver thought. It was too late, too futile, for that kind of nostalgic meandering. Finding out what Harold knew would help him achieve something more tangible.

He took the gun from the glovebox and wedged it inside his jeans, flinching at the coolness of the barrel against his bare skin.

***

Harold definitely wasn't home. Oliver knocked on the front door and peered inside. There were no movements, no sounds emanating within. He tiptoed around the side of the house, through a small walkway beside the fence that was draped with ferns and plants and had beach sand spiced along the path like cinnamon sugar. He walked up the steps, onto the rear verandah, and noticed—

The wood.

When Oliver had asked about Harold's hands, he'd answered, '*Oh, nothing. Just fixing some boards and staining the back deck. No one tells you your body becomes an apple when you're old.*'

Oliver crouched down and brushed the boards with his fingers. They were cracked and splintered. Lacquered they may have been, but they certainly hadn't been stained a week earlier. A year or two had passed since someone had last taken to them with polish. There was dirt and sand and mud congealed on a leg of the outdoor table; a kind of mess that could only accumulate with time.

He peered inside the house. There were so many paintings visible on the wall that they almost morphed into a mosaic. In the kitchen, he noticed a loaf of sourdough peeping from brown butcher's paper. The lid to the butter dish had been left to the side, the yellow fat melting and seeping down the edges, with the humidity, onto the bench. A sign that Harold had left in a hurry.

Harold wasn't home, but he'd be back. And when he was, Oliver would be waiting. He sat on one of the chairs and closed his eyes. For a brief moment, he thought of nothing; listened only to the bellbirds as they fluttered and chimed and flapped their wings.

***

Less than an hour later, the sun waning, the verandah steeped in grey, Oliver heard the garage door rattle and go through its movements. He stood up, opened his phone and began to record audio, before slipping the phone into his pocket. A minute or so passed before Harold entered the kitchen. He was dressed in suit pants, a navy chequered jacket and a patterned white shirt that was only half-buttoned. Oliver thought Harold would see him through the glass door, but he didn't; the gallerist was too busy cursing at the spilled butter, shaking his head while dancing around the bench, using paper towels to absorb the fat. Oliver then lost sight of him, until Harold reappeared in the kitchen with a bottle of wine and began extracting the cork. When he looked up, he jumped at the sight of Oliver standing behind the glass.

'Jesus fucking Christ,' he hissed, pulling on the handle. 'What the hell, Oliver?'

'Did I scare you?'

'I'm far too old and compromised for surprises.'

Oliver stepped inside and Harold walked further back into the kitchen. Beside the wine was a decanter and two glasses.

'What?' came a voice. 'I didn't catch tha—'

A woman materialised, evidently startled.

'Oh. Sorry, I—'

'Madeleine, this is Oliver. One of my oldest friends.'

Oliver nodded, and the woman stood there awkwardly, before saying tentatively, 'I was just going to walk down and grab …' She paused, clearly still crafting the narrative in her mind. 'Something for later. Would you like anything?'

'Don't go,' Harold said to her, peering into Oliver's eyes. 'Our friend here shan't be staying long.'

'I don't think a walk's all that bad an idea,' Oliver added, scowling at Madeleine. 'I think Harold and I could have a quick chat over a glass of that beautiful barolo he's just about to open there.'

Madeleine glanced at Harold, confusion veiled behind a polite smile. As she left, she gave an unconvincing wave. She appeared familiar to Oliver. He'd seen her before, he just couldn't quite place where.

Once the front door had closed behind her, Oliver said, 'That stain you did on the back deck didn't last long, did it?'

The sound of the cork leaving the bottle, like bubblegum bursting, was followed by silence. Harold poured the wine slowly into the decanter.

'What are you doing here?' he finally said.

'What's she doing here is the question,' Oliver said. 'She was gone faster than the babysitter's boyfriend after the car pulled up. I'm guessing she was hoping her visit was a little more covert?'

Harold bristled, poured some wine into a glass and swirled it in his hand. 'What the hell do you care? Since when have you given a single fuck about the morality of my relationships?'

'I don't,' Oliver said. 'Just an observation. What I do care about, though, is how you've been lying to me.'

'About what? Enjoying your barbera?'

'Killing Theo.'

Harold laughed. 'Oliver. I warned you about the fox. It's been a big week, mate, but you need—'

Oliver pulled out the gun and pointed it at Harold's head, his hands sweaty and shaking. Harold was more confused than scared.

'Sweet Jesus, what kind of historical junket is that?'

Oliver clipped the gun. 'Talk.'

Harold emitted a breath that turned into a groan. 'Come. Sit down.' He placed the wine on a glass coffee table. Something modernist. He sat, opened his palm and pointed at the chair opposite.

'I'll stand,' Oliver told him.

'Can you please just put the gun back in your pants? You're not a natural. And with your lineage, that's a compliment.'

'You killed him. Over the paintings,' Oliver pressed.

'I didn't kill him,' Harold said, taking a sip of wine. 'But I was there.'

Oliver tightened his grip on the gun. 'The night he died?'

'Yes, Oliver. The night he died. I came late that afternoon … you'd already gone. Your brother and I had a disagreement.'

'About the painting?'

'Paintings. It's been established already.'

'He wouldn't give them to you?'

Harold nodded equably. 'Correct. He said some unsavoury things about me, your twin brother.'

'Warranted?'

'I can understand why he wanted the paintings,' Harold said, swirling his glass, unaffected by the gun. 'But there are ways to do things. If he'd asked me for them, I probably would have just given them to him. But you don't steal from someone.'

'So, you were there. You saw who killed him?'

Harold looked momentarily confused. 'I have no idea who killed him. We had an argument, a couple of punches. He winded me, I slugged him right in the noggin. That would be the blood. We swore a little. It was a bit like something that happens after a big day at the races. Too much booze and testosterone. Silly egos. Not something I'm proud of. Anyway, I left straight after that.'

'So, you beat him and left him to die?'

'Jesus, don't you get it? We fought, he wouldn't give me the paintings and I left in a huff. At that stage whoever poisoned him or killed him moved in. I was long gone by then, in Orange by about nine. I stayed with a friend. You can confirm that if you want, Detective.'

Oliver wasn't sure what to believe; he wasn't expecting Harold to be so candid this early. He thought there'd be more resistance to admitting he was at the vineyard the night Theo died. Oliver had a bad feeling, in the pit of his stomach, that Harold was telling the truth. And that this would send him back to where he had started with Theo's murder.

'Why didn't you tell me?' he asked.

Harold looked at Oliver like he was daft. 'That I was there the night he had his throat slit like a sacrificial lamb? When I left, Theo was perfectly alive and well. I've given up on the paintings. I've told the police everything I've just told you. I'm not scared.'

Oliver returned the gun to his pocket. 'I don't know what to say, other than that you disgust me.'

'I think you need to trust the police. You stick with your wine, let them stick with this.'

Oliver moved towards the door.

'Oliver,' Harold called out, crossing his legs. 'Have you read Jack Gilbert's poetry? He poses the question, Why does everyone forget that Icarus also flew?'

'Goodbye, Harold.'

The gallerist grinned. 'Do you believe Icarus was failing as he fell, Oliver, or simply coming to the end of his triumph?'

***

Oliver had been to Terrigal beach a handful of times since he'd moved away. It was always filled with tourists and perhaps for that reason there was something about the suburb that felt distant to him, as though he was stranded in a country he'd never been to before. When he was seven, his family had moved from the city to the Central Coast, where – apart from a brief, temporary stint in the bush for his father's work – they'd settled. For a long time, the beach had felt wholesome; had been his escape as an adolescent. It had been home. Oliver had walked up and down the sand at Wamberal, a few kilometres away, paddled in the surf, letting his imagination run wild. Terrigal beach, after his encounter with Harold, felt like a tatty imitation of his childhood home.

Oliver sat on the brick wall between the esplanade and the sand and stared out to sea. The weather was warm, calm, a slight breeze ruffling his hair. He was only four hours' drive from the winery, but he felt as though he'd been away for weeks rather than hours.

A new feeling of resignation had seeped into his stomach. Harold wasn't guilty. He wasn't telling Oliver everything he was involved in – he knew now without a doubt that the man was as crooked as a dog's hind leg – but he wasn't a murderer. Oliver knew that much. He'd followed his intuition until he'd seen the look on Harold's face. One quick look – unknowing, perplexed – along with some admissions, had told Oliver everything he'd needed to know.

And yet, there was something not quite right. Something Harold was withholding from him. Oliver suddenly realised why Madeleine looked familiar. The woman, Oliver could have sworn, was the one in the photograph Everson showed him after Theo was killed.

Or was he just seeing patterns that didn't even exist? *You're tired,* he told himself. *Everything feels strange.* He missed Penny. For so long, he'd tried to be independent. After everything that had happened with his mother and father, and with Theo running away – and his ex leaving – Oliver had wanted never to rely on anyone else in his life again. Just as he was beginning to think he could trust Penny with everything, he was back to the start.

His phone vibrated in his pocket. He realised he hadn't even turned off the recording. Gabe's name appeared on the screen.

'Hey.'

'Glad to hear you're alive.'

'In the flesh. Not sure about the spirit.'

'Did you see him?'

'Yeah,' Oliver said. He wished he had a cigarette. 'It's not him.'

'Wouldn't confess?'

'He didn't need to. He was there, had a fight with Theo, but he didn't kill him. I don't want to believe him, but I do.'

Gabe stayed silent. 'Don't let that fool you,' he said eventually. 'I've met him before. I think that man lies for a living.'

'I had a gun to his head.'

'Good joke.'

'Do I sound like I'm in the mood?'

Gabe exhaled. 'I called because we have a problem. Something strange.'

'Something stranger than what's already happened?'

'I called Clare's winery, pretending to ask about an order. Apparently, the cellar door is open as usual today. The staff said it's strange that the dogs were left alone, but there was no sign of Clare. So, that means no one found any blood. And by the way they were talking, there was no body.'

Oliver tensed; a man jogging by clipped his arm without looking over his shoulder.

'Whoever killed her went back?'

'I'm guessing so.'

Oliver paused, racking his brain for something. 'I don't know what to think anymore.'

'You definitely saw her? Dead, I mean.'

'What?'

'Was she—'

'She was gone, Gabe.'

'I know, I'm just concerned. I think you should call Everson.'

'When I return. I'm going to stay the night here. I'm too tired to drive.'

'That could be the first smart thing you've said all day.'

'You don't have to worry about me, mate. I'm fine.'

Oliver heard someone else's voice in the background. A few bangs on a door. 'Sounds like you've got company.'

'Murray's here. And actually I need to go – I think someone's at the door.' He paused for a moment. 'Can I give you a call soon?'

'Don't let me interrupt your soirée. I'll see you tomorrow.'

'See you then,' Gabe said, words fading. He hung up the phone before Oliver could say anything else.

Dear Angie,

I've been writing about the past. I'm stuck, you know. Can't settle
in the present. Unnecessarily oscillating between what happened
yesterday and where to go tomorrow. I fear I'm missing out, Angie,
with this persistent toing and froing.

I've been thinking a lot about my twin brother. How I failed Oliver
in the past and, even now, how I can't seem to muster the courage to
see him. Last night, for the first time in years, I dreamed about him
and his first girlfriend.

Oliver first met Rosie Woods in high school. Back when we all
thought she was hiding something. Oliver could tell from watching
her in the playground; meandering about with her friends, whose tans
looked like they'd been dabbed on with teabags. She sat across from
him in maths and he found it impossible to take his eyes off her. She
was beautiful in this cryptic, furtive kind of way. Her skirt stopped
before her knees and her auburn hair draped her shoulders like a
stage curtain. Sometimes she'd see Oliver staring and he'd dart his
eyes away, hoping that she wouldn't notice. The girl seldom spoke,
but when she did the class sort of paused, hanging onto her words like
they were some kind of imperative.

I wasn't the only one who could tell that Oliver had a crush on her,
but after so many years of hiding his feelings, it was a welcome relief.

One night we went to a party that included a bonfire in a paddock,
an infinite line of utes and swags, and a keg of rum. Our friend threw
his eighteenth on the outskirts of town and everybody in Grade
Eleven showed up. It was pandemonium: crackers and kisses and fires
and empty bottles splayed across the slope of the property.

The moon was trying to lustre, but the paddock was black. Cars
and mobs of kids were sprawled along the driveway, and Oliver and

I sat on the back of a ute, taking turns chugging from a bottle of Southern Comfort. I told him it was the only spirit I could drink straight. But Oliver told me it was too sweet for him. I guess he had a pretty savvy palate, even then.

I was so drunk, I collapsed onto the ute's tray. Oliver took the bottle from between my legs and took a gulp. The kids that thought they were too cool for the party were parked in their own line. Oliver was staring at Rosie among them. They were laughing and joking and putting on the tough act. I remember closing my eyes, pretending to be asleep, and surreally, as if in a beer dream, Rosie was there, her soft hand clipping Oliver's as she pulled herself up next to us.

She took the bottle from Oliver's hand and swigged from it. Her lips were wet and gleaming in the light and a trickle of the bourbon slid from her mouth to her chin; she wiped it away and leaned back, gazing up at the sky. I knew that Oliver wanted to say something, but he couldn't. They shared the occasional conversation but they struggled to flow; each time they spoke it became a concerted effort to avoid an awkward silence. I wished I could have spoken for him.

She offered him a vodka-and-raspberry premixed bottle, and he took a sip. Before the bottle had left Oliver's lips, she was waiting. I turned away, but I could hear their tongues as they dovetailed in a feverish rhythm.

Someone called Rosie's name, but they continued to kiss for a little while until Rosie pulled away and kissed Oliver's cheek – a soft hand on his thigh as she jumped from the tray – and walked away without a word. Oliver glanced down and saw me pretending to have passed out, my head to the side with a drunken leer.

The problem was, though, Oliver had fallen in love with her. Things moved quickly after that. Oliver even held Rosie's hand whenever they'd walk home from school. He lost his virginity to her, on the beach, at an impromptu party. He stopped telling me any details after that night.

But then, when Mum was murdered, he stopped hanging out with her altogether. Rosie visited him after that, once or twice, but I'm not sure he really made the effort. I think he was too scared of what she thought of him. What she'd make of our family.

One night I stayed at Rosie's. Ended up drinking at the pub one afternoon – got blind with a bunch of mates. Wrote myself off. She was there somewhere, fully sober, dressed in a singlet top, denim shorts and a pair of thongs. She drove my ute home, with me barely conscious in the passenger's seat. The music was blaring. She told me I had to stay at hers as Robert Palmer crooned that I was addicted to love.

I tried to kiss her, you know? At that time, my life was a mess. Spinning, spiralling, untethered. She was the one who pulled away, who told me not to be stupid, that my brother deserved better.

I'm not sure I was a good person for a long time. I never told Oliver that I stayed with Rosie – that I passed out, slept beside her in my jocks. I'm not sure he ever knew, but after my group started hanging out with her, Oliver changed. Became cold. I wasn't sure whether it was because of everything else or ...

You know, as talented as Oliver is, he's a pretty shithouse talker. Never really says what he's thinking. Would never confront me about it. I confess: that's all I wanted. An argument with him, a fight: fists out, toe to toe, blow for blow, twin brothers in a blue. But he wouldn't provoke me. Not once. In some ways we've always been alike, and in other ways we've always been so different.

Forgive the rambling. I must visit him soon. Make amends. It's true: we hurt the ones we love most. I'm sure a criminal barrister sees it every day: betrayal, lost love, heartbreak. The extremities of the human experience. Sometimes, it's too much to handle, don't you think?

I must go, Angie. There's a joint to roll, a deck chair to collapse onto.

I'll write to you again soon.

Peace,

Theo

13.

Harold wished he had a joint. He was craving one, lying on top of the duvet, naked, cringing at the look of his pale and puckered skin. Sans a smoke, the experience felt like a three-course dinner without dessert.

'And what was young Oliver doing here?' Madeleine asked, straightening her jacket in the mirror beside the bed, before flicking the seam at the top of her stockings. 'I thought for a moment that Theodore had returned from the dead.'

'Yes, it feels that way sometimes,' Harold said, getting out of bed and reaching for his underpants. He leaned against the wall, keeping balance as he stepped into them. 'You have nothing to worry about.'

Madeleine picked up her bag from the dressing table and leaned in an inch from Harold's face. 'I know. But if anyone else finds out, you certainly do.'

Harold sneered as he walked into the living room, towards the kitchen. 'Hardly my fault that your beloved lost the bloody painting. And my paintings!'

'It can still be found, but the window's almost closed.'

'Someone can come and take the *Yallingup*. It's right here,' Harold said, pointing to Julia's canvas on the wall, mounted beside the hallway.

'It's too suspicious with the murder. We need the *Wadani*.'

'You screwed this up, not me,' Harold jeered, pouring a sip of barolo for himself. He left Madeleine's glass empty. 'You sent a kid in to steal his dead mother's painting. For someone with your intelligence, I'd say that's pretty fucking moronic.'

'Theo was good. We had no reason to doubt his motive or ability. How the fuck was I to know he was connected to your past? To an artist? If I remember correctly, you were supposed to bring the painting back, but instead he winds up dead?'

'No reason to doubt his motive and ability? Not only is the *Wadani* missing, he left the gallery with two that are mine! With sentimental value.'

'Julia Crespo's works?'

'No,' Harold lied. 'Someone else.'

'Sounds heartbreaking.'

'You'd have to have a heart to break it.'

'You or me?'

Harold took a sip of the barolo – wished he'd left it in the cellar longer. It was still taut and tannic. Taking a sip, he tried to gauge Madeleine's reaction, but her expression was impassive. Harold thought how different she looked. She'd recently cut her hair short, with a sharp fringe, but it didn't make made her face any easier to read.

'The detective working the case in Mudgee called earlier,' Harold said. 'Wanted to know about the painting. It sounds like they're connecting the dots.'

'Well, if the painting wasn't with Theo, they're not going to have it. They won't know it was him. They must know you were there before he died, though?'

'I told them I went to visit Oliver. I think they're suspicious, but they don't have anything concrete.'

Madeleine stared into Harold's eyes. A moment longer than was polite.

'What about the barista?' Harold asked.

'You mean barrister?'

'Whatever. The woman Theo was seeing.'

'They've checked her apartment. Found nothing.'

'I've swept the vineyard from top to bottom. I don't know what he's done with it.'

Madeleine walked to the back door. 'You know we're both fucked if we don't find it soon? I'm talking days. They're applying pressure. A hand gripping the neck.'

'We'll find it,' Harold said. 'It always works out in the end. Thank you for calling in, sweet.'

Madeleine opened the door and put one foot outside. 'Call me "sweet" again and I'll shoot you myself.'

Get in line, he thought. It seemed everyone was closing in on him. Theo. Madeleine. The police.

***

Later that afternoon, he noticed a silhouette peeking through his front window. He could see whoever it was brazenly looking in, hands over their eyes. He flung open the door just as she chimed the doorbell.

'Mr Keller.'

It was the voice of the detective he'd spoken to on the phone.

'Can I help you? I was just heading out.'

'Won't take too much of your time,' the woman said. She was alone, and he'd forgotten her name. Clarkson? She flashed her badge. 'Detective Inspector Geraldine Everson. We spoke earlier.'

'Yes,' Harold said, now smiling blandly. 'I remember. Please, come in.'

They walked into the sitting room and Harold directed her to the same seat he'd offered Oliver earlier.

'How can I help?'

Everson sat, crossed her legs and appraised the room, almost grimacing at some of the paintings. 'Just forming an air-tight timeline of the night Theo was murdered.'

'You haven't found who killed him yet?'

'Getting close,' said Everson, peering intently into Harold's eyes. 'Just to be able to rule you out, Mr Keller, it'd be great if you were willing to submit a DNA sample. Of course, it isn't compulsory. But it would be great to confirm that you're willing to cooperate.'

He shot his eyes away, her stare too rigid and uncomfortable for his liking. 'Of course. I can come to the station later today.'

'Perfect,' she said. 'Gosford station will be fine. I won't keep you long now. Just need to corroborate a few things and I'll be on my way.'

'Sure.'

She started writing something down; was silent too long. Harold didn't like unnecessary silence. He was feeling off his game, struggling to be his charming self. 'How are you finding Mudgee?' he asked after a while.

'It's nice to be posted to wine country for a change,' Everson said. 'If I'm sent out of the city it's usually way out in the sticks. Flat plains, red dirt kind of country.'

'Chasing missing girls?'

'Dead girls,' Everson said, without hesitation. 'And men as well. I work in homicide, Mr Keller. Not missing persons.'

'Right,' Harold said. 'Well. If you don't mind, I—'

'On the phone, you mentioned you'd called into the vineyard. Can you confirm for me what time you were there?'

'I left here at … twoish? I would have arrived in Mudgee after six. It was dark, I remember that. Ran over two bloody potholes on the way in.'

'What was the reason for your visit?'

'I was heading to Orange to drop off some paintings and thought I'd call in and say hello. I'm Uncle Harold, for all intents and purposes.'

Everson sat up. 'It's not really practical to call into Mudgee on the way to Orange, though, is it? Wouldn't you save a few hours by driving south towards Bathurst? Through the Blue Mountains?'

Shit. How had he been so daft?

'Yes, but I had another delivery in Mudgee. More urgent. Bit of a testy customer.'

'He'll confirm that you dropped the painting off that day?'

'The testy customer? She will, yes.'

'Name?' Everson asked, pen resting on paper.

'I'm not sure I should be giving my client's private details to the police. Although, I don't think she'd mind. She was christened as Kaylene Gregory, I believe.'

'So, you dropped the painting to Kaylene and then headed to the winery to see Oliver?'

'No, I visited first. Then dropped off the painting to Kaylene and headed to Orange.'

Everson sat back, looking towards the artwork again. It was as though she was understanding that silence made Harold uncomfortable. 'If she was a testy customer, wouldn't you have dropped the painting to her first?'

Harold paused for a moment; he was too smart to be caught in her web. 'I could have, although I would have had to drive into town and then come back out to the winery. It was quicker to nip into the vineyard first. Saved on time and petrol.'

Everson didn't reply, didn't nod, just scribbled down some words.

'I arrived in Orange by nine.'

'You told me that.'

Rude. But Harold felt sorry for Everson. She was always coming into people's lives when they were grieving, angry, evasive. Harold wouldn't take her job for all the money in the world.

He made a mental note to call Kaylene straight away and ask for a favour. God, she owed him more than one.

Harold broke the silence again: 'As I said, Oliver wasn't home, just Theo. We had a bit of a disagreement, if I'm honest. A little scuffle. I was pushed against the wall.'

Everson looked up. 'You didn't mention that on the phone.'

'I didn't think it'd matter, but I want you to know I'm willing to cooperate,' he said, opening his palms. 'Speak to Caroline Foxton in Orange. She'll confirm I was—'

'What was the disagreement regarding, Mr Keller?' Everson's voice was turning terse.

'Honestly? About the twins' mother.'

'Who died when they were boys?'

'That's right.'

'And?'

'Theo believed he was entitled to some of her prints,' said Harold, signalling the wall. Everson didn't look across. 'He thinks – thought – that I didn't do enough to save his mother. Basically, he insinuated I was the one who killed her through neglect. The twins' father did all—'

'Wait,' Everson said. 'Go back.'

'What?'

'You said he thought you were the one who killed her?'

Of course: Oliver and Theo had changed their names. Their grandmother had whisked them away the day after Julia disappeared and Harold was taken to hospital, worried for their safety. She kept them hidden from Miles while the court case was splashed through the papers, all over the nightly news. It had only been a few days, but how hadn't the detective discovered their past? All of a sudden, he didn't feel stupid.

'The twins' father, Miles Jones. He beat me to a pulp and killed Julia Crespo. The twins were then taken away and lived with their grandmother. They changed their names to avoid the controversy.'

Everson didn't reply. She snapped closed her book and hurried to the front door. *Lost in her head*, Harold thought. Angry at what she'd missed. If she wasn't trying to implicate Harold in Theodore's murder, he almost might have felt pity for her.

Dear Angie,

Meet me at Dear Sainte Eloise at Potts Point, this Sunday at six pm. I have a proposal for you. One that involves travel.

    Peace,

    Theo

14.

Oliver was almost anticipating an armed police squad to arrive. They'd either hunt him for Clare's disappearance or for holding up a revered gallerist. Everson hadn't tried to call. Surely, she would have heard about the strangeness in Orange. Another winemaker missing or already dead; one closely linked to Oliver.

It was only a matter of time.

He checked in to the hotel nearest the beach, having parked his Jag on one of the side streets. Sitting at the bar, he tipped down two neat whiskies. The bartender didn't seem surprised by Oliver's order, as though dishevelled men like him sat in the exact same stool every night, ordering from her the same drinks, getting tipsy to escape the same problems.

He should call Everson. His gut told him that she was a good cop, reasonable, likely to listen to his truth. If he told her about the paintings, and everything he knew about Theo, perhaps she would trust him. They'd simply started off on the wrong foot. He would tell her about having dinner with Clare, about returning to collect his phone. Almost being shot himself. He would volunteer his phone records and she could listen to his conversations with Gabe. All of his friends knew he was a terrible actor, entirely incapable of forging such an elaborate cover. He'd give her access to whatever she wanted. Why not cop the brush with Harold on the chin if he had to? If it proved he had nothing to do with the rest of the mess? Oliver was worried someone had seen his Jaguar leave the scene. It wasn't exactly a common car. A faded red sedan in Orange? Certainly. A bottle-green, restored Jaguar E-type? Not so much.

He looked around the bar. Everyone, even on the beach, seemed so debonair. Rolled-up jeans. The men slick, with pomade in their hair. The scent of perfume and cologne mingled together and made him feel ill. It was why he'd taken such a liking to the country: everyone was unique in some way. Dirty hands. Sun wrinkles. Sock tans. Cigarette-stained fingers. A distinct dryness to their voice.

Oliver remembered then, as the blood rushed to his head, that he'd barely eaten all day. A winemaker living on a diet of coffee and whisky.

Leaving the bar, he walked along the esplanade until he found a takeaway shop, where he purchased a couple of battered indulgences from the hotbox, along with a can of Coke. He sat in the Jaguar and ate; the grease bleeding through the paper bag, the salt and the syrupy sweetness comforting after everything that had happened earlier. The only other person who might have answers was Chase. Oliver wasn't convinced he'd even sent the letter to Theo, but he'd have to at least rule out the possibility himself. He'd let the invitation take a backseat when he should have tried speaking to Chase earlier. There might be something his half-brother could tell him that no one else could. The only problem was, he had no idea where he lived in Sydney.

Sitting alone in the car, Oliver had a small epiphany – an arbitrary stroke of luck. He remembered the Christmas card that he'd received towards the end of last year from Chase. It had been unexpected, but not entirely random given he'd visited the vineyard earlier that year. He hadn't really divulged too much about Chase's visit to Theo, thinking he'd share more once his twin had settled in and they'd had a chance to work out the nature of the invitation.

Like Oliver's twin, Chase had arrived out of the blue one weekend afternoon. Oliver was doing something in the wine shed, tinkering with his barrels, when a knock had reverberated through the tin panels beside the door.

'So, this is one of the country's cult wineries, hey?'

Oliver nearly didn't recognise his half-brother. Chase's features hadn't changed, but his hair was longer. Greyer. He was still lanky, perhaps even taller than Oliver remembered. He was nearly next to him before he worked out who it was.

Chase extended his hand. 'I'm in town for the weekend. Thought it'd be rude not to call in.'

They shook hands, slowly, gingerly. Oliver invited him into the shed and soon after offered him a taste out of the barrel. Chase seemed interested, intelligent. He probed with the right kind of questions.

'What are you doing with yourself these days?' Oliver asked.

'Believe it or not, I studied political science at university and moved to Canberra for a while. I've got a job in state politics now. Living in Sydney.'

'There you go,' Oliver said. 'Both done all right for ourselves, I guess.'

Chase nodded, looking around the shed. 'I drink your wine fairly often, to tell you the truth.'

Oliver was humbled, unsure what to say. He'd often wondered whether his brothers had sipped his wines and what they thought of his career path.

'Have you visited him?' Chase asked after a while.

'Miles?'

Chase nodded.

'Once,' Oliver admitted, filling his own glass. He did the same for Chase, who, despite earlier protesting that he needed to drive, continued to drink anyway. 'I wish I hadn't gone.'

'Me too. I've been twice. Mostly out of guilt. It's a hard one to work out. I stew in indecisiveness, rather than go and visit him. They don't really give you a book at school on how to deal with a murderous father.'

Chase hadn't changed his name after Oliver and Theo's mother's murder had been splashed across the news and the TV current affairs specials.

Oliver considered whether to tell Chase more about his visit. Standing with him then, he'd been sure what his father had said couldn't be true. He knew, looking at his half-brother, listening to the way he spoke, that Miles had fabricated everything; insisted he was innocent, when all the evidence pointed at him.

'He was in denial,' Oliver told him. 'Kept saying it was an accident.'

Chase mumbled something, then added, 'I can believe that. He kind of went off on a similar tangent with me.'

'I don't believe anything he said,' Oliver told him. 'I still believe he's guilty.'

Chase stared into Oliver's eyes. 'You did the right thing. I think you're brave for going to the police. The truth would have come out eventually. He dug his own grave. If he had nothing to hide, why did he move the body? Why beat up Harold?'

Oliver waited a moment before speaking. 'Thanks for saying that.'

'I'm sorry for everything that happened when we were kids. I guess it was my way of dealing with having a new family. Still, you know. Those weren't my proudest moments.'

Oliver changed the subject. Chase stayed for another wine. They talked about politics and grape varieties and how their childhood felt like a past life. The two men traded numbers, even though Oliver knew they probably wouldn't speak again. Not for a long time.

'Do you see Theo much?' Chase enquired as he hopped into his car.

'I haven't seen him since he went overseas.'

Chase smiled. 'He was always running away as a kid. You were on the piano, and he was off towards the mountains with his bag around his shoulder.' He started the car and wound down his window. 'Old habits die hard, don't they say? I've got your address now. I'll send you a Christmas card.'

When it arrived, Oliver had opened it in the car. The next day, when he was picking up Penny, he'd moved it from the passenger's seat and placed it in the glovebox; a surety against any future questions.

Now, he quickly swallowed the last of the potato scallop, swilled the remainder of the Coke, stepped out of the car and flung the rubbish into a bin. Hurrying back to the Jag, he sanitised his hands as he sat down, and took a deep breath before he opened the glovebox. There was some information on the car – its service history – and below, where he'd left it, an envelope with a Christmas card. On the rear, in Chase's own handwriting, was *15A St Pauls Street, Randwick 2031*.

The Christmas card was concise: *Merry Christmas, Oliver. It was great seeing you this year. I hope we can catch up soon. All the best, Chase*

Was it the same handwriting as the note Theo had showed him the night he arrived? Oliver scolded himself for not hanging on to it; for not remembering that he had the card in the car and that he could compare the sets. Perhaps they were the same, and Chase had sent the note?

Oliver twisted his key and the car roared to life.

***

After dark, it took just over an hour and a half to reach Chase's terrace in Randwick. Oliver parallel-parked along the one-way street and walked to the front door. He knocked but wasn't surprised to see the windows dark, no light spilling out from inside the terrace. It was entirely plausible that Chase wasn't home, but something was off.

Theo. Come to Oliver's winery. Search for Four Dogs Missing. You'll find me there. We need to talk. Chase

Oliver closed his eyes. Heard a bus shifting through its gears ahead; music spilling from a restaurant, a bar – sounds he'd long ago learned to live without.

Should he wait for Chase? What if he was away for a week? Oliver hadn't thought it through – had felt a shade intrepid after a few whiskies and got behind the wheel to drive, thinking when he arrived that all of his uncertainty – the doubt – would be sated.

When they were kids, living in Terrigal, Miles had always kept a spare key on the verandah's roof beam above the back door.

Oliver walked to the side of the terrace, opened the gate, and stepped into the small backyard. There was a covered deck. He looked through the window, but there was no one home. Maybe Chase was asleep inside? Oliver doubted it. He stood on a chair and pawed his way around a supporting beam for the spare key, just in case it was there.

The chair was shaky under his weight. He ran his hand along the top of the dusty beam until he felt something small, the brass cold between his fingers. Jumping down from the chair, he stood at the French doors, but the blinds were blocking his view.

After using the key, he pushed open the door a little and pulled aside the curtains. The house was dark and eerily quiet, the sound of a fridge beginning its hum the only disturbance. Flicking open his phone, trying to impose some kind of light, he moved into the bathroom. There was a towel flung over the shower glass, and a toothbrush resting on a tube of toothpaste. The bedroom showed the bed was unmade, the pillows piled together on one side. Oliver opened the wardrobe and noticed Chase's clothes were stacked and hung neatly.

Having found nothing, he walked back into the downstairs hallway. The kitchen light was on: everything wiped over and neatly kept. A clean pan sat on the stove. Oliver opened the fridge. Milk, since expired; six eggs; a couple of Heineken stubbies. A bottle of riesling. When he closed the fridge, he noticed a calendar. There was a long green line marked through the current week as *CROATIA*. So, Chase was overseas?

He walked out into the front living room and found that the glass coffee table had been pushed aside, left at a strange angle against the sofa. Careful not to touch anything, he shone the torchlight across it. There was a bottle of red wine. Oliver squinted and read the label, feeling dread creep into his blood: *Four Dogs Missing – Southern Block Cabernet Sauvignon 2015. Mudgee.*

Beside the bottle was paperwork. The state government letter-head. Above, a handwritten note with the words:

Chase. Here's a bottle of my wine. Theo is coming to the vineyard. You should join us soon. It's been too long. Oliver

Oliver grabbed the wine, walked down the hallway and opened the garage door. He guided his phone torch across to see Chase's Volvo, parked in darkness. The keys were hanging from a hook in the kitchen. Without knowing why, he clutched the keys, and made his way into the garage. Stopping himself in front of the boot, he took a deep breath. He imagined opening it and finding Chase inside, lying on his back. A smudge of vomit dried on his chin; blood seeping from his eyes.

He pressed a button on the key and the boot opened. It was empty. The scent of new upholstery. Before he could feel relief, a sharp shot of adrenaline coursed through him at a sudden thought. He found himself running out of the house to the Jaguar. He threw the bottle onto the backseat and grabbed the Christmas card. Taking it inside once more, he compared the handwriting. It was different, but the notepaper on Chase's table was the same as the one Theo had proffered to Oliver the night he arrived at the vineyard.

***

Oliver stepped back into the bar in Terrigal in time for last drinks. The drive had been necessary to clear his head, to tease out exactly what he'd discovered. Someone was unequivocally trying to pin this on him; he truly believed that now.

He tipped back a whisky and gave the bartender a nod as he walked upstairs to his room, holding the rail to support himself. It took a few attempts to get the lock to properly welcome his key card. Once inside, he pulled off his boots and collapsed on the crisp white sheets. Inhaled their smell; the faintest spoor of bleach in the fabric.

Surprisingly, he slept. And dreamed. Old memories that had morphed into dreams.

***

'Oliver, my name is Detective Hanson.' She was in her forties, with short hazelnut hair that bobbed at her shoulders. She always wore a suit jacket, with light-blue-striped shirts. 'Thank you for seeing me.'

'S'okay.'

She thrummed her fingers on the black vinyl tabletop. 'I'm going to cut straight to the chase. You're not here because you believe your mother disappeared by herself?'

'No.'

'Why don't you think that?'

He pushed his hair from his face. 'She wouldn't leave us. Me and Theo.'

Hanson offered a sad smile. 'Mate, she has stage three cancer. When people have to confront their death that closely, they can do things that we wouldn't normally think they'd do—'

'She wouldn't.' He cut her off. 'She didn't take her piano music. She wouldn't go anywhere without her music. Or mid-painting. I know she wouldn't.'

'What do you think happened?'

Oliver inhaled. He'd told himself, an hour before walking to the station, that no matter what happened, he would be strong. Would not cry.

'My dad killed her.'

Hanson was writing something on her notepad. Her fingers halted. Oliver expected her to refute him somehow.

'Why do you think that, mate?' she asked softly.

'We heard them arguing.'

'We?'

'My brother. Theo.'

'Does he think the same way as you?'

'Yeah. He doesn't know what to do.'

Hanson nodded. Every time Oliver looked up, her eyes were all over him.

'What were they arguing about?'

'They were always arguing. Dad has been worse than normal. A bit … controlling. We went to bed. The next afternoon, when we got home from school, Mum was gone.'

'Not in the house?'

'Yeah.'

'Where did your father say she was?'

'He said that she'd gone for a walk to get some fresh air. He didn't see her leave.'

'Did that sound right to you?'

'Maybe. She'd mostly been staying in bed, in the house. She drank a lot of tea and played the piano. She didn't have a lot of strength.'

Hanson was scribbling notes. 'She didn't come home later that night?'

'No. One of the cars was missing. The little blue Barina that Mum drives. It had been there that morning.'

Hanson leaned back in her chair and tapped the pen on the stretched skin between her thumb and forefinger. 'I've seen the report. She went for a walk, came home, packed and took the car.'

Oliver pursed his lips. What was he doing here? He knew, in the pit of his stomach, that his father was guilty, but admitting it to the police, pursuing the truth, was fraught with a raw danger he hadn't fully anticipated.

'There's blood,' Oliver blurted. 'In my dad's boot. A small smear in the bottom left-hand corner.'

Hanson frowned. A sad kind of frown. After they'd found the car burnt out in the bush, after they'd pinned his mother's murder on Miles, Oliver remembered the frown better than anything else. Without having to say it, Detective Hanson had said it all: *I'm sorry, Oliver. Your father killed your mother.*

* * *

Oliver opened his eyes a little after four am, parched, needing to piss. He was too lazy to move, too tired to get up and have a drink of water and find the toilet, so instead he lay there regretting his indolence, drifting in and out of variegated dreams. Sometime after the sun came through the blind, he heard his phone somewhere in the room. He patted the doona, the bedsheets, but realised the sound was coming from the floor. It was still in his jeans pocket. He was too late, discovering he'd missed three calls. One from an unknown number and two from Rocky. Oliver would have bet his last dollar that the unknown number was Everson.

She answered after two rings, saying only his name.

Oliver said, gravel in his voice, 'You must have heard me thinking about you.'

'Where are you?'

'On the coast.'

'What, taking a holiday, are we?'

'Something like that.'

Everson didn't say anything for so long, Oliver took the phone from his ear to check the call was still connected.

'You're really starting to piss me off,' she said.

'That's fair.'

'Blind Freddy could tell someone's setting you up. I had been giving you the benefit of the doubt, you know. Despite everything else.'

'What's everything else?'

'Despite the car, despite another disappearance linked to you. The black eye. Your own sudden disappearance. But now I'm not so sure.'

He thought of telling her she had a penchant for the word *despite*, but thought better of it.

'You said *holiday*. One tends to return at the end.'

'Cut the bullshit, I'm not in the mood.'

Oliver grimaced as he spoke. 'What are you after?'

'I thought you'd be in Mudgee after hearing the news. It brought me back from investigating elsewhere.'

Oliver sat up. 'News of?'

'Seems you've brought it all here, mate. You want to keep me in this shithole longer. Your neighbour's been flown to Royal North Shore on life support and your vineyard manager's here in hospital overnight. Bullet grazed his shoulder.'

'What!' Shock reverberated through him.

Everson gave a humourless laugh. 'Some of us take all of this pretty seriously.'

'What happened?'

'You tell me. I was hoping we could have a chat. We have a fair bit to catch up on.'

Oliver swallowed, deciding to grab water from the tap. It rushed out in a warm stream and then turned cold, and he scooped it into his hands, holding the phone between his ear and shoulder. 'So, Gabe's all right?'

'He'll live.'

'Fuck.'

'Anyway. That chat …' Oliver imagined Everson sitting in the car, next to Mulaney, Wayfarers on, lack of sleep causing dark circles around her eyes. 'By the time you get back to Mudgee, I'll be waiting on that nice Chesterfield you've got in front of the TV,' she said, a satisfaction in her voice that Oliver hadn't heard before.

'Really?'

'I've almost got a warrant, and I can't wait to use it. And when I leave the winery, you'll be coming with me.'

Dear Theo,

As you're aware, this is the first time I've put pen to paper for a while. I'm flying from Sydney to Melbourne without being able to use my phone, so I thought it might be time to resume our letter writing. After all, there was always something exciting about discovering one in the mailbox before we met.

It's hard to believe it's been a fortnight since our road trip. I know it's not hard to believe, but I seldom take a holiday. I suppose I get time off over Christmas, when the courts – the entire corporate world – curl into a forced hibernation. But crime doesn't take a holiday then, so of course I'm still needed. To actually put my phone on silent and drive away from the city, into the vineyards, was incredibly relaxing. And for that I'm grateful.

I can't decide whether I preferred the views and the wines in Mudgee or in Orange. They were both pretty and delicious for different reasons. After hearing about your twin brother, I can see why he settled in Mudgee. Despite being a beautiful place, it seems to have its own ongoing identity crisis. There are orchards and vineyards only a few minutes' drive from the mines. I remember seeing a Maserati parked beside a dinged-up, drug-filled Commodore station wagon. There are pubs that play the discordant song of poker machines and there are wine bars serving 300-dollar bottles of organic wines. Rich Sydney couples with their puffer jackets and a Porsche are sleeping only a street away from kids who have gone to bed without dinner. It's almost like a suburb of Sydney has separated and drifted away into the bush, being swallowed by what existed before.

I knew, from the second night we met, at that quaint wine bar in Potts Point, that you were a good man. You'll remember I ordered for us a bottle of riesling, one from Austria that I'd tried earlier and enjoyed. By arriving first and ordering the wine – by sipping it when you arrived – I was telling you about the baby without even having to have the conversation. I suppose it's not something you want to talk about on a second date.

We haven't discussed it much since, and to be perfectly frank I haven't really felt like talking about it. I don't regret my decision and I respect you for respecting my choice, and for taking a nonchalant stance. I might have chosen an average wine the night I met you, but at least I chose a decent man.

Yours,

Angie

15.

Three and a half hours later, Oliver slipped the empty Luger into Rocky's 44-gallon-drum mailbox on the way to Mudgee Hospital. He tried to call Penny, but the service was patchy; he could only find her message bank.

Gabe had been transferred out of intensive care, into a room on the other side of the building. Oliver realised, as he walked towards Gabe's room, just how antisocial he'd been since moving to Mudgee. He'd lived there a decade and had no idea who anyone at the hospital was. His father – even Theo – would have made friends with people in town. Found connections and charmed people in the right places. If he'd walked in with Penny, she would have known someone. He wasn't sure whether his reclusiveness helped or hindered him in these kinds of situations.

Gabe was in a white robe, bandage over his shoulder, arm in a sling.

'You scared the shit out of me,' Oliver said, pulling up a chair and sitting down.

'God, you look awful,' said Gabe.

'Think one of us must have killed a Chinaman in the last life.'

'You can't say that anymore.'

'Can't say anything. What happened here?' Oliver fiddled carefully with the bandage; he could see blood swelling through the fabric.

Gabe sighed. 'Nothing to do with you or Theo, I'm pretty sure.'

'Something to do with Murray?'

Gabe closed his eyes. Oliver noticed his lip quiver.

'Long story. The drugs are making me drowsy.'

'No hurry,' Oliver said. After a minute, Gabe closed his eyes and appeared to be in a light sleep. Oliver heard the sound of buzzers, squeaky wheels and nurses laughing. The swish of tyres outside, the perpetual monotone of machines.

When he was alert again, Gabe said, 'We owed money, Oli. Got in a little deep.'

Oliver straightened in his seat. 'A little? With whom?'

'Doesn't matter.' Gabe opened his eyes. He was gazing out the window, longing for something in the distance. 'Horses. Syndicates. Partying a little too hard in the city. It's easy to go too hard.'

'So, they shot you because you didn't have what you owed them?'

'They beat me up. Hit me in the guts. Murray was worse. He walked to his ute as they were leaving and pulled his shotgun. Then, well …'

'For fuck's sake. So, it was definitely related to gambling?'

Gabe stared at the ceiling, refusing to make eye contact. 'I don't know. Perhaps. They weren't familiar.'

'Do you think it was the same people that came for Clare? Gabe, I need you to tell me what you remember. Were they driving an old red car?'

Gabe immediately shook his head. 'Black four-wheel drive. Dark, expensive.'

'This is my fault. Ever since Theo came, everything's just ...'

'Don't blame yourself, Oli. We both know the messes Murray's been in before. I'm sure it's to do with that. It makes the most sense, doesn't it?'

Oliver tapped Gabe's thigh. 'You're not allowed to die on me. At least not till I'm rotting in prison.'

'Everson doesn't like you much.'

'Some days less than others. Reckons she's got a warrant for the vineyard.'

'There's nothing to fear from my cottage,' Gabe assured him. 'She doesn't come across as the religious type, so she shouldn't be offended by some "curious straight friends experimenting together" kind of porn.'

'I thought you'd be into big and black?'

'Has to have some kernel of possibility.'

'You're a good-looking man,' said Oliver. 'Don't sell yourself short.'

Gabe exhaled, stifling a giggle. 'At least we can still joke about it.'

'If we didn't keep our humour, what else would we have left?'

Gabe was staring out of the window. 'Some days, my friend, I'm not too sure.' He closed his eyes and after a moment appeared to be asleep.

A nurse walked into the room and frowned. Gabe didn't stir. She looked Oliver up and down and said sternly, 'Make sure he drinks water.'

Before Oliver could reply, he heard Gabe's voice: 'Prefer a gin martini if you've got one. Dry, with an olive.'

***

In the car, Oliver placed his forehead on the warm steering wheel. Had he ever been this lonely before? He felt forlorn. Sad and angry and full of adrenaline, all at once. He tried Penny for the third time, but she seemed to be ignoring his calls. He hadn't asked Gabe whether she knew about the shooting. It had to be connected to him, Orson and Clare, didn't it? Gossip would travel through Mudgee with unpredictable urgency, granules of truth sprinkled somewhere in the mix. *Did you hear that the reclusive winemaker shot his neighbour and vineyard manager? The one he's gay with? The poor girl who owns the wine bar. How could you face it?*

Oliver hated gossip. And his vivid imagination even more.

He remembered his trip to Martinborough with Penny a year ago. How far in the past it seemed. Sitting beside the fire, drinking pinot noir and picking at pâté. They were with Rocky and Penny's brother, Clint, both of whom had gone to bed earlier.

'Let's brave the cold for a cigarette?' said Penny, standing up and snatching the packet from the table. It was bleak outside, but after living in Mudgee they'd grown accustomed to the cold. Oliver had loved New Zealand. He'd enjoyed the trip and the company.

He placed the cigarette to his lips, ready to light, but Penny plucked it away and kissed him. They finished the rest of the bottle before they were on the boards inside, her breath warm over his neck. It sent a shiver along his side. He could still remember the way the dim light reflected onto her body, how it looked and felt as she moved up and down. The little noises she made, trying to keep quiet, as she came. Her palm pushed to Oliver's mouth to mute the groan that vibrated along his chest. The warmth of the fire as they lay together, naked.

Bringing himself back to reality, Oliver started the car and drove to Four Dogs Missing. He was surprised to find the gate still closed.

PRIVATE.

There was no police tape at Gabe's cottage. He drove down and parked in the driveway and opened the door to his house.

It smelled stale, like something had turned in the kitchen. A couple of indoor plants drooped with neglect. He checked his phone, but Penny still hadn't called. There wasn't much battery left. He scrolled through his contacts until he came across Gabe's sister.

Vicky worked in a bank in Sydney. Oliver wasn't sure she was close with Gabe, but he thought she should know her brother was in hospital. Both of their parents had passed away, and as far as Oliver knew, it was just the two of them left. There wasn't much service on his mobile, so he dialled the number on the landline.

'Vicky speaking.'

'Hey, it's Oliver.'

There was a pause. 'Oliver. Right. From the winery?'

'Yeah. Look, I'm just calling about Gabe. He's doing all right, but he's been shot.'

'Shot?' She sounded neither shocked nor surprised, merely curious. 'What on earth happened?'

Oliver twirled the phone cord and stood looking out onto the balcony, watching the sun bathe the cabernet vines that ran from the front to the back of the property. It felt like only a few weeks ago they were green and bushy; now they were maple brown and almost leafless. Everything felt oddly quiet as he struggled for words.

'I'm not exactly sure. A bullet grazed his shoulder at his cottage last night. He's in hospital but he's doing okay.'

215

'He's conscious, then?'

'Yes.'

'Smells like trouble to me,' Vicky said. It sounded like she was on a train; Oliver heard the whoosh of movement, voices in the distance, the signal cutting in and out. 'Just be careful, Oliver. He's got himself in deep.'

'What do you mean?'

'With money. That's what it's about, surely? It has to be. Horseracing. He'd hate to know you've called me, because there's the chance I'd tell you he owes me more than thirty grand.'

'Really?' Oliver said, surprised. At that moment, he was glad he hadn't taken the paintings to Gabe. 'I'm sorry, I had no idea.'

'Just be careful,' she said again. 'I doubt I'll ever see the money again. Gabe is a good salesman, but I knew one day he'd get himself in too deep.'

'Anyway,' Oliver said. 'I just thought you should know.' Before she could hang up, he said, 'Sorry, Vicky, just one question. Do you think Gabe could hurt anyone?'

'What do you mean?'

'As in shoot someone. Murder them.'

She was silent for so long, Oliver wondered whether the service had dropped out. 'I would have said no for a long time, but when someone's desperate to save themselves, they'll do all kinds of things.'

'Even murder?'

'Well,' she said. 'Gabe is myopic when he needs to be. I don't think he would …' Vicky paused. 'No, he wouldn't. But, it's true that desperation does funny things to people.'

'Yes,' said Oliver, taking a breath. 'I guess it does.'

***

In the kitchen, Oliver poured himself water from the tap. As he took a sip, the house phone started to ring. He stared for a good few seconds before walking over and grabbing the receiver. The sound of someone breathing.

'Who is this?'

There was a click. A metronome. One hundred beats per minute.

He put the phone down and swiped open his laptop and the camera app, but it was taking too long to load, so he walked outside as fast as his legs would carry him. He made it to the wine shed, opened the padlock with his key and went inside. After pulling the lever, the lights kicked on, but there was no one around, so he walked into the piano room. Also empty. He looked under the tables, behind the wine barrels, in the small toilet, but the building was vacant. Then he walked over to the piano and saw his metronome sitting on the piano, moving back and forth.

Tick.

  Tick.

    Tick.

      Tick.

        Tick.

          Tick.

            Tick.

Dear Angie,

I've been thinking a lot about my father. Thinking too often about the signs, thinking about what I could have done to prevent things. How life could have been (which is a waste of time). Although I do wonder if it's helping me go easier on myself, in relation to leaving Oliver behind.

I think we both faded into the world in the only way we knew how.

While in theory I want to remember my father as a murdering piece of shit, there are so many good childhood memories. The problem with criminals, and I'm sure you understand this better than I do, is no one is ever mercilessly evil. As a kid, Oliver and I would hang out at our father's pharmacy and laugh along with the staff at the jokes he used to tell. The customers, especially the old ladies, used to love him. When we were younger, I'm positive, too, that my mother still loved my father. Sometimes it's a snap, other times it makes sense over time. I wonder whether we were too close to see all of the signs?

You asked me in Orange, though, if I remembered the first sign. A warning. There was an ominous and obvious one, clearly full of foreboding. I can see that now, with the benefit of hindsight – although you'll have to forgive me for not being able to connect the dots the day we turned ten.

I remember brooding clouds, a full moon, even before dusk. That afternoon, the three of us loped through the long grass, flecked with mud after the biggest storm I'd ever seen. The earth squelched between our toes: it was cool, especially for the first week of summer. La Niña, our father said, stomping behind us in gumboots. 'Do you boys know what it means in Spanish?' he asked us. 'The girl. A cold event. A fuck ton of rain.' Miles decided he was taking his twin sons yabbying and hunting, something to pass the time together in our

218

new backyard; something country people did to celebrate another lap around the sun.

We'd only been in the bush for a few months and we'd been told, ad nauseum, to prepare for the heat. Our father had packed us into the car and taken us five hundred kilometres west of Sydney, our mother anxious as we drove along the barren landscape that refused to recede into anything more than dust and sporadic gums. The destination: a town of eight hundred people so desperate for a pharmacist they agreed to pay my father twice his city wage.

Miles kept a small butane stove on the back of the ute. We'd parked beside a farm dam and he tossed a live yabby we'd caught into a stained silver pot that spat boiling water. The yabby had barely been in there twenty seconds when he pulled it out with his fingers and seared the knife down its middle. Only then did the claws stop wriggling. Sometimes, even now, the same crunch permeates my dreams – an image of my father standing over me, the crack of the knife plunging into my ribs. He squeezed lemon over the flesh and handed one half to me, the other to Oliver, telling us, 'Better than the shit at home. Enjoy it, won't you?'

It was one of the best things I'd ever put in my mouth. It was a tad dirty but tender, sweet, nothing at all like the overcooked pasta and stewed meat we normally ate.

Once we'd finished, I was allowed to drive us – in second gear – around the paddock. I'm not even sure who the land belonged to, or if our father had permission to be there. Oliver sat quietly in the back seat, uninterested in taking his turn. When we pulled up, the two of us sat on the tray and watched our father shoot at boars and kangaroos as the sun waned behind the flat earth. I can still hear the high whirr of the bullet leaving the chamber.

I remember one particular kangaroo leaping towards us. It turned away when it saw my father draw his shotgun and aim, and it began hopping frantically towards the trees. I was desperately hoping it would escape, that Miles's shot would miss – but our father pulled the trigger and less than a second later the animal dropped dead.

'Come on. Let's have a look,' he told us. 'Might be able to slow-cook her. Best way to nibble our coat of arms.' Oliver and I ambled dubiously behind our father.

'Check this out,' Miles said, pointing to a joey, still alive, cushioned in its mother's pouch. It was only a few weeks old. Completely helpless. Oliver and I shared concern. Maybe we'd take it home with us? Keep it as a pet, something we could raise before releasing back into the bush. Next thing we knew, Miles pulled the joey from the pouch, held it by the tail and forcibly struck its head on a rock – once, twice, three times. Blood mottled the wet grass. He tossed the dead joey to the ground as though discarding a spent cigarette.

I stared at my twin brother: any bit of existing colour had leached from his skin. Our father laughed. 'Oh come on, boys. How would you feel if I killed your mother and let you starve out here alone?'

The ebullient laugh still echoes from time to time. It was almost thirty years ago, but it still enters my skull some days without warning. Without reprieve. It was a sign, wasn't it?

I know that now. And how did I ignore the others? What should I have done differently?

(trying to find) Peace,

Theo

16.

Oliver sat at his dining table, reviewing the recorded footage on his laptop. A man wearing a hoodie entered the frame – his movements taut, athletic – before the camera cut out. The intruder had obviously found it and turned it around, facing into darkness. So much for a subtle placement. For a moment Oliver wondered if the figure might have been Chase, but quickly convinced himself that he was simply being paranoid; Chase was probably overseas, so how could he be snooping around the winery? Something told Oliver his half-brother wasn't involved, and like Orson and Clare and Theo, had unknowingly become caught up and entangled in some devious plot that Oliver couldn't yet unravel. Even though his mind was messy, he could only think about properly reconciling with Penny.

She arrived home a little after eleven pm. Her car lights grew brighter as she parked behind Oliver, who sat waiting in the Jag. Chopin played through the stereo – or, rather, someone played Chopin through the stereo. Penny stepped out and closed the car door gently, then stood waiting, with her arms folded.

Getting out, Oliver said, 'Pretty good game of phone tag there.'

'What a week.'

She approached him and they hugged. He had definitely missed her smell: wine and sweat and sweet shampoo.

'Is Gabe okay?' Penny said.

'He'll live.'

They walked inside. The house was messy, littered with dirty clothes, and food-smeared plates were stacked precariously beside the sink.

'You're both the talk of the town. I think more than half the tables tonight came in to find out about your brother or Gabe.'

Oliver sat on one of the dining-room chairs. 'One thing I hate about country people is how nosy they are. You can be dying on the street in Sydney and no one looks at you twice. Out here, it's no one's business and they want to find out the intricacies of your fridge.'

Penny sighed as she put two glasses down on the table and removed a bottle of red from her bag, leftover from the bar. 'I should have listened to my father,' she said. 'The place's cursed.'

Oliver nodded, mumbling something that sounded like agreement.

'He doesn't like coming here, you know? Says he can feel the bad vibe.'

Oliver had read about Aboriginal massacres in the region, the little information that was available online and in books. Often he stared out across the vineyard and wondered how many people had died, how many had disappeared without anyone in the past bothering to even keep a record.

'I'm still working out how spiritual I am. Craig believes in it. Says you can feel it. The history creeping through your bones.'

Oliver took a sip of wine. 'Do you think a place can do that?'

'Of course. A place can feel unlucky,' Penny said. 'Surely, you're feeling that now. Maybe the place itself isn't cursed, but the memories it encourages can be.'

'I don't know what to think anymore.'

Penny let out a protracted breath. 'I'm not sure how much longer I can stay here, Oli. I wanted to believe everything people said about Mudgee was bullshit.'

'What about the bar?'

'I like running a swanky bar in a wine region. Telling rich white eastern suburbs hedge-fund babies in their puffer jackets that no, I'm not Israeli or Spanish or Fijian, I'm black. And yes, I'm the owner. Even if half my family looked down on me for choosing Mudgee. But the wines? They're great. And I'm close to everyone here.'

'Well, keep doing it. You're good at it.'

Penny rummaged through her bag, picking out another half-opened bottle of wine, pouring a taste before deciding which one to drink. 'I don't think people know how hard I work. How much I saved to start my dream. Sure, I had help. But I work harder than anyone I know. Sometimes, though, I hate being so tied down. You're the same. When you're tied to a business, you can't just up and run.'

Oliver understood. Even though she owned a business, sometimes Penny would disappear for a couple of days. Pay staff to look after the place in her absence. She wouldn't take her phone, or if she did, she wouldn't turn it on. Oliver, more than anyone else, didn't begrudge her need for time away.

'I've always felt safe at the winery,' he said. 'Like it's the only place in the world that hasn't been … tarnished. Not sure about that anymore.'

'Since Theo?'

'Yeah. Since this all started. Someone's fucking with me. They keep calling the house phone. I'm pretty sure they're on the property.'

'That's creepy.'

'Tell me about it.'

Penny looked Oliver dead in the eyes and he was worried about what she was going to say.

'Tonight, let's drink wine and talk. I'm not saying it's always been hard between us, but, Oliver … I can't keep us alive if you don't open up to me.'

Oliver grabbed the bottle and topped up their glasses. 'That's why I'm here.'

Penny was staring off into space. 'Why don't we just go,' she said. 'Leave the winery. I'll get someone to take over the bar. Gabe can look after the vineyard.'

'What?'

'I'm serious, Oli. Let's take the paintings and run. You can make wine in France. We'll go to farmers' markets in the morning, read books, drink wine, be away from it all.'

It was certainly an appetising proposal. Leaving the country, the police, Harold and the memories of his father behind. Starting from scratch. A new winery. Something burgeoning. It wouldn't be easy, but Oliver wondered if Penny was right; tapping into his own desires to run.

Penny placed her glass on the table, took off her jumper and moved towards him. Something in her demeanour had shifted. She sat on his lap, wrapped her arms around Oliver's neck. 'It's been a shit time, and I'm ...'

They kissed, a larghetto rhythm, his hands moving down her waist. How was he doing this now? It was a reminder that one's libido didn't play by rational rules. As he slipped Penny's singlet from her shoulders, his phone lit up on the table. It was a local number, one he didn't recognise.

Reluctantly pulling away from Penny, he answered.

'Before you start to worry, I'm fine,' Gabe said. 'Other than the nurse refusing to fix me a gin and tonic.'

'You don't have your phone?'

'No. I got rushed here. It's sitting at home with a dead battery.'

'Is everything okay?'

'All good with me. I just got a call from Mary next door.'

'About Murray?'

'No. Apparently, there are police at the vineyard, Oli. Lights on in your house and mine. Both of them lit up like cruise ships.'

'Everson,' Oliver deduced. 'She kept saying she was going to get a warrant.'

'Well. With or without it, she's definitely there. I'm guessing you're not?'

'I'm with Penny.'

'Well, let me know.'

'Will do.'

Oliver tried Everson's mobile, but she didn't answer. It went straight to voicemail: no service.

'Can I borrow your computer for a sec?'

Penny jogged to the bedroom, came back and handed him her laptop. Flipping open the screen, he logged in to the camera software and saw a man in a police uniform walking around the cellar.

Shit.

He called his landline, but there was no answer. He waited thirty seconds and tried again. Someone picked up without saying anything.

'Is that Everson?' Oliver asked.

'Hi there,' she said. 'I was hoping you'd be here. We're trawling through your things.'

Oliver stood up. 'Wait. I'm coming now.'

'I don't mind if you come,' Everson said brazenly, 'but I'm definitely not going to wait. It's much too late for that.'

17.

Penny throttled her Corolla, while Oliver rode shotgun. He wished
he was driving because he wanted to get there faster. After the call,
Penny had grabbed her car keys and rushed out the door, Oliver
following behind, unquestioning, grateful. Until now. *Why hadn't
they just taken the Jag?* Penny was only a little over the speed limit,
a busted muffler offering the illusion that they were travelling
faster. The night was dark and the moon was gibbous, veiled by
clouds, and the thought of Everson touching his things made him
twitch.

'I'm sorry to drag you into this.'

Penny exhaled. 'Look at us, rushing to your vineyard because
the police have a search warrant. Murders. What the fuck is going
on?'

'And Gabe. Bullet through the shoulder.'

'I thought it only grazed him?'

'I think it's more serious than that, from what I saw at hospital.'

'What happened?'

Oliver checked the road. They were only a few minutes from

the vineyard. 'Gambling. Money borrowed, money owed. I think he and Murray are in a little bit of debt.'

'Shit timing. Is Murray all right?'

'It's touch and go. Apparently, the men who attacked them were leaving after delivering the beating, and Murray pulled a shotgun from the back of the Cruiser. When one of the men tried to wrestle it off him, the gun went off and hit Gabe. Then they beat the shit out of them both again.'

'For fuck's sake. Murray's such a typical second-generation winemaker.'

Oliver's gaze flicked to Penny. 'What does that mean?' He realised how much he had missed her. Her unpredictability. The nuance she brought to each conversation.

'There's kind of an old doctrine. The first generation builds it, the second fucks it, the third fixes it.'

Oliver was surprised to find himself laughing. 'Wait, who's the third generation?'

'Murray's sister, Haley. Her sons.'

'True,' Oliver said. 'Forgot that. Probably my Alzheimer's kicking in after inhaling all of the Vernons' nasty pesticides.'

Penny shot Oliver a sly smile. 'Maybe if you tried to get on, you might realise you have more in common than you think.'

'Sorry,' Oliver said, 'but I could never be friends with anyone whose signature wine is a moscato. In Mudgee.'

Penny spat as she laughed a little, shaking her head. 'You're funny. And not wrong.'

***

The gate had been left open, and as the Corolla turned into the driveway Oliver saw that there were bugs everywhere. They circled around the car's headlights before being consumed by the bonnet.

Oliver couldn't stop swallowing. His Adam's apple felt like it was going to dislodge itself and topple down his throat. There was nothing for Everson to find, but he hated the idea of the police trawling through his things.

Two police cars sat in the dark beside his cottage, which had the lights on in every room. The sight made Oliver squirm. As soon as Penny parked the car he rushed into the house, but it was empty, the overbrightness of the place making it look cloaked in the tones of a nightmare.

They were all down at the wine shed.

Oliver and Penny walked together, almost breaking into a run. There were police congregating near the door, some peering around the barrels.

'Don't open them. There's only wine inside,' Oliver said.

Everson came from the piano room. She had a bottle of wine in her hands. 'Nice of you to join us. What's outside near the vines?'

'What do you mean?'

'What have you buried out there?'

Shit. He knew how it would sound. A barrel buried in the ground. Just before Theo had arrived they'd dug another hole, and it was there, empty.

'A wine barrel,' he said.

Everson raised her eyebrows, placing the bottle beside the door. 'Why have you buried a wine barrel?'

'It's a biodynamic procedure,' Penny interjected. 'If you knew about winemaking, you'd know it was pretty normal. It keeps the temperature of the wine stable.'

'Funny you say that,' Everson retorted, stepping closer. 'No one seems to think anything out here is particularly normal.'

'Yeah, well, no one else around here can make wine like Oliver.'

'So, they're jealous?'

'What does this have to do with your search?' Oliver asked. Everson made eye contact, held it, and waited for him to break it. Oliver wondered exactly how old she was; where she lived in Sydney; whether she was married. He realised she'd nearly traipsed through his entire life and he knew nothing about her save for her name and what sunglasses she wore.

Before she could answer, a noise came from the piano room. Everson turned and walked towards it. Oliver and Penny followed. Sergeant Mulaney was standing over the piano, wearing gloves, looking inside. Everson was doing the same.

'What's that you're hiding down there, Mr Wingfield?'

'A bottle of water,' Oliver said. 'Half full. It stops the wood from cracking.'

Everson leaned in, and when she came up, she was holding a handgun. Different to the one he'd dropped in Rocky's mailbox, but it wasn't fake. It was real. Before Everson said anything, he knew that it was the same gun the man had used to shoot Clare.

'I'd be saying half empty if I was you,' Everson countered. 'Is this registered?'

'It's not mine.' Oliver looked at Penny, whose face was all panic. 'I've never seen it before in my life.'

Mulaney took a pair of handcuffs from his belt. 'Oliver Wingfield. You're under arrest for the possession of a prohibited firearm.'

***

Having never been arrested before, Oliver realised he knew very little about the judicial system. He had no idea how to apply for bail, and a few facts were illuminated almost immediately: if a senior officer objected, you had to wait to see a magistrate. If you were arrested late on a Friday, you weren't getting a call until Monday morning. Oliver had been taken to a cell, but after a couple of hours a cop he didn't recognise came in and took him to the room he'd been interviewed in twice before, where he sat and stewed. Eventually, Everson and Mulaney entered and sat down.

'I'm in here all weekend?'

'I don't make the rules,' Everson said, flicking through her small notepad and finding the page she was looking for. 'And it appears you don't follow them. A firearm stashed inside your piano, a murder linked to your winery, a business associate presently missing. Might be time you started following said rules. And time to get used to a cell.'

'Can I speak to a lawyer?'

'Sure,' Everson said offhandedly. 'You can make a call for one right now, before I drill some questions into you. It's worth noting that as far as I'm aware, your lawyer can't get you a bail hearing until Monday regardless, so I'd get cosy in that cell.'

'Maybe Gabe could help, I don't—'

'You don't even have a lawyer, do you, mate?' Mulaney chided. 'You come across to me as someone who has the kind of ego to represent themselves. This is all pretty serious stuff.'

'It's not my gun,' Oliver said. 'I'm just trying to get to the bottom of what—'

'See,' Everson said, moving close to Oliver. 'This is what I don't understand. Everyone told me that you're some kind of recluse, a snob who makes fancy wine and doesn't talk to anyone. That you mind your own business and stay in your own little world. Burying your barrels, summoning the moon or whatever weird shit it is that you do. But you know what? Ever since I've been here, you've been nothing but a pain in the arse.'

Everson paused, then closed her notepad. She started counting on her fingers as she spoke: 'You've withheld information, openly lied to me, and have been so suspiciously close to everything that you're making it almost impossible for me to look anywhere else. I really tried to trust you, Oliver.'

'You can.'

'You can't keep everything to yourself without suffering any consequences.'

When Oliver didn't reply, Everson hit a button on her device and began spouting the same platitudes about recordings and inducements as she had in their first ever interview.

'And you're refusing a solicitor, Mr Wingfield?'

'I don't wish to say anything at this point in time.'

'Just for the record, Mr Wingfield has refused to make a call for legal representation and is electing to represent himself.'

'Could I at least have a glass of water?'

Mulaney grunted, stood up and left the room. Was gone less than a minute and came back with a styrofoam cup half filled with cold water that tasted like it'd been scooped from a chlorinated pool.

'So, tell me about your business partners,' Everson said. 'In this technology company.'

'No comment.'

'I called Orson Denver a few days ago. Just to acquire some kind of character witness statement for you. Considering you're a bit quiet in Mudgee, I thought he'd be a good place to start. So when I called Orson's mobile, I was surprised when his wife answered. Do you know what she told me?'

Oliver knew exactly, but didn't offer a response. He could feel sweat sticking to his palms.

'Just for the benefit of the recording, Mr Wingfield is refusing to comment. Valerie, lovely lady, told me that shortly before he died, her husband had been drinking wine. Not just any wine, but specifically the samples you sent over a few weeks ago.'

'Orson had a heart attack,' Oliver interjected.

'One that was induced by the same poison we found in your brother's whisky glass,' Mulaney said, sliding what Oliver presumed were Theo's autopsy findings halfway across the table. He glanced down but couldn't make sense of anything.

'Exactly,' Everson added, pointing to the piece of paper. 'Some interesting results there. I'm guessing when Orson's autopsy arrives from the US, we'll see much of the same. Can you tell me, Oliver, why people close to you and your wine are winding up dead?'

'No comment.'

Everson leaned back in her chair. 'Oliver, where's Clare Jacklin?'

'I don't know.'

'If she's alive, and you know her whereabouts, it's not too late for us to come to some kind of agreement. Her welfare is paramount at this point.'

'I don't know where Clare is.'

'Tell me what happened. Did you and Clare plan to take over Orson's share of the company once you'd poisoned him? Did Theo stumble upon it by accident, and you had to kill him to keep him quiet?'

'You have a vivid imagination,' Oliver said.

'I don't think you could write a book about this. So, when Clare has grown frightened and she's told you that things have gotten out of hand, you've had to shoot her to keep her quiet? To stop her from coming to us?'

'I have never shot anyone.'

'We'll see about that,' Mulaney said. 'Ballistics are running tests on the weapon as we speak. Silencer and all. I reckon Theo must've brought the gun. Is that why he came to Mudgee?'

'No.'

'Ballistics are pretty good these days. We'll be able to tell when the weapon was last fired. Do you reckon there's a chance that was a couple of nights ago? The same time Clare Jacklin was last seen?'

'This is all bullshit.'

'Is it, though?' Mulaney said.

'No comment.'

'No comment is still a comment, especially in court,' Everson said, frowning as she looked at her bare watch-tanned wrist. 'Friday night. Still haven't had a beer. Supposed to be in Sydney tomorrow for my daughter's birthday, but I don't think that's going to happen.'

I don't want to be here any more than you do.

'I thought you were being set up at the beginning,' Everson said, settling back in to her interrogation. 'But your brother, both of your business partners. Not going to tell me about your father? Or worried I'd realise you were following in his footsteps?'

Oliver froze. How did she know?

'See, initially, I may have taken your surprise as innocence. But now I see it as hubris. You thought that you were just too clever for me. That there was no way I could have known about it already.'

'Hubris is a big word.'

'That's why I don't like you, mate. I've met a lot of bullies and idiots in my day, but you know what? I've never met a dumb detective.'

'I didn't suggest that.'

'Sure,' Everson said. 'Although, I did one stupid thing. I believed you when you said both of your parents were dead. But why would someone lie about that? I suppose they would if they had something to hide. I found out that your grandmother tried to protect you from your father by changing your name through the courts.'

'No comment, no comment, no comment.'

'Are you working with your father, Oliver? How's he involved?'

'The three no comments were for the next two ludicrous questions I knew you'd ask.'

'I've been running some scenarios in my head based on the evidence. Tell me if I'm close. Last week, Theo comes home and you go to Penny's for the evening. You drive back to your vineyard in the middle of the night to make sure he's succumbed to the poison you put in the whisky. Things get messy, so you're forced to slit his throat. A week or two earlier, you sent a poisoned case of wine across the world to your mentor in California, who – allegedly, for now – dies by ingesting the same poison you gave Theo. You go to Orange to talk through the plan of attack for the company with your remaining business partner, but something goes wrong, so you end up shooting Clare and moving her body. No other witnesses, only people who saw a bottle-green Jaguar in Orange on the night of the murder. Then hidden in your piano we find a gun that's looking like it's definitely involved in this whole debacle. For someone who's pretty stupid, mate, even I can join the dots ...'

'I didn't fucking kill anyone!' Oliver yelled.

Everson moved close. 'You weren't on the coast when I called you this morning, were you? You beat Murray Vernon to a pulp last night. Let's wait until he wakes up and can tell us what's going on.

A good question is, though, Oliver … why is Gabe still protecting you? Is he in on all of this, too?'

'I'm not saying another fucking word without a lawyer.'

Everson slid a folded piece of paper across the table. It was a printout of a newspaper article.

'Interview terminated at ten-o-two pm,' she said, before pressing a button on the recorder. The sergeant stood up first, and the detective followed.

'I'll see you on Monday,' said Everson, a sudden iciness to her tone. 'I'm going to triple-check I've got enough evidence together so you'll never have to bury another body or barrel ever again. You sick fuck.'

Central Coast murderer receives 32-year sentence for killing well-known artist wife and assaulting local gallerist

A man who killed his wife – who had been diagnosed with cancer – and later assaulted her manager, was sentenced on Wednesday morning to twenty-nine years. The judge ruled the Terrigal pharmacy owner won't be eligible for parole until at least 2025.

Miles Raymond Jones, forty-six, was on Tuesday sentenced to a maximum of twenty-nine years in prison for the murder that Justice Catherine Nott called 'callous and clumsy'.

Jones was found guilty of killing Julia Crespo by a NSW Supreme Court jury earlier this week. He is also being charged for assaulting Crespo's manager and gallerist, Harold Keller, who was only recently discharged from Gosford Hospital, where he remained for weeks in a critical but stable condition.

Crespo was an award-winning and celebrated artist, known on the Central Coast and all over the world for her abstract paintings of coastal landscapes.

Jones allegedly struck his wife over the head and killed her on the afternoon of 6 October. He disposed of the body in the ocean before returning home, where he lived with Crespo and his teenage twin sons.

Despite the verdict, Jones maintains his innocence. He took to the stand, emotionally telling a jury that he discovered his wife, who had been battling lymphoma, dead on the floor; he claims he only moved her so that his sons would not discover their mother's body. Jones then angrily sought answers about his wife's death from Crespo's manager, Harold Keller, who he claimed had been at the house earlier in the day. The court was told an argument ensued, leading to Keller's hospitalisation.

'We will certainly appeal. My client maintains his innocence in the death of Julia Crespo, and has shown an unbelievable degree of remorse for the assault of Harold Keller,' Jones's lawyer, Edward Bridgers, told reporters.

Whoever informed police of key evidence that led to the search of the accused's vehicle, eventually leading to the conviction of Jones, has not been identified.

18.

Of course he'd scrunched up the article. Torn it to pieces. But sitting in a cell made him think of his father. Oliver had visited him once. As far as he knew, Theo had never gone to see him.

Visitation was akin to television in some ways and different in others. It was a quiet drive to the prison outside of Lithgow. The day Oliver mustered the courage to go it was pouring rain. He wished he'd taken Theo or someone else along for the ride, to help him escape his own head. Even remembering an umbrella might have helped.

Oliver made sure he arrived on time. A burly-looking man scanned his body and clothes for weapons. Oliver had to fill in a form. He was ashamed to write that Miles was his father, but there was no point in lying. Sadly, Miles wouldn't have been the most macabre man in the jail.

Was he wearing heels higher than five centimetres? Motorcycle gang 'colours'? He ticked 'NO' to everything and checked over the form umpteen times to make sure he hadn't missed something that might ruin his chances of heading in. He knew that if he stumbled on a technicality and had to leave, he wouldn't return.

After a few minutes of waiting, he was led to metal-topped table. Oliver sat there for fifteen minutes before a guard brought his father through, hands cuffed, and seated him on the opposite side of the table. There were a few other people visiting at the same time. Some sat quietly, barely talking; others angled together as closely as possible and whispered like they were getting paid per spoken word.

Miles hadn't changed much; but he had lost some weight, and his skin had a sickly pallor.

'You came,' were his first words.

The guard moved behind them and stood with arms crossed, looking bored.

'Yeah.'

'Missed you and Theo at the trial. I looked.'

'I know. We wanted to. Be there, I mean.'

Was that true? *Had* he wanted to be there? No, of course he hadn't. He'd had no desire to sit still while the prosecution drilled their facts and theories into a jury, disproving everything he'd ever hoped to believe about his father. He *wished* he believed that Miles was innocent. Wanted to more than anything else. A pang of guilt vibrated, somewhere, internally. Should Oliver have been one of those loyal family members, sticking by the accused until the sentence was handed down?

Miles didn't speak for what felt like a long time, though it would have been only seconds. 'I know that you think ...' He paused, scratching his moustache vigorously with his thumb and first finger. 'That I did it. But we're going to fight. They think there weren't enough internal injuries to suggest a beating.'

'Dad.'

'As far as I knew, she had months to live. A murder doesn't make sense.'

Oliver thought of the newspaper reports: *Crespo had been responding well to chemotherapy. The prosecution argued Jones killed Crespo for insurance, as her cancer hadn't progressed to …*

'Harold's lucky to be alive.'

'Prick.'

Oliver inhaled, looking down at his lap.

'I have a temper,' Miles whispered, 'but I'd never hurt your mother. Do you really think she would have stayed with me all of these years if she thought I'd hurt her?'

Oliver spurned his words, dragging his fingers over his eyes. 'It's too late now.'

He could only think of the night they were told their mother had died, how they had come home to find Miles sitting on the lounge, drinking beer.

'I came home. I knew Harold had been there 'cause I'd called her earlier to check up. But when I got home, she was dead.'

'You were watching TV. Laughing at a comedy after she'd died. Look, I don't want to talk about this.'

'No pulse. Skin cold. Blood on her skull. What was I going to do, Oliver? Call the police and tell them she'd had a fall? Let you and Theo come home and see her like that? I had to carry on like normal for you two.'

'You should have told the truth. You can't play God.'

'Don't fuck with me. I did the human thing and panicked,' Miles spat. 'I was worried about you. I was distraught. Angry. I shouldn't have beaten Harold, but the things he said …'

'She told you she was going to leave you,' Oliver said. 'And the next day she's dead.'

Until Julia's murder, Oliver might not have thought of his father as a terrible man. He had never been a good one, but a murderer? A psychopath? Oliver knew that Miles had controlled his mother too much; wouldn't let her buy everything she wanted, even though she earned more than he did. That he silenced her, probably stopped her from seeing her friends and family. *A chauvinistic manipulator*, Harold had called him once. Eventually, Julia had begun to fade away, despite Oliver and Theo's best efforts to support and love her.

'Do you know what's funny?' Miles said, leaning forward in his chair. 'You live your life. Try to be a good man. Run a business, raise a family. You make one snap decision to move a body, put someone at peace, and then it all implodes. It's like every good deed you've ever done disappears into some abyss. It was a mistake. Two mistakes. But have you ever even thought about that, Oliver? What it's like to be in my shoes?'

Oliver stood up, signalling for the guard. 'I'm glad I'm not in them.'

Before he turned towards the door, he looked at his father's face – the moustache neatly trimmed, sideburns, skin white, no time in the sun. Miles was completely and utterly devoid of any empathy. Oliver wanted, more than anything, to believe that his father was telling the truth. But he couldn't, and he never wanted to see his face again.

He turned around for one last look and said, 'I told them about the blood. In the boot.'

Oliver thought he heard Miles reply. A word, maybe two. Almost a whisper. He was already halfway to the door, holding his breath, and he did not turn back to check.

In the car, he punched the steering wheel: once, twice, three times before he registered any pain. Anger and grief shot through his veins.

It felt like a dam had burst, surging through his body, aggressive enough to take anything in its path.

***

Sometimes, when Oliver couldn't sleep, he would think of his father.

He wouldn't think of the gruesome things that Miles had done. Instead, he thought of his father in his cell, sleeping, hair gone grey, alive and existing in that same, present moment.

Hundreds of kilometres away.

Alive and breathing, despite the life he'd taken away from the world.

***

Now, as Oliver sat in the police cell, a memory of his mother came to him. They were making risotto, Oliver sitting on the bench, ladling stock into the rice while Julia stirred. There was music, some kind of classical jazz, and there was a candle burning on the bench. Theo was at the beach. Where was Miles? His mother hovered the spoon around his lips. Oliver blew on the contents and swallowed the rice on the spoon.

Salt! he screamed. *All I can taste is salt!*

Julia tasted too, spat the mouthful into a paper towel and laughed. *I said one tablespoon. How much did you put into the stock?*

Oliver fumbled for the recipe. *You said cup, not tablespoon!*

Julia hunched over, laughing, as steam rose from the saline stock. Her hair was long and brown and wavy around her shoulders. Was this perhaps the most potent memory he had of his mother? Their laughter as they cooked together? Even now, sometimes, he could conjure the taste of salt. Somewhere in the distance, a mile along his tongue.

***

Saturday morning began with a visit from a stranger.

'I'm not sure I know you,' Oliver said to the woman sitting opposite him. When Sergeant Mulaney led him to the interview room and told him that someone was here to see him, he was expecting to find Gabe or Penny at the table.

'We haven't met before,' she said, opening a folder. 'You don't look too well.'

'I'm fine. Did Gabe organise this?'

She sat back and twirled a pen between her fingers. She was clearly a lawyer. Oliver's age, or a touch older, with ginger-tipped chestnut hair and maroon lipstick, dressed stylishly in a tartan suit and glossy cream high heels.

'You'll have to forgive me. I don't know who Gabe is.'

Oliver exhaled. 'I'm sorry, but I have no idea who you are either.'

'My name is Angie Proctor,' she said. 'I'm a criminal barrister and I'm here to help you.' There was a pause. 'I knew your brother. Theo.'

'Really,' Oliver said. 'That makes one of us.'

'I'm aware that you two were estranged. Didn't speak often.'

'Not at all.'

'Although in my experience, estrangement isn't the preponderant motive for murder.'

'I haven't killed anyone.'

244

Angie nodded. 'I know. But it seems you've certainly pissed someone off.'

Oliver couldn't deny that one. He thought of all the bodies – Theo and Orson and Clare – piled on top of each other. Two of them poisoned in some way – bleeding noses, vomit-stained clothes, bloodshot eyes. One with their throat slashed. One with gunshot wounds to the head and chest. An image fit for nightmares. Did they all know in their final moments that they were going to die?

'How did you know Theo?'

'We met at a wine bar. He was sitting beside me. Told me that sauvignon blanc is a yummy mummy's drink and that I should try something better.'

Oliver smiled. 'Not wrong.'

'Guess you're twins, after all.'

'So, how well did you know him?'

Angie started making notes. 'Well enough.'

'A few people in Orange thought they saw me with a woman with ginger hair. Would that be you with Theo?'

'Sure,' she said, without hesitation. She was quick to answer questions. 'Theo and I travelled, spent time together, before he came here.'

'Why did he take the paintings?'

Angie looked surprised, but continued quickly: 'Let's speculate after we get you out of here.'

Oliver nodded. 'How did you know that I'd been arrested?'

'I do this for a living, Mr Wingfield. You might also say that I've been keeping a close eye on things since Theo's murder. Although I will admit, standing in front of a magistrate in the Mudgee courthouse on a Saturday morning is a new highlight.'

245

'Everson told me I wouldn't get a hearing until Monday.'

'She lied,' Angie said. 'We've got one today. I've rushed it. It's best to catch them off guard and make this as casual as possible.'

'How's it casual?' Oliver asked.

'You'll be in front of a registrar on a Saturday morning, along with a couple of wife beaters and drink drivers. There's only one thing I need to know.' Angie paused, and the silence engulfed every corner of the room. 'The gun. Is it yours?'

'I've never used a gun. Not even for vermin control at the vineyard.'

'No, I need a simple answer. Do you own the gun, or have you ever touched it?'

'No.'

'Very good.'

Oliver nodded, sat back in his chair and folded his arms. 'Why are you helping me?'

Angie was quiet for a moment, staring past him into the distance. Perhaps at the door behind Oliver, or the clock on the wall.

'How about you stop asking so many questions and let me get you out of here? Some of us want to ensure whoever's legitimately responsible is prosecuted to the full extent of the law.'

***

Oliver saw how Theo would have been in thrall to Angie. She was undeniably bright and quick-witted, the tone of her voice sanguine and comforting. There was something about her eyes. Unlike his brother, Oliver would have been too nervous to approach her at a bar on Elizabeth Street.

When it was time for the hearing, Oliver was led to Angie, who was waiting outside the courtroom. He couldn't help but notice, as he looked down Market Street, towards town, how pretty Mudgee was in the late autumn. If he was a tourist, visiting for the first time, he might have appreciated the post office, famously pink, across from the park, where claret ashes were losing their red and bronze leaves. Punters were already perched on stools out the front of the adjacent pub – the aptly named Courthouse Hotel. Though the days were cooling down, the sun was still warm on Oliver's skin.

The sergeant walked inside with Everson, whose appearance was far more casual than usual. Her dark hair was oily, loose; it was the first time Oliver hadn't seen it pulled into a ponytail. She wore jeans and a puffer jacket.

The registrar sat at the front of the courtroom. She had grey hair tightly wound into a bun, and did not look up from writing her notes as Oliver followed Angie inside and sat down.

'Wasn't expecting this,' Angie whispered. 'Female registrar and no prosecutor. You won't have to say anything. Just have your biro and chequebook ready. Or are they still in that nineteen-sixties car you left outside your girlfriend's place?'

'I'm not sure I can afford you. We haven't discussed fees.'

Angie groaned. 'I'm talking about bail. Happy to get you out of here, but judging by the price of your wine, I've made the assumption that you won't be needing a hand with surety.'

Oliver looked perplexed.

'Surety. A financial guarantee. I don't think we'll need one today, but keep your ears open.'

The registrar spoke. 'Are we ready, Sergeant?' Her voice was bristly, a coarseness achieved through a lifetime's dedication to cigarettes.

'We are, thanks, Your Honour,' said Sergeant Mulaney, his name printed in capitals on his badge. The police officer's tension was clearly evident. He kept his hat in his hands, which were shaking slightly. 'While—'

'Let me interrupt you there, Sergeant. Just to save anyone else the trouble as we continue today. I'm a registrar of the court, and while it's an honour to be here on this fine Saturday, I'm not a magistrate, so you can call me "registrar".' She smiled at Mulaney and then waved a hand in the air.

'Yes. My apologies, Registrar. It's been a big week.' Mulaney grimaced, but composed himself again as the registrar smiled smugly. 'Owing to the seriousness of the crime, and the evidence we're currently verifying, we believe that Mr Wingfield is a danger to the community and especially those close to him. We oppose bail.'

'Okay,' the registrar said, taking her own notes. 'Ms Proctor?'

Angie stood and signalled for Oliver to do the same. 'Registrar, my client strenuously denies the accusation that he is a danger to those close to him or the wider community. He has no prior criminal record or any history of weapon possession or violence. The alleged gun was located by the police in a wine shed that is accessible to other employees and tradesmen. One of the benefits of regional living is that one doesn't have to be hyper vigilant when it comes to keeping doors locked. Unfortunately for my client, leaving—'

'The firearm was loaded and is potentially linked to a disappearance,' Sergeant Mulaney interrupted. 'We believe releasing Mr Wingfield poses a significant danger to those who know him, and the wider community in general.'

Angie fired back rapidly: 'Sergeant, an adult disappearing, potentially of his or her own volition, is not a crime.'

'Yes, but we are collecting evidence that we believe will eventually, uh, lead to the discovery of a body.'

Angie's features tightened. 'Registrar, I'd remind the court that there is no evidence to support this crime, or further crimes, having been perpetrated by my client. The police case is entirely circumstantial. The only matter before the court today is a firearms charge.'

'Thank you, Ms Proctor,' the registrar said, glancing at a piece of paper in her hands. 'However, Sergeant Mulaney is correct that we are talking about a serious offence, possessing an unlicensed and prohibited firearm.'

'Registrar, we could understand the opposition if my client was caught firing the weapon, or even with a gun in his direct possession. However, Mr Wingfield denies knowing about the weapon at all, and as I've indicated, multiple other parties have access to the premises. My client hasn't had so much as a driving offence before. My client has cooperated with the police and has on multiple occasions made himself available to answer questions. I submit that my client poses no risk to the community and should be released on bail.'

The registrar looked at Angie, then at Mulaney. She repeatedly flicked a pen between the skin of her thumb and first finger. 'I'm inclined to agree, Ms Proctor. Mr Wingfield hasn't been convicted of even a minor misdemeanour in the past. I also know he does make some of the region's more boutique wines. He runs a busy business and supplies locals with their much-needed evening tipple.' She grinned then, revealing a straight set of wine-stained teeth. 'With all of this in mind, I'm going to offer bail, but with some conditions.'

The convivial moment passed and she paused to read her notes. Oliver noticed Everson was typing something furiously into her phone, which she hid furtively in her lap. 'Obviously, with other ongoing police investigations, Mr Wingfield must remain on his property at all times, leaving only to report to the police station every day before five in the afternoon. These conditions will remain in place until a committal hearing, or, of course, if the charges are dropped.'

The room was silent. 'Oh. Surety. We don't normally ask for it unless it's in relation to a financial crime or is tied to the accused ...' The registrar looked at her watch, then out past the police to Angie and Oliver and the others sitting behind them, waiting for their turn. The registrar paused and cleared the gravel in her throat. 'And that about wraps it up. If I had a gavel, Sergeant Mulaney, this is when I'd bang it.'

19.

Harold heard from Madeleine that Oliver had been released on bail. Later that night, sitting on his deck, looking across to the ocean, a whisky in hand, he found his thoughts drifting to Theo. The night he died.

It was almost dark as Harold dodged potholes on the gravel road, passing a kangaroo, battered, flattened, bloody. The wind was whipping leaves over the windshield, tousling the trees, a cold snap moving through from the mountains. As he turned off the road into the vineyard, he noticed the Jaguar wasn't there, but he saw the navy kombi van – the same one Theo had turned up in when he'd come to Harold's house the week before.

The job was supposed to be straightforward: break into the Bateau Bay gallery and take the *Wadani* painting. Madeleine would move it and Harold would receive a chunk of the insurance money. The only problem was, Harold hadn't known Madeleine and her guys had sent Theo to commit the theft. If he'd known that was the plan, he would have told them no. Warned them away.

Theo had nabbed the *Wadani*, but he'd also found the other

paintings. Julia's unfinished works. Canvases she'd started for the twins' eighteenth birthday. Theodore Wingfield had taken both and run. Destroyed his phone. No one could find him, but Harold had a pretty good idea of where he'd gone.

A few days after the theft, Harold decided to pay Oliver a visit. He had a feeling that Theo would have gone to the winery to see his brother.

One of the twins answered the door.

'Hello, Theo.'

'How do you know it's not Oliver?' the man said, an open arm to the cottage behind: exposed wooden beams, a fireplace, Julia's paintings hanging from the wall.

'Don't insult me. I've known you both since you were kids.'

'The painting isn't here, if that's what you came for.'

'I don't think you're being honest with me,' Harold said. 'The multiple paintings you stole from me. I need them back.'

Theo stood to the side, allowing Harold to step into the house. 'Would you like a whisky, Mr Keller?' he asked, closing the door to keep out the cold.

'No. Just the paintings, thank you. Then you'll never have to see me again.'

'I'd like that. Afraid I don't have them, but.'

Harold looked around the house. Tidy, a black-and-white film on an old television. 'Where's your brother?'

'With his girlfriend. Met her?'

'I'd have to know that he had a partner before I could meet one.'

Theo took a sip of whisky. 'That's right. You'd actually have to give a fuck about us to know anything, right?'

'Oh, please,' Harold said, moving towards the kitchen. He was scanning the cottage, searching for anywhere Theo might have stashed the canvases. 'Don't act like the money you inherited didn't come from me. Don't act like I haven't done everything for you both, when I could have quite easily pissed off. Who supported you financially for six months while you finished school? While they were recovering from being beaten nearly to death?'

'It would have been nice if you had. Given a fuck.'

Harold remembered walking up to Theo. Grabbing his shirt. Jostling him to the wall.

'Cocky little shit,' he hissed through gnashed teeth. 'Thinking you can do as you please. After what I've been through.'

Theo's face twisted into a humourless grin. 'So, it's okay to steal my mother's art if you're going to profit from it … but not if it's private? Is that what you're saying, old boy?'

Harold punched him. Straight to the jaw. A line of blood spurted across the room. Theo crouched, shielding his face. Harold adjusted his glasses, a sharp pain searing his knuckles, along his fingers. He walked down the hallway into what seemed to be Theo's guest room. Clicking on the light, he began foraging: under the bed, in the wardrobe. He found nothing.

'You can keep whatever other shit you stole from Madeleine, Theodore,' he yelled. 'But you're going to give me the canvases you brazenly took with you.'

'You're wasting your time,' came the reply.

Harold threw a pillow from the bed: pegged it to the wall in frustration. He was puffed. In all of his life, he'd never lost his temper like this. Had never hit anyone before. But Harold knew if he didn't come up with the *Wadani* soon, he was toast. Knew it on an elemental level: like someone staring into the eye of a gun knew they were going to die.

'I don't even know what paintings you're talking about.'

Harold inhaled, a big breath. Held it in then let it out. 'You had your chance, Theo. You made your bed.' He walked past Theo, to the door, and looked back. 'She'd be disgusted.'

'Not sure she'd be proud of you, either. Drive safely,' Theo said, holding a wad of tissues to his face, the whisky in his other hand. 'Would hate for you to collect a roo. Don't want too many insurance claims this month, old boy.'

Harold left without replying. He remembered the sound of his boots on the bare boards, the chilly breeze as he stepped outside, his engine kicking over and the lights illuminating the trees. The anger fermenting inside him.

Harold remembered: a full moon above.

20.

'They'll have already tapped your phone. Maybe your car. If you haven't intimated you committed a crime, they can't arrest you. Likely, from your own words, they're worried that you are innocent and they have no other leads.'

Oliver stood very still. Angie's heels echoed through the wine shed as she inspected the barrels, the notes scrawled on each one, bending down and peering underneath.

'Why did you become a winemaker?' she asked.

Oliver picked up a pipette, sucked wine from one of the barrels, sniffed in the glass and passed it to Angie, who smelled it briefly before handing it back.

'Why not? You get to turn fruit into something special. Something that gets better, different, with age. And it changes in the bottle. You get to put your personality into every glass. You get pissed and you call it work. And you have to be patient,' Oliver said. 'Which I had to practise. It takes years. Sometimes, I won't make a vintage if I'm not happy with the grapes.'

'Why Mudgee?' Angie called. Oliver followed her into the piano room. She was inspecting one of the bottles.

'It was cheap when I moved here a decade ago. And it's a great spot. Underrated. It has a Spanish climate, akin to Rioja. Similar to Sonoma. No one took it as seriously as they should have. There are some great producers here.'

Oliver wanted to ask her if she had loved Theo. How close they'd been. Angie appeared to conceal her emotions – packing them into her bag and not removing them again until absolutely necessary. He wanted to ask if it hurt to have to look at him knowing that he wasn't Theo. It was all too cruel, meeting his brother's lover like this. And just as cruel having Penny so close to meeting Theo but being deprived of the chance. Oliver couldn't stop thinking how close he'd been to reconciling with his brother. He'd long wondered whether that would ever happen in his lifetime.

'How do you know I didn't kill Theo?' he challenged.

Angie smiled and placed the bottle of wine back onto the table. 'Because you two are more alike than any two people I've ever known. Not just physically. And the Theo I loved was naive and got himself into trouble. But I can't see him as a murderer.'

'You're probably the one person who's ever said we're alike. Other than our appearance.'

'For someone who plies their trade with logic, words and reason, I'm not even sure I can explain it to you. Let's call it a feeling.'

'And you're confident we're not killers?'

'I've defended a few murderers in my day. What was refreshing to me about Theo was his sensitivity. He was a true empath. He carried lots of guilt and didn't love talking about his past. Am I striking a nerve?'

'I suppose you do this kind of character analysis for a living.'

Angie paused. 'I feel like I never properly got to say goodbye.'

Oliver inhaled, scratching at the edge of his fingernail. 'You and me both.'

'I know what he was caught up in. We never spoke about it overtly, but we didn't have to either, if you catch my drift.'

'The drugs?'

Angie rocked her head. 'I think the drugs were a cover. The cops always know about that. I think there was more to it. Fake art, jewellery. Something rotten. My intuition says Theo found himself in too deep and wanted to get out.'

'He was like that,' Oliver said. 'Went wherever the wind blew him.'

'Whatever happened on that last trip wasn't good. He said he was going to see you afterwards. But I didn't hear from him again. All calls went straight to voicemail. He left a message at my office, saying he was going to post me a letter, but I never got it.'

'Post you a letter? What?'

Angie smiled. 'He didn't want to attract attention. And that's how our relationship started. In an epistolary manner.'

'You got Theo to send you a letter?'

'Several. We met in the city, and the only way I could track him down was from his home address. So, I sent him a letter and he wrote me back.'

'Did he mention anything about stealing any paintings?'

Angie folded her arms. 'He didn't, but any artwork could be related to his work? One would assume.'

Oliver nodded in agreement. 'So, something's gone wrong?'

'Well, I've never seen Theo drive that kombi before. Randomly showing up out here, allegedly hiding stolen paintings and then winding up dead? I'd definitely say something's gone wrong.'

Oliver went to the barrel and filled two glasses, then passed one to Angie. 'To Theo,' he said. They clinked the glasses together.

'This isn't going to kill me, is it?'

Oliver swirled the wine and took a sniff. 'I can think of worse ways to go.'

Angie took a small, careful sip, swished it around her mouth, before moseying over to the spittoon and directing the liquid inside. *Fair call*, Oliver thought. *I don't think I'd swallow it, either*. Maybe sending Angie to Oliver was Theo's final gift from the grave. While the thought of having to spend time in prison terrified Oliver, the fact that he would be in there for something he hadn't done would leave him seething, bitter, for the rest of his life.

'That's straight cabernet,' Oliver said. 'I'll blend it with some bush-vine barbera before putting it into the bottle. In Italy they call it a "Super Tuscan".'

'The fruit is lovely.' The barrister put her glass down on the table and walked the short distance from the shed into the piano room.

'I wish I'd spent more time speaking with him the first day he was here,' Oliver said. 'Actually asked him more questions.' He paused briefly. 'Why didn't you visit when you went on a road trip to Orange?'

'Theo said that he should see you, but he wasn't ready. I didn't want to push it. I knew that he'd come around eventually. I'm glad you got to see him before ... well, you know.' Angie walked back towards the barrels and stood across from Oliver.

'So, Theo's poisoned first. Your old mentor in California dies the same way. Your other business partner is missing, and your vineyard manager ends up in a tussle and gets shot.'

'Yep. What are you thinking?'

Angie raised her eyebrows. 'That we can almost rule out a coincidence.'

'Yep.'

'Sounds like someone wants to set you up. Lock you up. Piss you off. If they wanted you dead, they would have done it already.'

'I know Harold, our mother's old gallerist, saw Theo here. But he wouldn't kill him.' Oliver thought of the woman from the mugshot who he'd seen in Harold's house. 'He's dodgy. Might be involved in shonky art deals, but he's not a violent man. I don't think he'd kill Theo. I've known him for thirty years.'

'Don't say that. Anyone can kill someone. Just wait until they're desperate enough.'

'And yet you still believe I didn't kill anyone.'

'I have a superhuman ability. This inkling that's always right.'

'I see.'

'Keep me posted. You've scored yourself a new lawyer.'

Angie moved towards the door, warming up to leave. Normally Oliver wanted to be left alone, but the thought of stewing in solitude made him uneasy.

'What do I do now?' he asked, almost as if it was a question for himself, looking past her to the barrels, the hoses, the open door into the piano room.

'I don't know,' Angie said with a flat smile. 'Stay safe. Be careful what you drink. Don't leave the property. Let the police do their digging. They'll find a big dirty bone, eventually. If they try to arrest you again, I'll be here. Please just don't say another word to the police without me present.'

'Yeah,' Oliver said. 'Well. Thanks.'

Angie looked at her abandoned glass, as though she was pondering one more sip-and-spit. 'I know it hasn't been easy for you. Theo told me about your father.'

Oliver flinched. 'What did he say, exactly?'

Angie moved closer to him, placed a hand on Oliver's shoulder. 'About what happened. Why he's locked up.'

'I don't want to talk about that now.'

'I understand,' Angie said. 'Your father's a bad man, but you and Theo aren't like him.'

'Oliver, what's going on?'

A voice from the entrance: Penny.

Oliver flinched, turning towards her. 'I've been trying to call you.'

'I came out as soon as I got your messages. I brought Gabe home from the hospital.' Penny stared at Angie, shifting her eyes to Oliver. 'Why was your father a bad man?'

Angie's brows shot up. 'I best be off,' she told Oliver. 'I need to get back to the city.'

'Oliver,' Penny said, a sternness to her tone. 'What's going on?'

'Let's talk outside,' he said, but before he'd even finished the sentence, Penny had disappeared.

***

'Why are you being like this?' Oliver said. 'I've just gotten out of jail, for fuck's sake.'

The only sound came from the leaves scrunching beneath Oliver's feet as he followed Penny. She stopped at the door of her Corolla and turned to Oliver, her face filled with rage. 'Why *is* your father a bad man, Oliver?'

'Why are you being like this?' he repeated.

Penny opened the car door and went to get in, but suddenly stopped herself. 'Did you hear my question, Oliver? Why IS your father a bad man? Present tense. Why would a man who died of cancer over a decade ago be a bad man?'

Oliver froze. He felt the same kind of paralysis as when the police had come and carted his father away in handcuffs. 'I promised I'd tell you everything and I will. I just can't do it right now, after this. I need more time—'

'Just answer me this,' Penny said. 'Did your father die of cancer a decade ago or not?'

Oliver exhaled, and his reluctance to answer the question betrayed him. He watched Penny's face morph with anger into something ugly. In that moment, he imagined Craig's face when his soon-to-be mother-in-law told him no daughter of hers would ever marry a black man. He imagined Katrina's face when Craig disclosed he'd had too many affairs to count on two hands and was leaving her to raise three children alone. And now Penny, looking at him like this, for lying terribly about his past.

Penny shook her head and sank into the car, slamming the door. The Corolla kicked up dust and gravel as it tore down the driveway towards the road.

21.

The beginning of winter. Usually one of Oliver's favourite times in Mudgee. You could feel it in the air. Something energising, the opposite of the humidity he'd grown accustomed to in his adolescence. He loved the trees being stripped of their leaves by the cold, as was happening now with the Japanese maples dotted around his cottage. Loved the shorter days, the cooler nights. Standing among the vines, Oliver could feel the snow-tinged breeze moving in from the mountains. He listened to a crackle of cockatoos chatter and squawk in the morning light.

His bail conditions stipulated that he couldn't leave the vineyard. That he had to stay within a certain radius. He was warned there would be random police checks to ensure that he was complying with his bail. In truth, he was surprised they didn't have some kind of draconian bracelet strapped around his ankle.

Penny had stopped answering his calls. Maybe she'd just left? She'd discussed it with him before he'd been arrested. Running away to Europe, escaping the present. But Oliver's lies about his family had been the final straw. He had been so close to confessing everything that night in her terrace, but then the police had arrived at the vineyard and Angie had, well … And here he was.

Oliver sat on a chair outside the wine shed, looking up at the mountains. Gabe wandered over, Luna loping in his wake.

'I called the bar. She's gone for a while,' he said.

Oliver inhaled. 'You sure?'

Gabe took off his glasses and wiped them with his shirt. 'Well, she went in and saw them.' A magpie Oliver sometimes fed darted from a branch and began pecking at the grass near their feet. 'She's gone, Oli.'

Oliver stood up, walked over to Luna, leaned down and scratched her sternum. 'I don't know what to do anymore,' he said.

'I know.'

As soon as his hand had left Luna, she began whining for another pat. 'Heard from Murray?'

'He's still in a coma. They're thinking fifty-fifty on recovery at this point.'

'Fuck. I thought the year of a global pandemic might have been the worst one for a while.'

'You'd think so. But this one is definitely worse.'

Oliver heard the sound of car tyres on gravel before he turned around. A small white SUV was making its way up the driveway, past Gabe's cottage, towards them. It wasn't Penny, and it didn't look like a car Everson had arrived in before.

'Looks like you've got company. I'll come back later,' Gabe told him.

'Do you know who it is?' Oliver asked, surveying the car to see who was behind the wheel.

'I have a feeling,' Gabe said, as the vehicle rolled towards them, 'that it's Penny's father.' Gabe waved at the man, whose car was crawling down the driveway towards Oliver's cottage. The engine died suddenly and Craig Williams stepped out. He smiled at Oliver, but it wasn't the same all-encompassing beam that Oliver was used to from Penny's dad.

'Craig.'

'Hey, mate. Just a check-up. Heard you've been having a shit time.'

Oliver pointed towards the house. 'Cuppa?'

'I would,' Craig said, 'but I hear people who drink shit around here get taken away on their backs.'

Despite everything that had happened, Oliver snickered.

'Sorry, mate,' Craig said, walking to Oliver and firmly grabbing his shoulder. 'That was a bit on the nose. English breakfast, with some sugar.'

***

Craig stirred four lumps into his tea. Oliver tried not to flinch at the scrape of the metal spoon on china.

'Have you seen Penny?'

'Yeah, mate,' Craig said, taking the spoon and placing it on the coffee table. He blew into his cup, now only an inch from his lips. 'She's doing okay. Just having some time away from the bar, you know?'

'I thought that.'

'Not sure she ever told you, but I never wanted her to do it.'

'The bar?'

'Yeah.'

Oliver nodded. 'Why not?'

'I'm proud of her, don't get me wrong. It's just a lot of stress.

And pouring piss alongside a lot of stress ain't always a match made in heaven.'

'I think Penny's sensible,' Oliver said.

Craig took a sip of his tea and nodded. 'Not debating that, but she's fragile. You know that. I hope I don't have to say it's best you give her a bit of time at the moment.'

'No, you don't,' Oliver said, trying not to fidget in his chair.

'I like you, mate. You make a good beer and a nice drop. From all reports, you treated Pen right.'

Past tense. Oliver nodded; could see where Craig was taking it.

'The local cops don't like you much, but. Not your biggest fan.'

'I've been getting that vibe.'

'Half of 'em are a bunch of pricks, so I wouldn't worry too much.'

Craig worked in the Central West as a police liaison officer. He was the conduit between the Aboriginal members of the community and the police. Oliver had always maintained that to say it was a tough gig would be a gargantuan understatement.

'I don't even want to try to understand what's going on,' Craig said. 'And we all keep secrets.' He paused again.

The thing about being serious with someone was that you invited them into your emotional life. Penny knew Oliver's pressure points. Where to push, squeeze, when to press and when to ease up. Sending Craig to have a conversation with him was a very clear signal that while things weren't necessarily over, Oliver certainly needed to back off.

Craig reclined, opening his large palms. 'Mate, I don't think it would hurt to just let things run their course. Wait until all this shit has passed before you talk again, you know what I'm saying?'

Oliver did. The truth was he wouldn't be a good partner to Penny if she was here right now. He was drinking, trying to imbibe so much that he'd numb the nightmares, the memories, the rogue thoughts he'd let his imagination conjure. What had Clare told him after Theo had died?

I know how far into your own head you can disappear.

'I understand what you're saying. I appreciate you calling in.'

'Seriously though,' Craig continued, 'don't let those local cops give you a hard time. You have any problems, you call me, all right?'

'I will,' Oliver said, as Craig stood to leave.

'That's it,' Craig said, shaking Oliver's hand with such brute force he'd surely fractured something. 'Good bloke.'

***

'What did he want?' Gabe asked.

'How would you feel about opening some of the museum bottles?' Oliver replied.

Gabe grinned, scanning his watch. 'That bad, huh? Well, to be honest … a couple of wines at two in the afternoon? After the last week, nothing would make me happier.'

A few minutes later, as he was pouring a glass for Gabe, Oliver said, 'He was just checking in, I suppose you'd say.' They sat on the back of the work ute, which was parked to look across the mountains. 'And very subtly and kindly suggested I should leave Penny alone for a while.'

He missed Penny. Regretted fucking things up so badly. Did he really believe that he'd be able to shield her from his father's past forever? He knew that he couldn't, but the thought of having to detail what Miles had done – to actually discuss his mother's murder – was enough of a challenge to delay. Humans, Oliver knew, tended to do what made them comfortable. He should have ripped the bandaid away earlier, but he'd let things fester until it was too late. How many times had he watched a film and wanted to scream at the protagonist for keeping a secret from their partner? He knew that it was inevitable they'd find out, just like it was ineludible that Penny would discover the truth about his father.

Watching Craig's car drive away, he'd wondered whether he'd ever see him again. Which seemed crazy to him right now, because in the weeks before Theo had arrived and everything turned to shit, Oliver had been pondering proposing to Penny. He'd imagined Craig walking her down the aisle. He'd imagined children, a new house built somewhere else on the vineyard. After a few wines, he begun to paint a picture: kids inside, his records playing – something bluesy – Oliver searing beef in the pan and Penny decanting a magnum of red wine. It was something he thought he didn't deserve, something he thought his father had ruined for him, but now that it was looking less likely, he was realising just how much he'd been yearning for a different kind of future.

Halfway through the bottle, Oliver said, 'Mate, if you're in trouble, financially or whatever, you can talk to me about it.'

Gabe gazed down into his wine; lifted it up and scanned the glass, as though if he read the liquid in a certain way it might carry the answer to whatever question he was struggling with.

'It's not really something you rush to talk about with your boss. How bad you've been with money.'

'Business partner,' Oliver corrected him. 'You've got shares.'

Gabe nodded once. 'You know what I mean. Muz and I haven't paid a bloke in one particular syndicate. One of the horses we owned outright died last year. The insurance company is taking their time to pay out. It'll all be fine, there're just a few cashflow issues. Once they pay, we'll be back in the black.'

'Sounds like this bloke's impatient?'

'He's been forgiving enough,' Gabe said, straightening his glasses and frowning. 'We're just scraping the barrel.'

'Murray,' Oliver said. 'Forgive the assumption, but I didn't think he was necessarily short of a quid?'

'All tied up. In the company. What's the saying? Asset rich, cash poor.'

'You can ask me for a loan,' Oliver said, and waited a beat. 'You know that, don't you?'

Gabe sternly shook his head. 'There will be no muddying of the professional waters, Mr Wingfield. They've sent their message. If you don't mind, I'd rather we leave it alone.'

Oliver topped up their glasses. 'There's a lot we need to leave alone. The community for a little while, for one.' He looked out at the vines, the trees in the distance. The glass was blurry, everything turning itself abstract. How tipsy was he?

After a moment, Gabe said, 'There's something I don't think I've ever asked you.'

'What's that?'

'The name. Four Dogs Missing. Was the sign really there, or did you put it up?'

Oliver smiled as he took a sip of wine. 'I didn't see this question coming, if I'm being honest.'

'Sorry,' Gabe said, 'I've just always wondered.'

'It was there. First thing I noticed. The agent who sold me the property told me that the guy who owned the vineyard was a nutter. His father had been a decent winemaker, but the son had given it up. Just drank all day. Sold some of the fruit, but most of the vines had gone to shit.'

Gabe raised his eyebrows before taking a sip of his wine. 'I remember that part. So, a nutter with a lot of dogs.'

'Four missing. I wonder if that was all of them, or whether he had more? The cottage didn't smell like dogs.'

'Still, I'm glad you changed the floors and painted everything. I don't think you would have wanted to live in the same space he had.'

'I don't think he was that bad,' Oliver said. 'Just a loner who loved his dogs. The agent told me he'd walk up and down the road looking for them. Wouldn't ever ask anyone for help. Never drove anywhere. He wanted to do everything alone.'

'Jesus,' Gabe said, 'sounds like it runs in the place.'

'I'm getting better, aren't I?' Oliver asked, finishing his final mouthful.

'You don't actually want me to answer that, do you?'

***

Three bottles later, Gabe lurched back to his cottage. Oliver flicked on a few lights around the house and checked his reflection in the mirror: yellow teeth stained deep purple at the edges. Pillars to a dock eroding, ready to sink. He walked around the house, unable to settle himself. Thought about dinner; just gazed into the fridge but couldn't think of a single thing he felt like eating. The wine with Gabe was supposed to calm the nerves, but instead he was shaky.

The piano? No, he wouldn't be able to focus. Ida would be annoyed with his lack of progress. Even with a decent excuse. And that's why he liked her so much.

Heading outside, he slipped on a pair of sandals and trudged through the vines. He should have donned a jacket. There was a bitter breeze moving in from the mountains. He patted his pocket but he'd left his phone back at the house, or maybe in the wine shed. Not that it really mattered anymore. Who was there left to call?

He tried not to think about Clare. Her body on the floor. He wouldn't be able to cope with that yet; it would be entering an inescapable labyrinth.

Deviating from his usual route, he approached Murray's vineyard and then stopped. His neighbour was arrogant and loudmouthed and involved in bad gambling circles, but he wasn't a killer. It was obvious to Oliver that Murray hadn't orchestrated the murders, but that didn't mean he wasn't complicit somehow.

Suddenly brimming with Dutch courage, he climbed across the wire fence. Holding it down and stepping over, he realised he was properly drunk. He'd barely eaten anything. As soon as he had the thought, his stomach growled in acknowledgement.

Oliver straightened up and walked towards the house. What was he looking for? Curiosity beckoned. An amber security light kicked on and a kennel of dogs began barking and howling and snarling. The sound of chains stretching.

No, he wouldn't be able to get into the house. He meandered past the cellar-door entry, across the cobblestone path. There were trees with drooping branches and old bird baths. Even though the wine was shit, it was a decent view, he'd admit that.

Oliver moved towards the shed and tried to open the door, but it was locked. Ditto around the side. Closing his eyes, he listened to the constant natter of crickets and buzz of bugs, the sounds of life that came from the trees.

There was a larger shed at the rear of the winery, towards the vines; well away from the house and the cellar door and everything else on the property. Easy to access from the back roads. It had once been a storage shed, housing equipment, Oliver assumed. The roller door wasn't locked. Without a torch, Oliver had to wait for his eyes to adjust.

A wheelbarrow filled with junk. Jerrycans. An old ride-on lawn mower parked to the side. A rat, or at least a large mouse, scuttled past Oliver's foot. He searched the walls for a light switch, but it became clear that the shed wasn't powered.

There was a car parked at the back. A couple of paint-stained sheets covering the shape of a sedan. Leaning against the car was a large shotgun with a polished wooden grip. Oliver picked it up.

'Is there anyone here?' His voice echoed through the room.

Oliver walked over and pulled the sheet away. Though his eyes were still adjusting, he felt a pang of panic grip him. Even in the dark, he knew it was a red sedan. Old and faded. The same car he'd seen speeding away from Clare's vineyard.

Driven by the man who'd shot her dead.

***

It made sense, didn't it?

Clare knew Murray, so she would have let him into her house. They would have chatted. Shared a wine. When Oliver knocked on the door, Murray had panicked and shot her dead. He'd probably planned on shooting Oliver as well, but he'd got away. Or perhaps he'd wanted Oliver to live?

Oliver moved back towards his vineyard. Squeezing the gun tightly between his arm and side, he pushed down the top of the fence and stepped over.

Shit. If Murray was involved, Gabe had to be as well? No, surely not. Couldn't be. In some ways it was logical that the plot against him was Gabe's idea – but Oliver had known him for too many years; Gabe was one of the only people in the world he still trusted.

What would drive Gabe and Murray to murder? Well, money, for one thing. Something they clearly needed. But why would they kill everyone when they could have just asked Oliver for a loan? That motive looked murky at best. Maybe they'd moved money out of Oliver's business accounts. Gabe had direct access to the funds and Oliver seldom checked them properly.

If they'd killed Orson and Clare, it was obviously so that Oliver would be a sole shareholder in the vineyard technology company. And if they'd killed Theo and tried to poison Chase, it was so that Oliver didn't have any family left.

But why had they let him live? To torture him by killing everyone he loved? *No*, he thought. To plan what had to happen next. It was all about money. Gabe's sister had said it best: people did crazy things when desperation had them by the throat. They'd killed Orson and Clare so that they wouldn't inherit Oliver's business interest, and they'd killed Theo so that he wouldn't take the winery.

Were they after his vineyard? If Oliver died without any family to contest the will, Gabe would inherit everything. The technology company, probably valued at half a million dollars. The vineyard, which included the winery and acreage, was worth well into the millions.

Jesus.

How hadn't he seen this earlier? He was too preoccupied with the dead end that was Harold Keller. All of the travel he'd done for nothing.

Oliver started a slow jog, wishing he'd brought his phone, even given the shitty service. He needed to call Everson, call Penny.

Where *was* Penny? He couldn't believe she would abandon him now; he understood she was mad at him ... but with everything else going on? None of it made any sense.

Should he confront Gabe? Use the shotgun to elicit a confession from him? No, that was a terrible idea. He couldn't do it. He would get back to the cottage, go straight to the landline and call Everson. He was probably breaching his parole, admitting that he had been on Murray's property, but that wouldn't matter.

No. He needed to know why Gabe would do it. Why wouldn't he just ask for the money ... Just how deep in shit was he?

Oliver saw the house in the distance, the living-room lights a beacon. He started to run faster. He was puffed already, but he didn't have far to go now.

Looking at the house, and still drunk, mind a mess, he'd forgotten where he was. His right foot slipped and twisted, and his left didn't catch ground. With a thud, he fell headfirst into the bottom of the hole he'd dug for his barrel.

22.

A sharp heave and there he was: nestled in the damp earth, rain sporadic and finding him in spatters. It was dark and cold and still night-time. Oliver had fallen and passed out. Had been dreaming too, but thankfully the images waned as he woke up. He could feel the nightmare still in his body, along with the understanding that his reality had become one.

His ankle. A new lump, protuberant, an egg, large and throbbing. At the very least, it was a welcome distraction from the cold. He opened his eyes fully and looked up to the sky. There was a strange smell in the air. There were no stars. Just a grey blackness and the grumble of thunder. If he could stand, he might be able to climb and reach up enough to be able to jump ...

No, he realised. He'd dug too far. Theo had even commented on the size of the hole, and Oliver had explained you needed it to be deep enough so that once the barrel was buried, you'd be able to maintain a consistent temperature.

He reached for his pockets, knowing the action was redundant. They were empty and his phone was sitting on the kitchen bench, probably out of battery. Once he climbed out, he'd crawl back to the cottage. He was only fifty metres from his front door. When he got to the landline, he'd call the police. Get them out to the property and explain what had transpired. He didn't trust them – wasn't sure he trusted anyone – but there had to be someone he could tell. He'd call Angie and detail everything.

Unexpectedly, he started to cry, but he slapped himself back to reality. His throat was parched and he needed to piss. Rolling over, and with a groan, he felt something solid under him. Murray's shotgun. He tried to pull himself up, but he could barely move.

His father. Miles Jones.

Why did he always come back to him? It was annoying that he was thinking of Miles now. He could blame him for the past, but he couldn't blame him for this. His mind in overdrive, he looked up and saw him standing on the earth above his grave. Miles peered down, kicking gravel and rocks and dust onto his son. He was older, but he hadn't changed much physically. Oliver closed his eyes and groaned. When he flicked his gaze back up towards Miles, his father was gone.

He rolled over again, ready to lift himself to the ground. His fingers made contact with something in the mud below. It was hard and cold. He pulled it out and towards him. Although he couldn't see perfectly, as soon as his fingers grazed the object he knew it was a human hand.

Shit.

Oliver dropped it straight away. Someone was buried at the bottom of the trench. Fuck, not Penny? The body wasn't there when the police had scaled the place days earlier. He picked up the hand again and examined it as closely as he could bear. The first finger was long, white, the nail painted with crimson polish. Oliver breathed in and tried not to cry.

He checked the shotgun's barrel for bullets. It was loaded, three shells inside. Snapping the chamber closed, he stared into the cold night. Cocked the weapon. He'd keep two bullets for later; he'd need some leverage for getting Gabe to come clean. If Gabe didn't want to call the police about the body, he'd know that he was setting him up. That he wanted to find a way to dispose of Oliver so he could inherit the vineyard. Frame him for Clare's murder.

Oliver waited a moment, and when a few large drops of cold rain slapped his cheek, he held the gun as far away from his face as he could. His temple throbbed and his heart beat like the metronome. Taking a deep breath, ignoring his scratchy throat, he screamed, 'Gabe!'

And then he pulled the trigger.

***

Luna arrived first, running excitedly in circles. She whined, regarding Oliver, too scared to approach the edge. He held the gun into the air, and soon after he heard the crunch of footsteps.

'Jesus, Oli. What the hell happened?'

Gabe was flashing a torch into the hole. The light irradiated the dark-brown earth; wet, slimy worms wriggling around the rocks. Oliver's clothes were covered in dust and dirt and mud.

'Whoa,' Gabe said, standing back. 'What are you doing with a shotgun?'

'I was hoping you'd tell me,' Oliver said, his voice raspy.

'Tell you about what?'

'The gun.'

Gabe kept the torch in his eyes. 'What are you talking about?'

'It's yours, isn't it? Or Murray's. That's where I found it.'

Gabe pulled the torch away, leaving it at his side. 'Murray's gun was taken by the police.'

'I found this in his old garage.'

Gabe was silent for a moment, then his demeanour shifted. 'What were you doing in Murray's garage?'

'It's not right, Gabe. I need ...'

Before Oliver could finish, he heard Gabe's footsteps move towards the wine shed. He arrived back a few minutes later and slid a ladder towards Oliver. With the gun still in one hand, Oliver winced in pain and began to pull himself up.

***

'You need to shower,' Gabe said. 'I'm worried you'll catch pneumonia, stuck down there as you were in the rain.'

Oliver burned his mouth gulping tea. It felt good to be swathed in a blanket. The sun was beginning to rise while a fog rolled across the vineyard.

'I need to know why,' he said.

Gabe was growing impatient. Oliver was still holding the gun, ready to point it at Gabe if he came too close. 'What the fuck are you saying?' Gabe took off his glasses and tossed them onto the bench.

'Whoever killed Clare left in the car that's now parked in Murray's garage. How do you explain that?'

Gabe stood, cup of tea in his hands, looking out at the sunrise. 'I don't know. The family have all rushed to Sydney to be with Murray. It's probably an old paddock basher, Oliver. I doubt it's the same car.'

'I just don't think Murray could do it without you knowing. You're not telling me everything.'

Gabe put his tea down on the bench and said seriously, 'Murray was with me for dinner the night Clare died, Oliver. Then he went into town for a winemakers' meeting. With witnesses. He wasn't in Orange. Murray's an idiot, but he's not a murderer.'

It might have been true, but that didn't mean that Murray and Gabe hadn't organised someone else to kill Clare. Perhaps the same people who had come back and bashed them. Oliver wondered if gambling debts were even the cause. How far into the chasm were they?

He looked at Gabe. Had his best mate and Murray orchestrated everything so it was just him left standing? Oliver had no family, and then when they'd killed him, Gabe would be the logical next step in his will. The only person left in his life.

'There's a dead body at the bottom of the trench, Gabe. It's Clare.'

Gabe immediately turned his head to Oliver. 'Jesus.'

'We need to call the police. Right now. It wasn't me, there's none of my DNA on the body. Well, I touched the hand. Just to make sure it wasn't Penny.'

'We can't call it in,' Gabe said, strangely calm, sipping his tea. 'If we call Everson and tell her there's a body at the bottom of the hole, you're being dragged in for murder. And you'll never get out of jail again.'

'But I didn't do it!'

They were both yelling now.

'Oliver, someone's setting you up! These thugs associated with Theo. Someone wants to take you down and they're doing a bloody good job of it. If we call it in, they'll win and you'll be locked up!'

But they'd have to get away with it first. Get away with all of the murders, for that matter. They'd already done a good job of convincing Everson that Oliver was the one who'd poisoned Theo and Orson. They'd planted the gun that made it appear like he'd shot Clare. It was a clever plan: have the police think he killed his friends and family because he was unhinged, mentally ill, and then he'd feel guilty; there would be a wave of remorse to wash through him and then he'd commit suicide. Leave a note next to his dead flesh. Would they shoot him or poison him like they had the others? Oliver remembered his phone call with Vicky, the icy tone of her voice: *You know that desperation does funny things to people.*

Oliver twitched. Stood up.

'Where are you going?' Gabe said, taking another sip of his tea.

Oliver looked at his cup on the table and wondered whether it was spiked. 'I'm sorry, mate,' he said, and with all of his energy, battered Gabe over the back of the head with the barrel of the shotgun.

***

Oliver needed a cigarette. He felt ill. His heart was flouncing about in his chest, and he had to lean against the wall to steady himself. Hobbling down the hall, he used the gun for support, as a walking stick. When he got to the study, he reached for the cigarettes – they were probably nearly stale. Taking one from the pack, he looked out the window at the sunrise. A small shaft of light was reflected onto his desk, and a stack of books caught his eye. The books Theo had put there the day he'd arrived.

'*By the way, I put a few things out on the desk in the office.*'

Among them was a Donna Tartt novel, and a desk diary with loose papers stuffed between its pages and the cover. They were letters, Oliver realised. He slipped them out of the diary and started to read.

Angie,

This latest instalment is being penned from a café in Mudgee. I'm guessing from the friendly service that this is a place Oliver frequents. Although, I've been told in town he's a bit of an oddball. The term 'recluse' was used twice. The tobacconist has never heard of him (or his wines), but the barista said he doesn't come into town often. She said he is more than likely 'agro-phobic'.

I'm sorry I haven't returned your text messages. I couldn't get onto you; I probably tried calling when you were in court. Anyway, I left a message to let you know I'd be writing to you, in the same format you first used to woo me.

Another confession: I haven't been entirely honest. You're perhaps the smartest and most perceptive person I've ever met, so I'm sure it will come as no surprise, but I'm not only a bartender and courier. I realised over the last few weeks that stealing art, wine – moving drugs – isn't what I was put on this earth to do. Don't get me wrong, crime certainly pays. We both understand that, I'm sure. But I'm on the wrong side of the fence, and it's time to change. Perhaps meeting you has helped me to understand. Helped me to realise that I need to be better; that running away doesn't always solve everything. Oliver and I have missed over a decade of our lives; the highs, the lows and everything in between. I need to run back to him for a while.

We'd spoken about starting again: me getting out, you taking time off. Doing some proper travel. Getting a kombi and going up and down the coast and drinking and swimming in the ocean and making love in the caves. The dream. Shit we've always wanted to do but have been too distracted by work or life or whatever we tell ourselves to help us sleep.

Wish me luck. I've got the kombi and I'm about to drive to the vineyard to see Oliver. A note arrived at the bar from our half-brother last week, saying he was going to Mudgee, and it feels like the right time to reunite. It will be the first time I've seen Oliver in fifteen years. Four Dogs Missing, he's called the winery. Two Brothers Estranged would be just as catchy. Thank you for helping me to decide it was something I needed to do. As always, you're right. I probably should have done it with you so you could give me emotional support. But anyway. Once I've settled in at the vineyard, I'll call you again and we'll work out a time to catch up.

PS – I'm at Oliver's alone. He's off with his girlfriend, who I'm keen to meet. I was ready to send this but then I got a call back from Chase, who didn't end up coming. Apparently our father was released from prison a month ago. Quite a few years earlier than the law said he should be. Not too sure how I feel about that. At least being here with Oliver now is definitely right. I'll let him know, and then Chase said he'll touch base when he gets back from Croatia next month.

Lots to discuss.

Looking forward to seeing you again soon.

Peace,

Theo

23.

Oliver was halfway down the hall, digging at his temples, begging that Gabe was okay, when he fell over. *Shit.* He'd left the gun in the office. He hobbled back and snatched it from the desk.

Everything was shimmering and spinning: Miles was out of jail. Why hadn't Theo said anything when he'd found out? He should have called Oliver immediately. If Oliver had known that, he wouldn't have wasted time.

He was livid with Theo, but it wasn't his fault. Oliver had to move swiftly now. He stood at the door and looked into the hallway. The house was quiet. No sign of Luna – Gabe must have taken her home before he'd come to make tea. A cockatoo shrieked in the distance. In his head, he formulated a plan.

He would make sure Gabe was okay. Tend to the gash on his head, ensure he was conscious. Then he'd go straight to the landline. Call triple zero and tell them that Gabe had fallen. Ambulance and police, immediately. That would get Everson's attention. Did he have Angie's number? She'd given him her card;

it had to be somewhere. He needed to get to Gabe. Get as many people as possible to the vineyard before Miles appeared.

There were no sounds of movement, which meant Gabe was still unconscious.

Jesus. What had he done?

24.

Consumed with fury, it was inevitable that Harold fell into the memory as soon as he lay down.

He shouldn't have left Four Dogs Missing empty-handed that day, that was for sure. Shouldn't have let Theo speak to him as he did. Looking out the car window, he noticed the rust-grey moon was still scintillating in the sky. Harold's hand throbbed as he drove away from Oliver's winery and into town. He hadn't lied to Oliver, the police – he *had* gone to Orange after his fight with Theo. Eventually. But he'd stopped the car first and veered to the side of the road. There was no music playing, only the sound of the blinker, incessantly ticking.

No, Harold thought. *If you won't give the paintings to me, I'll make you find them.*

He turned the car around and began driving down the gravel road once more. He passed the battered kangaroo again, live ones prancing between the olive trees in the distance. *Was this what getting old meant?* When he was younger, he would have kept driving, run away, started somewhere else, gone to the police. He would have entertained a melange of scenarios. But he wasn't sure he had the energy to do anything more than this.

Theo was mopping the floor when Harold stormed into the cottage. A bucket, scent of bleach, beside the mouth of the hallway; the boards wet as he moved towards the spare bedroom. He heard a wheeze. Theo was clearing his chest, inhaling a deep breath.

'Are you all right?'

'Never better,' Theo said, but his face had turned pink. Was he choking on the whisky?

'If you don't give me the painting, we're both dead. You know that, don't you?' Harold tried to reason with him.

'I'll take my chances.'

Harold remembered he'd bunched his fingers into a fist; sliced his palm with his own nails.

'You knew Miles did it,' Theo accused. 'You knew him better than we did. What he was capable of. You were older and wiser and you were an ambivalent motherfucker. You let it happen. You lived and she died.'

'What?'

'Maybe she'd be here if you'd been a better man.'

'Fuck you, Theo. You know that I was millimetres away from dying as well?'

'Probably.'

'Definitely. And you treat me like the villain?' Harold said, anger burning, brewing in his stomach, pushing itself into his throat. Heat in his mouth.

Theo coughed again, then took a slurp of the scotch. 'And yet you're alive and still profiting from her. Fucking prick.'

Feeling his temper taking over, Harold grabbed Theo's throat. The younger man's eyes were bloodshot. Out of nowhere, Theo swung the whisky bottle, clobbered Harold over the head. It shattered across the floorboards as they both fell to the floor.

Theo grabbed Harold into a headlock, and they twisted together on the ground. Broken glass pinched Harold's skin. He felt the pressure around his neck, like he was going to suffocate, throw up. Gasping, he reached out, fingering a large piece of glass. He didn't remember how, but he swung his arm, trying to hurl Theo off him, and instead he raised his arm and cut Theo's throat open.

Theo coughed and gurgled, blood the colour of dried currants disemboguing from his neck, dripping across his chest.

Harold inhaled sharply and stood up, looking at Theo on the ground. He didn't have children. Had never settled down long enough to want them. Life had been too busy to entertain the notion. But out of all the young ones in his life, Theo had been his favourite. Slightly rebellious, intuitive, witty. Naive enough to experience life without fretting about failing. There was so much of Julia in him. He wished that he'd tried to keep in touch with Theo when he went overseas. That he'd done more for the boys after their mother's death.

Now, Harold stood over Theo's body and watched the blood ooze from his neck, over his chest, and trickle onto the ground. He sighed.

Harold touched his head. Surprisingly, there was no mark there. But his hands, he noticed, were covered in scratches. He plucked a small phone from Theo's pocket. It looked like a burner; a cheap pre-paid model that no one would know about. Harold slipped it into his jacket and frowned at all of the blood. He needed to clean up. Leave the cottage. Wipe away anything. The next few hours would be hell, but he needed to go.

***

While Oliver was languishing in the hole, Harold had woken on the couch, red wine rising from his gut; phone hot, vibrating on his cheek. It was still dark. He burped, whacked his chest, then pulled the phone up and answered.

'Yeah?' he croaked.

'The favour you called in,' Madeleine said. 'Miles Jones was released a month ago. He ticked the boxes and he's a free man.'

'Shit.' Harold sat up. 'He's not meant to be released for another few years at least. What time is it?'

'Twenty past five.'

'Shit,' he said again, rubbing his eyes. Getting up, he headed towards his bedroom.

'Anything else?' Madeleine asked.

'I'll call you back.'

Grabbing his old address book, he found the landline number he'd coaxed out of Oliver for the vineyard. It rang continuously, without going to any kind of message bank. He hung up and tried again.

'Come on. Pick up.'

The line kept ringing. Harold gave up and dialled Madeleine.

'Yeah?'

'I'm going to talk to him. He needs to know. I'll get the painting, I'm getting close.'

'Too slow, Harold. I've got men heading over today. You just need to focus your loyalty and pray that they find it.'

'I told you I'd get it back.'

'You know, Harold,' Madeleine said, a splice of smugness in her tone, 'there are people who say they *will*, and there are people who actually *do*. Do you understand the latter?'

'This isn't on me! If you hadn't sent Theo in the first place, none of this would have happened. If you'd told me it was him, I would have avoided this!'

'I'm not sure if you're a religious man, Mr Keller, but if I was you, I'd be on those arthritic knees praying my little fucking heart out that they find that painting.'

***

'Hello?' came the voice.

'Oliver?'

'Who's this?'

'Harold. I'm almost in Mudgee. I've been trying to call you all morning,' he said, pushing the sedan as fast as it would take him. He kept the phone to his ear as he drove. 'Listen, I'm coming to see you. I'm worried. I think your father has something to do with everything. He was released quietly a month ago and no one has seen him since he finished his parole. I know why you thought it was all me. He's making us turn on each other.'

Oliver said nothing. Harold moved the phone from his ear but saw the call had dropped out. He tried calling back straight away, but before the line connected, a computerised voice gave him a message he'd heard a hundred times before: *Your call could not be connected. Please check the number and try again.*

Fuck.

He drove. Harold knew that he should call the police. That he should have confessed to killing Theo. An accident, an act of self-defence. That's what it was, wasn't it? A misunderstanding. Greed that had turned into a calamity. He needed them to know how dangerous everything was.

But he could only think of Julia. How much he missed her; how he'd helped her succeed so well in life, but how he had failed her so miserably in death.

Harold started to sob but soon pulled himself together and pushed on the accelerator, hardening his grip on the wheel. He needed to get to Oliver before anyone else did.

25.

Miles was standing a few metres away: pistol in one hand, wine bottle in the other. He'd cut the phone line, obviously. Oliver heard Harold's voice before it dropped into a mid-word abyss. A minute later, his father was standing in his cottage.

'Hey, mate,' Miles said, still the same inflections in his voice, as though he'd only been with him in Terrigal a short time ago.

Gabe started to sputter on the ground. Grabbing the kitchen bench, he attempted to stand up. Immediately, Oliver extended his hand, helping to pull him to his feet.

'Who are you?' Gabe said, now fully upright.

'Who am I?' Miles mocked, a slight grin at the edges of his lips.

'I thought I dreamed you were standing above me this morning,' Oliver said. 'But you really were there.'

'Someone found my hiding place,' Miles said, reaffirming his grip on the gun. 'Changed my plans.'

'What's going on?' Gabe asked.

'Shut the fuck up.' The tone was icy.

The three men stood in silence. Nobody moved.

'Stand very still for me,' Miles said.

Oliver was strangely calm. His father hadn't changed much in nearly two decades. Slightly skinnier, grey hair now white. Same thick moustache. Oliver and Theo had inherited his nose. Luckily, the rest of their features were more like Julia's.

'The paintings aren't here,' Gabe said. 'You're wasting your time.'

'The fuck?' Miles said. 'I'm not here for artwork.'

'Let Gabe leave,' Oliver said. 'He won't involve the police. We'll work this out between us.'

Miles snorted; ugly, uneven bursts of laughter.

'What's that, mate, you're ashamed of your old man?' he said, stepping closer. 'Now, Gabe, make yourself useful and grab two of those nice crystal wineglasses from up there.' He pointed the gun at the cupboards. 'Place them down on the bench right there in front of you. If you try anything stupid I'll shoot your thick head that many times no one will be able to identify your body.'

***

Miles shuffled towards the kitchen bench. He unscrewed the lid from the bottle and poured a glass. Oliver could tell, just from looking at the liquid, that it was his own southern block cabernet. The wine had a particular purple hue he'd observed hundreds of times before.

'I really don't understand how this shit sells for so much money. In saying that, I remember hearing inside that these days people pay an exorbitant amount of money to drink coffee that's been shat out of a monkey.'

Miles walked to the small wine rack Oliver had beside the

kitchen bench and pulled another bottle of the cabernet and cracked it in front of them. He held the neck of the bottle above the other glass for a moment, before tipping his wrist and letting the wine pour. Oliver's red wine from the old vines outside. Nothing more than fermented grape juice. A few drops splashed and slid down the outside of the glass, pooling on the table.

Miles grasped the base of the glasses and sent them screeching across the bench: one towards Gabe, the other to Oliver.

'The world's gone fucking mad,' Miles said.

'You're fucking mad,' Gabe retorted, but Miles only moved his eyes; offered a look of contempt.

'Both of you. Close your eyes. And no peeking.'

They did as they were told. Oliver couldn't sense a whole lot of movement; he only heard the base of the glasses shifting on the marble bench before them.

'I've been wanting to play a little Russian roulette with you both for a while now.' Miles moved back towards the dining table, pulled out one of the chairs and sat down. 'My initial plan was to kill you in front of Oliver. And then make it look like Oliver killed himself. You know, feeling bad for killing his brother and his business partners.'

'Why are you doing this?' asked Oliver.

'When you're in jail for nearly twenty years, you have a lot of time to think. What's the old saying? You either get better or you get bitter? I suppose when you're already bitter, you're only going to get worse.'

'So, it's been you? All of it?'

'Well,' Miles said. 'I was released a month ago. Early. Good behaviour. Finished parole. Only problem is, you don't leave jail with much money. Although, it's pretty easy to find an old pub in the bush and walk behind the counter, take some money from the pokies till and not look back.'

He straightened up and kneaded his nose with his palm. 'Then I bolted to Mudgee. Found the abandoned shed. Watched the winery and everything that was going on. Didn't hear a peep from anyone in that shed next door. I brewed some poison and stole some wine. You really should lock your cellar more carefully, you know. No one in Mudgee locks anything. Anyone can just walk in there in the middle of the night and grab whatever they need ...'

'You drove the Jaguar back here to Theo the night he died?' Oliver already knew the answer, but he wanted to hear it from his father.

Miles smiled. 'That was another improvisation. Theo had enough poison to very slowly kill him. He should have still been alive when you returned in the morning, but there was a commotion. Cars leaving the vineyard. So, I came across and found him dead. I didn't want to waste the opportunity to pin it on you, just like you didn't waste any time throwing me to the dogs all those years ago—'

'You killed Julia,' Oliver said. 'We just—'

'I didn't fucking kill her!' Miles yelled. He smiled, composed himself, then shook his head. 'I beat the shit out of Harold because I was angry. When I came home, she was already dead. She must have fallen. You know how weak she was, when ... well.'

'Why didn't you just leave her there?'

'For you or Theo to find? I moved her because ... it wasn't fucking right that she died like that. I panicked. Took her to the ocean. Harold saw her last, and I wanted answers. I wasn't thinking straight.'

'So, Theo cut his own throat as well? All very convenient.'

Miles grunted. 'Believe what you want to believe, Oliver. Why the fuck would I lie to you now, with a gun in my hand?'

Oliver blenched. The pain was so bad that Theo had cut his own throat?

'The body in the ditch,' Gabe said, as if following Oliver's train of thought.

'Your business partner. Probably should have been your half-brother, but he's holidaying in Croatia, by all reports.' Miles frowned, looking Oliver in the eyes. 'You all abandoned me, and I did nothing wrong.'

'And the man I saw on camera, that clearly wasn't you. The one sneaking around my wine shed? Someone working with you?' Oliver asked.

Miles seemed confused. 'Not sure who else you've got snooping around out there, but I'm too old and broken to trust anyone else with my work. No one knows where I am, as far as I know. Haven't yet connected the dots: a killer on the loose, one they made a free man on the assumption that he was rehabilitated.'

They stood in silence. Oliver heard it first: the sound of tyres on gravel. A car coming up the driveway. Was it Everson, arriving to check Oliver was adhering to his parole? He hoped it was. Or was it Penny, coming to apologise for leaving yesterday? Or to berate him for being a lying bastard all this time?

Oliver looked at Gabe. Having worked with him for so many years, he could read his mind.

Please don't let it be Penny.

***

'Follow me. Try anything stupid and I'll put a bullet through your temple.'

Oliver and Gabe did as Miles instructed. They moved slowly towards the front door in the living room. A moment later, as if on cue, there was a thunderous knock. The sound of the handle jerking. It wasn't Penny, for she had a key. Unless she'd driven over on the spur of the moment and had left it behind. Miles, keeping the gun pointed at Oliver, moved to the door and twisted the lock. Whoever was there waited a moment before turning the handle.

The door opened and two men stood there. Oliver recognised one immediately: long curly hair, the tattoo creeping onto his neck. The mugshots from his first meeting with Everson. He was obviously in charge of the attempted break-in, reaching out his arm to stop his bald-headed companion from moving further into the room.

'Who the fuck are you?' Miles said, pointing the gun at the art thieves, who continued to stand, stupefied, like they'd walked into a room and witnessed something they shouldn't have. Oliver checked the kitchen, wondering whether he'd be able to limp over and get the shotgun. And do what? He'd have to kill his father. He could talk the two men down; let them know he had the artwork.

'We've got your woman, mate,' the bald man said to Oliver. 'She's with the boss and we're not letting her go until we get the *Wadani.*' Then, instinctively, he moved his hand towards his jeans.

But Miles was too fast. With one click of his finger, a bullet left the pistol's chamber and entered the man's forehead – he jerked and fell into the other intruder's arms. Using the dead man as a shield, the tattooed thief shuffled backwards, towards the van they'd arrived in, but Miles walked a few steps closer and fired the gun again. Only one more shot. Oliver closed his eyes and heard the sound of two bodies collapsing onto the ground outside his front door.

***

Keeping the gun by his side, Miles turned to Oliver.

'Who are they?' he demanded.

Inhaling deeply, Oliver tried to steady his breathing. He felt a prickle of heat slide across his skin. 'I don't know who they are. Art thieves, drug dealers. They worked with Theo.'

Miles laughed. 'No one's going to be making a big song and dance about two thugs, eh?'

Penny. *They had Penny.*

But why wouldn't she tell them where the paintings were? What was the *Wadani*? She knew Oliver didn't hold too much sentimental value for the unfinished paintings; he already had his mother's art on the wall, and if it was going to put lives in peril, it wasn't worth it. Perhaps it was a bluff? After all, Penny wasn't at home earlier. Unless she'd arrived home to pack and they'd pounced? Tied her up and waited for the call to say that Oliver had paid the henchmen with the paintings before they'd consider releasing her? He remembered Everson's face when she had first showed him the black-and-white photographs of these people. Could still remember the clicking of the woman's high heels in Harold's house, the coldness of the gun's barrel against his skin.

Miles muttered something to himself and walked towards them. Oliver needed to find a way to slip into the kitchen and grab the shotgun; his father hadn't noticed it there.

'Right. You're going to help me lift these two bastards,' Miles said, pointing the gun at Gabe. 'We'll put them into their van. I'll take it somewhere later and burn it.'

Gabe didn't say anything. Only put his chin down towards his chest and followed Miles to the door. Oliver gazed at the kitchen, but his father's voice interrupted his thoughts. 'Oliver, walk with us. Or hobble. Whatever it is you have to do.'

While Miles and Gabe moved the bodies, Oliver kept hoping for the moment when he'd be able to return to the kitchen. He felt a steely bravery move through him. If he got the gun, he would have no hesitation when he pointed it at Miles's head.

As Miles slid the van door closed, he said, 'Oliver, there's someone coming up the driveway.'

He pushed the butt of the gun into Gabe's spine, and they all moved inside. There was a small splash of blood still on the footpath outside, but Miles didn't see it.

Don't be Madeleine holding Penny hostage, Oliver silently prayed.

Miles shot him a look. 'You're going to tell whoever this is to leave, quick smart. Or they'll be joining your friends in the van.'

26.

Harold fidgeted in the seat as he steered the BMW up the driveway. The gate was already open. Passing Gabe's cottage, he kept driving, until he reached the end of the gravel road. There was another van beside Theo's kombi. The reconnaissance mission that Madeleine had ordered to retrieve the *Wadani*.

Harold killed the ignition and took a breath. He thought of turning the key, starting the car and driving away. It was ludicrous that he'd turned up here again.

He stepped out of the car and quietly closed the door. The air was so much crisper in the country. The sound of cars was far in the distance as a flutter of sparrows skipped between the small gums. He admired how peaceful everything was. Maybe he should have chosen a life like this for himself?

Putting his phone in his pocket, he straightened his jacket and walked up the path to the door.

And knocked.

***

Oliver opened the door. A smidgeon. Enough for Harold to tell that it was him, but barely any more.

'The phone dropped out,' Harold began. 'I tried calling back, but I couldn't get through.'

Oliver didn't say anything. Just stood with the door ajar, refusing to make eye contact.

'Oli, I think that it's time we had a chat about—'

'What are you doing here?' Oliver cut him off. He opened the door and stepped outside and pushed Harold along the verandah. He was dressed in shorts and a T-shirt. There was dirt besmirched across his clothes, smeared over his jaw.

'Why are you so dirty?'

'I'm a winemaker. Getting dirty is what I do. Not as squeaky clean as famous gallerists.'

Harold didn't take the bait. 'Can I come in? There are things I need to tell you. Important things.' He glanced at the van, then at Oliver. He knew something was wrong with Oliver; he was grimy, rattled, almost panicked. He wondered whether Madeleine's men were searching the cottage, armed, and Oliver had been told to send Harold away quietly.

'It's really not a good time,' Oliver said, but his eyes were a plea for help. Harold looked across to the van once more. There was a faded sign that said *Preston Painting Co.* on the side.

'Whose van is that?'

'One for work.'

'Okay. Well,' Harold said, stepping back, surveying the mountains, thinking about what to do next. 'I'm worried for you. Clare is missing, did you know that? It was on Facebook today. The police shared it.'

Oliver said nothing.

'Where's Gabe?' Harold asked.

'How should I know?'

'He wasn't at his cottage.'

'He's lucky to be alive. Did you know he nearly died?'

Harold sighed. 'I'll come and see you later.'

'I don't know why you decided to come to Mudgee, but I told you before I don't want anything to do with you.'

'A cup of coffee later. Please. There are things you need to know.'

Oliver didn't speak. He just stood there, doing whatever he could to silently communicate his desperation.

'I'll come and see you later,' Harold repeated.

Oliver only nodded and, without another word, shuffled inside and closed the door.

***

Harold headed down the driveway, towards Gabe's cottage. He took care to park on the sandy area of the drive – around the side, so that his vehicle wasn't visible from Oliver's place – and got out of the car as noiselessly as he could manage. Approaching the door, he noticed a greyhound sitting outside the cottage. It stood up and walked towards Harold, who, having never liked dogs, pretended it wasn't there.

Harold knocked, but he knew there wouldn't be an answer. The dog barked, once, in acknowledgement. He checked his pocket, making sure his phone was there, and began walking back towards Oliver's cottage. 'Stay,' he told the dog, which looked perplexed, frozen. While he knew Oliver was eccentric, on the fucking spectrum, he'd been reading people long enough to know that something was off with him. Oliver Wingfield was hiding something.

Instead of trying the front door again, he ambled towards the rear verandah. Almost tripped stepping up. Everything was clean: a wooden table and chairs, either handmade or converted from old church furniture. Pot plants. There were French doors leading into the kitchen. Harold had searched under the house for the paintings but hadn't found anything there before. He moved towards the corner and peered inside. He could see Gabe and Oliver. Could hear the voice of someone else. An ugly laugh. Who would be there with them? He needed to get the painting first. Deliver it to Madeleine. Save his skin, make things right with Oliver.

He thought of knocking, but that approach hadn't got him too far. He turned the handle to the door, expecting it to be locked, but instead it swung open in front of him. Its speed almost made him jump. Stepping inside, he saw Gabe and Oliver standing between the living room and the kitchen, mouths agape, looking ... worried?

Harold went to speak, but another man, older, brandishing a pistol, stepped in front of Oliver. He recognised him immediately: Miles.

Before Harold could even turn around and walk back out the door, before he could register how dire the situation was, Miles pulled the trigger and shot him straight in the chest.

27.

'That's what happens when you don't knock, Mr Keller,' Miles said.

The shot had flung Harold into the kitchen. He lay on the floor, coughing, crimson blood pooling beneath him. He was only just conscious, clutching his chest, dazed.

'I think I'll let you bleed out slowly. I've been saving the best till last. One of my deepest regrets was leaving you while you still had a pulse all those years ago,' Miles said, moving closer to Harold. 'I knew you'd come back after speaking to Oliver. I listened in, and thought I'd give you a chance to leave and never return. But you can't help yourself, can you, mate?'

Oliver gazed at Gabe, whom he expected to look scared, maybe horrified. Instead, his friend seemed resigned – defeated, almost.

Please see the gun, Oliver pleaded silently. It was a desperate thought, a long shot. But would Harold even know how to use it? He flashed forward to an image of Harold sputtering on the ground, discovering the gun, taking it in his bloody hands and brazenly pointing it at Miles, only for his father to quickly raise the pistol and shoot Harold – twice – through the head. And then

Oliver would have no chance of finding the artwork. He needed to shoot Miles, drive into town and make sure Penny was safe. Oliver found himself thinking in only essential moments: *Kill Miles, drive to town, return artwork, save Penny.*

'Oliver,' Miles said, 'time for you and your friend to drink your glass of wine.' He put the pistol in his waistband, collected the glasses from the kitchen bench and moved towards the dining table. Placing both glasses down, he instructed Oliver and Gabe to sit. Miles took a sip directly from one of the bottles of cabernet.

'Don't get me wrong. Smooth and all. Especially after not drinking for two decades. But I can't see what's so good about it. As in the price. Come on, have a sip for me.'

Oliver picked up the glass and swallowed a tentative mouthful. It was still tannic, as it hadn't been opened long. He looked across at Gabe and noticed the gash on top of his friend's head, a smear of blood. Gabe still hadn't moved to pick up his wine. Oliver closed his eyes and took another sip. Was this how Theo and Orson had met their demise? What was it going to feel like? God, he hoped it was him. He couldn't sit and watch Gabe die in the same way. When he reopened his eyes, he saw Gabe slowly reach for his own glass and then hesitatingly drink the barest possible amount.

As Oliver took a third sip, a realisation slapped him with clarity: he was no longer scared of his father. He didn't want to die, but his father, as a criminal, a memory, a fucking totality, no longer scared him. Why had he let himself fester in his fears for so long?

'I don't think anyone is going to believe that I shot the two men in the van. Or Harold. This is getting too messy for you,' he told Miles.

'I'll get rid of them. It'll just be you and your boyfriend left.

A bit of a sad story. I'll disappear. Start from scratch somewhere, under the radar.'

'They'll know it wasn't me. It'll come back on you.'

'Not this time, mate. You're not on your high horse this time. You know, it could have been so different. We could have kept on. Your mother was all but dead as it was. But you had to ruin it, didn't you?'

'You fucking disgust me,' Oliver said, before coughing. 'Why would the police think I poisoned myself?'

'Why not?' Miles said. 'We'll make sure it's all in a nice, typed-up letter. Maybe you felt guilty about shooting Gabe here, so you drank some of the poison you used to kill the others. Or if your glass wasn't poisoned, you were sad about killing your mates and decided to shoot yourself. It's fun to let chance tell the story sometimes. Don't you think?'

Oliver glanced across at Gabe, who had put his almost-full glass back down on the table, and calculated that he could only have taken two or three small sips of wine at the most. This was good. Was Gabe's glass even affected? Oliver didn't know what was going on anymore; he just knew that whatever Miles had given him wasn't only wine. He felt his chest begin to beat arrhythmically. It was happening.

And then, suddenly, there was the sound of a gunshot in his ear.

28.

Myriad stars, followed by whiteness. Then he was in the dark, locked in his childhood bedroom. Why was he here? Harold could taste blood: something metallic at the back of his throat, like he was going to throw up wet coins. Sharp pain turning numb down his chest. He reached towards his shoulder and could feel a painful stinging move up and down his side. It was sodden with blood.

He'd been wrong. Miles had arrived before he'd had the chance to. He must have taken out Madeleine's men. Harold could feel the phone in his pocket, but doubted he had any service. He would have to try to prise it out and call someone. There was no way he was dying here, on Oliver's kitchen floor. Harold opened his eyes and stared at the white ceiling. Too bright.

Feeling the blood in his mouth again, he groaned softly, not wanting to draw attention to himself. After a moment, he turned his head and looked towards the three men. Miles stood above Oliver and Gabe, who were both sitting at the dining table. Miles swigged from the bottle. Maybe he thought Harold was dead? Then, clutching at his chest, something caught his eye. A glint of silver, coming from an object tucked away beside the fridge. It was a shotgun, akin to the one his father had used to shoot kangaroos and boars when he was a boy back in Tamworth. He'd used it many times. He remembered the hills, the open fields of his family's land. The fresh air, riding motorbikes and sliding down dirt roads …

What was a shotgun doing here? Obviously Miles hadn't walked into the kitchen; didn't know it was there.

Harold squinted across to the men. They were engrossed in conversation. Oliver coughed once.

Slyly, quietly, Harold rolled over – blanched without making a sound – until he was in a position to reach the shotgun. He took a brief breath and, seeing that Miles was facing away from him now, he reached for the gun. He would have to trust that it was loaded. He cocked the weapon slowly, tacitly, and pointed it at Miles's back, immediately in line with his heart. He thought of how everything had become so acidulous. How he'd killed Theo by mistake, because of a painting he should never have let go. *You knew Miles did it. You knew him better than we did. What he was capable of. You were older and wiser and you were an ambivalent motherfucker. You let it happen. You lived and she didn't!*

Blues and greys and reds, terrible greens, flooded his eyes. Harold could feel his strength waning, his eyes betraying him. Before he lost himself fully to sleep, he closed his eyes, the gun pointed at Miles, and pulled the trigger.

29.

'Oliver, stay with me. We're going to the hospital.'

'No,' Oliver said, holding his chest, struggling with his words. 'They've got Penny.'

'Harold needs a doctor right now or he's not going to make it.'

Oliver noticed then that Harold had dropped the shotgun and collapsed against the fridge. His white and navy striped shirt was entirely painted in his blood.

'Can you help me lift him? An ambulance will take too long. We'll get to the car. Stay with me.'

'I don't feel too good.'

'You're both going to be okay,' Gabe said, grabbing Harold's arm and lifting it over his shoulder. Oliver helped him get to his feet and they began floundering towards the door. Despite his head wound, Gabe seemed to be walking well. Oliver felt a tinge of guilt. When he glanced down, he saw Miles on his stomach, a massive hole below his shoulder, trickles of blood merging into a pool abutting his face. His left eye was open, empty, and Oliver forced himself to look away.

'The Jag,' Oliver said, grabbing the keys from the hutch. 'It's the fastest.' He began to cough, feeling like he needed to vomit. 'I'll drive.'

'No. Help me put Harold in the car.'

Less than a minute later, Gabe was roaring down the driveway so fast that when Oliver looked in the rear-view mirror, all he could see was a smog of dust and dirt rising to the sky above.

***

At the hospital, Gabe pulled Harold from the car, now wearing half of his blood.

'Oli, you need to see a doctor right now. I'm not losing you.'

'I've got to get Penny first. I'm all right. I didn't drink much.'

Gabe shook his head, sternly. 'No. Please. Just come in.'

'We'll be quick,' Oliver said. 'You go drop Harold off, we'll get them the paintings, Penny will be okay and I'll come back. I promise. I won't be able to settle in there knowing I've sent you into my own mess. If anything happened to you and Penny ... mate, I've got nothing left.'

Gabe nodded reluctantly. Oliver knew he'd understand. He felt further pain in his stomach.

'Wait here. I'll take Harold inside quickly and we'll go.'

Oliver dipped his head in acknowledgement. As Harold and Gabe disappeared through the hospital's glass door – he saw two nurses run to them immediately – Oliver clambered across to the driver's seat and turned the key in the ignition, the engine roaring to life.

Everything seemed brighter than usual, but he was able to focus on the road. He felt time passing by slower than normal. Or was it moving faster? It was hard to tell; something, he couldn't put his finger on what, didn't feel right.

Turning onto Penny's street, he could see there was a black Mercedes sitting right behind her Corolla. She was home. And the others were there, also.

Oliver parked, not even taking the keys from the ignition. Hobbled as quickly as he could manage up the path and to the door. Not bothering to knock, he turned the handle and prayed it would open. Seconds later, he was inside Penny's living room. It was empty. He walked into the kitchen and saw Penny sitting at the head of the dining table, tied up, tape across her mouth.

Before he could approach, someone leaped from behind the door and grabbed him tightly, pressing a knife to his neck. He felt the coolness of the blade across his skin. Was sure, if he could have looked down, it would have drawn a small stripe of blood. Then he heard the sound of high heels click-clacking on the boards.

'Where are my men?'

'Winery. I came here to get Penny.'

Penny was trying to speak through the tape, but Oliver could only hear her muffled words. Pleas, almost, like howls from under the water.

'We've already got two of the paintings,' Madeleine said. The woman from the mugshots, the one Oliver had met briefly at Harold's. She checked her watch. 'They were supposed to be bringing you here to me so I could talk some sense into you both. Make no mistake, we will find the *Wadani*.'

The man let go of him. Oliver started to cough, before falling to his knees and vomiting at the woman's feet.

'Please,' he heaved, 'leave her out of this. We don't have any others. Miles killed the men. Killed them both. They're in the van.'

'Fuck,' Madeleine said. 'Let's go. Cut her loose.'

Oliver sat down on the ground, everything spinning, before collapsing on his back. The man with the knife walked over and ripped the tape from Penny's mouth. Oliver watched the way he moved – sprung, agile – and with his last trace of lucid thought he knew it was the same man from the security footage who'd been standing in his shed. The man he had thought was helping Miles. Then he heard Penny scream his name. Could feel everything starting to drift away from him.

'Oli! We need to get him to a hospital!'

Penny left the room. Oliver could hear her calling an ambulance. He heard the sound of the thieves swearing, slamming the door, the driver moving through the gears as they sped away.

Penny was alive.

He tried to stay awake. Focused intently on keeping his eyelids open. He could smell Penny, feel her warmth in the room. He loved her, and he couldn't lose her now. Smiling dumbly, he felt a tear sliding down his neck. As his eyes drooped closed, he realised he could still taste wine on his tongue.

Salt.

Something, in the distance.

30.

Oliver opened his eyes. Bright-white lights above, floating, incandescent. The smell of the theatre. Some kind of performance space. Perfume tinged with popcorn. There was a grand piano beside him and he was dressed in a tuxedo. Something he'd never worn before. Tidy black bowtie. He felt a lightness move through him, a giddy sense of pride. Like he was drowning, but death didn't come.

His mother was in the front row, paint smeared over her hands.

Beside Theo.

Penny.

Orson.

Clare.

Gabe.

Ida.

Harold.

Oliver walked and sat down at the piano, then inhaled a big breath. Listening to the silence, the hum of the white lights, his fingers skimmed across the keys. When he peered up, he expected to see his father at the back door. And he was there, standing with his arms folded. A hole through his shoulder. Blood-daubed – drenched and filthy. Oliver went to pause, to stop playing, but his hands continued, the music floating through the sultry air, and when he had finished, the crowd applauding, he saw that his father had opened the door and faded onto the busy street outside.

Dear Oliver,

What a relief to hear that you're alive and on the mend. Drowsiness and confusion are to be expected after such an ordeal. I will be honest and let you know that I read about everything in the paper and online. For someone who claims to be a recluse, you've done an egregious job of staying out of the spotlight. Although, like everything, it will blow over and be forgotten in a few days. In Sydney, at least. I'm no authority on the duration of small-town slander.

Thank you for attaching Theodore's final letter. It was certainly – for us both, I'm sure – the final piece of the puzzle. I won't lie – I burst into tears when I saw his handwriting again, with words I hadn't read. I'll never be able to see them for the first time again, but it's certainly helped fill a tiny part of a rather gargantuan void.

I'm truly sorry to hear about your father and everything he's done. What he's put us all through. May I please remind you, Oliver, that the man I met – and whose twin brother I loved – is nothing at all like the murderous man I've been reading about. It's a tawdry tale, an all-too-familiar one. Everything that's happened has really made me rethink the work I do and those I help. I hate the thought of people like Miles slipping through the cracks. I hate the thought of people like Miles being released early because they have enough money to fight in court. I don't know about you, but I've been pondering how complicit I am in everything. Oliver, is our stubborn refusal and inability to change causing us inherent damage as we age? Sometimes, we have to be fully lucid and conscious to make true progress. I'm not envious of what lies ahead, but I do want you to know that I'm here for you. Especially considering Harold's still in a coma, unlikely to wake up. A shit stroke of luck.

You're right – I will definitely have to make the trip to wine country sooner rather than later. Sip some wine and scatter Theo's ashes through the vines. At sunset?

PS – I have a painting of your mother's here, at Chambers. It arrived via registered post a week after Theo died, with a note that read, 'For us, for later.'

When I opened it, I cried. Recognised it immediately as your mother's work. Lovely thick oils on canvas. I wanted you to know it's safe in storage here. I can't quite look at it yet. If you need me to send it to you, don't hesitate to let me know.

With love,

Angie

31.

It looked as though they'd buried a body.

Oliver stood next to Gabe above the barrel they'd just lowered into the ground, leaning on the shovel.

'I didn't think we'd ever do this again,' Gabe said, sitting on the chair of the bobcat.

'Well …' Oliver reached into the bobcat and took a bottle of Pommery from a small esky. He pulled the cork, took a sip and passed it across to Gabe. The winter wind was punishing. Over the hill, the vines had lost their leaves and the grass was tinged brown. The sun peeked through a cloud and Oliver closed his eyes, letting the serenity grip him. 'I guess we all almost checked out for a minute there.'

'I don't mean that,' Gabe said, sipping and then sending the bubbles back to Oliver. 'I just thought after everything that had happened, you'd find somewhere else. Something different.'

'I thought about it,' Oliver said. 'Now, though, it's like a burden's been lifted from my shoulders.'

'So, you don't want to sell?' Gabe looked seriously at Oliver. 'Sorry. It's been a week. I had to ask.'

He smiled. 'You can keep your cushy gig.'

Oliver was lodging with Gabe for the moment. He wasn't superstitious, but he didn't want to live in the cottage again. He'd already planned on building something else, closer to the wine shed.

'I was sweating that you'd actually make me find a real job. Next thing, you'll tell me you're going to build a cellar door.'

'I've done up some plans at the house,' Oliver said, and Gabe spat the champagne from his mouth. 'I'm joking. After all the shit in the media, I'd prefer we never mixed with the public ever again.'

'No objections here.'

Oliver passed Gabe the champagne bottle and went for a walk. Through the vines, across the hill; he needed some time to clear his head. He was recovering well, the doctor being happy with his progress, but he needed to take things slowly.

On the way back, beside a row of pines, he noticed a small lump of fur. He bent down, confirming that it was a joey. There was no sign of another kangaroo. The joey was tiny, the size of a kitten. Dirty brown fur, with mottled pink skin peeking underneath. It twitched slightly as Oliver approached.

Taking off his jumper, he delicately scooped the joey into the fabric, into his arms.

Gabe was still sitting in the bobcat when Oliver arrived back.

'What have you got there?'

'Little Jack's lost her mum.'

Gabe leaned over and peered down into the jumper, raising his eyebrows. 'Lucky to be alive.'

'Me or her?'

'Both.'

'I'll take her inside,' Oliver said. 'Hopefully, she'll make it.'

Oliver let out a deep breath, before taking in a draught of air through his nose. He looked over the mountains at the trees and the vines and the grass trying to fleck green after the rain.

'What are you thinking about?' Gabe asked.

'Sounds pretentious, but how fickle breathing is. How lucky we are to be here right now.'

Gabe got down from the bobcat and grabbed Oliver's shoulder. 'Every breath is a gift, no matter how fickle … Anyway,' he said, 'I'm heading home. I'll call someone about the joey.' He turned towards the driveway. 'It looks like you've got a visitor.'

Oliver pressed the animal's warmth closer to his body as he gazed towards the driveway. Penny stood beside her little white Corolla, parked near the house. After a moment, she offered an awkward wave. Gabe was already halfway to his cottage, walking with his head down.

'Can I help you?' Oliver called out.

'I think I'm lost,' Penny said, moving closer and stopping a few feet in front of Oliver. 'I was told there was a bed and breakfast out this way.'

'Ah, I'm sorry to be the bearer of bad news, but it hasn't been operational for a number of years.'

Penny frowned. 'Well, I can see there are some vines around here. Are you by any chance the vigneron?'

'Yes,' Oliver said, 'matter of fact I am.'

'Well,' Penny said, proffering a bottle of red wine, 'I had this old Brunello di Montalcino just rolling around in the car. Thought I could tempt you to let me stay. Maybe share it with me?'

'A ten-year-old Brunello? I suppose we could always make an exception.'

'You told me a few things in hospital.'

Oliver feigned a grimace. 'I don't remember any of them.'

'In fairness,' Penny said, 'you were pretty drugged up.'

'Did I tell you that you're the best wine-bar owner I know?'

'A couple of times. You groggily proposed twice. Said if I came out with a good bottle of wine, you'd cook me dinner and tell me everything. You might have even mentioned that whatever's yours is mine.'

'I really said that?'

'Which means I can come and teach myself the piano whenever I like?'

'Sure.'

'And I can open up some vino from the cellar, if I'm here alone?'

'You know you can.'

'And I can take a few bottles of the Pavillion Rouge du Chateâux Margaux on a girls' weekend next month?'

'Well,' Oliver said, pointing to the wine shed before leaning in and kissing Penny's cheek. 'There's yours and mine, and then there's taking the piss.'

'If our chat goes well,' Penny said, sliding open the door, 'I'll settle for a single André Jacquart Blanc de Blancs.'

'Did I really propose in hospital?'

'Four times. I said twice before, but now the Margaux's off the table, the truth's tumbling out.'

Inside, Oliver held the joey close and rinsed a couple of glasses with one hand. Closing his eyes, he almost smiled at the pop of the cork as Penny pulled it from the bottle.

Acknowledgements

I would like to acknowledge the Kamilaroi and Wiradjuri people, on whose land I lived while imagining and writing this novel. I pay my respects to their Elders past and present.

For their prowess in matters of policing, law, medicine, art and piano, my utmost gratitude to Trevor Robinson, Abby Millerd, Jacinta Merten and Graeme Compton. Any inaccuracies and deviations from fact are mine alone.

James Manners answered the myriad wine questions I threw his way over our morning coffees and afternoon beers. A deft winemaker and a great friend.

To my early readers, thank you for your feedback and encouragement. In particular, Virginia Lloyd and Tara Cairnduff for their recommendations and eager encouragement on early drafts, and to Carla Baxter for her friendship over the last decade.

My brilliant agent Gaby Naher immediately believed in this story and fought for its place in the world. I'm grateful to be in the hands of the team at Echo Publishing. Thank you to Juliet Rogers for taking a punt and always believing in Oliver's story, Diana Hill for the entertaining emails and astute comments, and Emily Banyard and Lizzie Hayes for launching the novel out into the hands of readers. I must also thank Alexandra Nahlous for her considered suggestions and eagle-eyed editing, Josh Durham for the wonderful cover, and Shaun Jury for turning those loose manuscript pages into a beautifully formatted book.

The love, support and guidance of my family cannot go without mention, even though it feels far too great to be distilled into a single sentence.

A big thank you to Courtney for reading every version of this novel and for strolling with me when I needed to leave the desk. And to Gus, who led us on every walk and chewed any book left within reach. With four dogs in the title, you were hoping for at least one to be mentioned at the end, weren't you?